Cut Action Murder

By Rebecca Kalyani

I0609978

1

Acknowledgements

A special thanks to Jan Hogan for all your love and support throughout this process. Many thanks to Jere and Alexandra for helping me edit this book.

Thanks to everyone who encouraged me along the way. I couldn't have done it without you.

Prologue

June 1st

Tap... tap... tap... went the sound of the keys as he typed. The dim light from his desk was the perfect setting to finish the script. It was a story like no other, he thought. For three years it had been his baby, his everything. Granted, his life was already good. Molding minds was fulfilling. But this, this work of art, this was his pride and joy. He couldn't wait to see it come to life...

June 14th

The day was hot as Cassie Garrison drove onto the lot. She wished it wasn't so full. She had to park further away than she was comfortable doing. She scanned the space. There were lots of other cars driven by lots of other hopefuls, who, like her, shared the mutual dream of breaking into "the industry." Once again, she was going to be late for her acting class. She knew how her teacher, Marco, felt about that. Cassie clenched her teeth in frustration. She didn't mean to be late; sometimes it was impossible in Los Angeles not to be. Snatching up her keys, she eased her tall frame out of the car, brushing back the blonde tendrils that threatened to block her vision. As she raced toward the classroom, she failed to notice she was being watched.

Chapter One

Cassie was eager to begin class. She swung open the bright red theater door. Her teacher, Marco, had an office down one hall; the doors into the bigger space where they practiced stood closed in front of her. She opened them slowly, then crept down the darkened aisle as quietly as she could. She smiled when she spotted her friend, Lindsay Jones, who waved for her to come and sit. *What a bright spot in a hectic day,* Cassie thought.

She leaned down and gave her friend a side hug, then took a seat beside her. The two young women looked very much alike. Some said they even looked like sisters. Lindsay smiled back at Cassie and tapped her fingers on the copy of the script they were working on.

Cassie had practiced her lines over and over in an attempt to master them, but she was having a hard time getting into one particular scene. Normally, she loved this stuff. But this scene dealt with a serial killer who was committing the perfect murders. *Yuck,* she thought. Just reading the bold letters gave her the creeps. Despite her deep discomfort with the subject, Cassie did her best to get past the creepiness and worked hard at mastering her role. She was determined to make a name for herself in the industry. She sure as heck hadn't moved to LA from Kansas ten months ago for nothing. She had a great life back home, a family who loved her, and lots of friends. She missed them. The ache in her heart felt almost physical. It had definitely taken courage to move so far away.

She was lost in thoughts of her former life when Marco's voice brought her back to the present. "Alright, let's begin. Cassie, I'll start with you." Cassie rose reluctantly from her chair, script in hand. The knot in her stomach grew bigger. Marco was impatient. "Ok, Cas, your character is walking into her house." As he narrated, Cassie walked through a prop door and onto the stage. "She drops her keys and her mail on the counter. She's had such a long day; she doesn't even realize he's watching her." Marco continued. Cassie nods in agreement. "She has a lot on her mind." Cassie planted a weary look on her face. "So tired she yawns." Cassie glanced down at her script. Marco's voice boomed almost gleefully: "She doesn't even realize he's in the house." She heard a small chuckle from the audience. "Our beautiful young star makes a simple dinner of a tuna melt and salad and slides into the chair

4

at the onset dining table to enjoy her dinner. She cleans up her kitchen. Performing the mindless task of washing dishes helps her zone out. Nothing is out of the ordinary." Cassie, in character, started getting ready for bed. She loosened her hair binder, releasing her blonde hair to fall across her shoulders. She washed her face and brushed her teeth. "Thinking about the day ahead, she's excited to go to sleep. She climbs into bed and lets sleep overtake her."

The next moment, Marco was standing over her holding a play knife. Cassie involuntarily shuddered; to her, the knife looked real. She knew this was just acting; so why did she feel so scared? She laughed uncomfortably, attempting to ease her fear. *Get back into the role*, she told herself. In character, her eyes flew open and on cue, she let out a loud, piercing scream. Marco narrated: "The killer makes his move and slits her throat. Cassie's character dies. Once the killer is satisfied she is dead, he grabs his knife, makes sure he has left no prints or blood of his own behind and slowly eases his way out the door, locking it with a key he had previously taken and made a copy of. No forced entry, no perpetrator's blood, no fingerprints. It's the perfect murder. Ok, cut." And just like that, the scene ends.

Marco smiled at Cassie and gave her the thumbs up. "Great job! Great job!"

"Thanks, Marco. I'm working on it. That's not an easy scene to do, but I'm working on it. I'm sorry I have to leave a little early. Shelly, one of the other waitresses at the diner, called in sick. I promised to cover for her. Hope that's okay."

Marco glared and rolled his eyes. Contrary to his expression, in a pleasant voice, he said, "Of course. It's disappointing you won't be joining us for the entire class. But do what you need to." Other than that snarky ending, the praise felt good. Cassie couldn't hide the smile on her face as she speed-walked out the door.

Chapter Two

The smile remained on Cassie's face all day as she thought about the scene and the way she had improved. *I'm really starting to feel good about acting*, she thought. It had taken a while for her to think, much less feel, that way.

Her day had been long. The sun had just about set. The sky looked incredible. Cassie watched the pink and orange colors fade. She heard a rumble and almost laughed out loud as she realized what it was: her stomach. Guess I'd better eat, she thought. She opened her car door and climbed in, started the engine and glanced in her rearview mirror as she backed out of the diner parking lot. Her feet ached. She reached down with one hand to rub them. Being a waitress required lots of running and lifting. She hadn't realized how hard the work was before she took the job. This was her first real full-time job. Her parents insisted she focus on being a teenager and then on community college. She was not to worry about money. *They're the best*, she thought.

Cassie Garrison glanced at the large clock display in her car; it was now eight p.m. Despite the long hours, she loved her job and her co-workers. The diner featured several Broadway shows as a background setting. It had a fun, show-time atmosphere to it. Still, it really had been a long day. She'd covered for Shelly and then worked her own six-hour shift. A loud yawn escaped her lips. She was really tired. Hopefully her boss at the diner would give her a raise soon. She was always covering for people, working really hard. *It's that mid-western work ethic*, she decided.

Cassie drove through several different neighborhoods on her way home, pondering what it would be like to own a house one day. Of course, the prices were out of this world in LA. She knew her job waiting tables wouldn't cover anything close to a down payment. For now her small apartment would do just fine. She pulled up to the complex and got out of the car, checked her mail, tucked it under an arm, and proceeded to her apartment. She unlocked the door, opened it, and walked in. With a thud she dropped her mail on the counter, grateful to be home. She could sort through it later. Perhaps she would sleep in tomorrow. Her body told her she could sure use it. Cassie opened her fridge and pulled out the mayo and bread. Her last meal was courtesy of the diner. Now, she only had the energy to make something simple. She found a can of tuna and started making herself dinner. She loved tuna. She laughed aloud, thinking how, if she could, she would eat it every day. It tasted great. Cassie was the type of person who found joy in little things, including, but not limited to, a tuna sandwich. She ate quickly, glanced once again at the stack of mail, then stuck to her original plan to go through it later. She was just too tired to tackle it now. "Whatever it is, it can wait till tomorrow," she mumbled.

Cassie checked her phone messages: one missed voicemail. She hit the button and put the receiver to her ear. "Cassie, it's Mom and Dad. We are just calling to say hi and that we miss you and love you. Call back soon, sweetheart." Tears filled her eyes as she heard those familiar voices. The ache in her heart was back. She couldn't wait to go home to visit. She thought about that as she got ready for bed. She took her hair down from her binder, letting the strands fall over her shoulders. She brushed her teeth and washed her face. For a while she sat in bed leafing through a fashion magazine. Her head bobbed up and down. She put the magazine aside, lay back, and closed her eyes. She tucked the blankets around herself and breathed deeply. The pleasant thoughts of her parents lulled her to sleep as her breathing slowed.

Chapter Three

June 18th

I looked up from the mound of paperwork on my desk. "How did this stack get to be so high?" I muttered. And people think that being a police detective is easy. I swear, half of my job is filling out reports. That's the part I dislike most. "If only there wasn't so much…"

Maybe it was my words, or the way I looked—I'm not sure, but something caused my partner, Matt Parker, to look up from his own stack.

"What is it now, Detective Blade?" he asked with a smile.

"As if you don't already know," I replied.

"Ah, the usual, huh? Don't worry," he teased, "only twenty more pages to go."

I rolled my eyes and looked back down at the stack of papers. *He really is a great-looking guy*, I thought. Matt was tall, well built, and had a thousand-watt smile. The blue of his uniform shirt brought out the color of his eyes; they were almost the same shade.

Matt was a great partner. He was the sort everyone in our office wants to have, an officer who was dedicated, professional, easy-going, with just the right amount of intensity. To be perfectly honest, there was just something different about Matt Parker. He was so kind, a lot more so than anyone I'd ever met actually. When I say kind, I mean to everyone. Sometimes I felt a little jealous. What was it about him that—

Our captain's voice jolted me back to the present. "Blade! Parker! You're up." Matt and I exchanged glances; we knew what that meant: a homicide. "The call just came in." I always feel a knot in my stomach when it's our turn. It usually signifies we have the end of a life to investigate. Still, that's what we do in Hollywood Homicide. Our Captain, George Mendoza, had been on the force for almost thirty years now. He had broad shoulders and huge muscles. He was fit, athletic, and one of the best officers I knew. Anyone would be lucky to call him their boss.

Captain Mendoza continued: "This one is at 11572 Fountain Avenue. Landlord by the name of Lanisha Bons called it in. She reported lots of flies and a bad stench coming from one of her tenant's

8

apartments. I told her I'm sending two of my best." Captain Mendoza nodded toward Matt and me. "That would be Apartment Five".

"We're on it, sir," I said, as we flew out the door.

"Let me know what you find out."

"Got it," we responded in unison as we hurried toward our vehicle.

I pulled the keys out of my pocket and jumped in the driver's seat of the squad car; Matt quickly dove into the passenger side. We sped off with lights flashing and siren roaring, feeling fortunate to have a modern cruiser. For the most part, I do the driving, probably because I like it. Even in LA. Something about it just calms me. Matt understands that, although my driving can make him a bit uneasy. "We're not on a high speed chase, so please—just get us there in one piece. Ok?"

I laughed. Still, the tension in me increased with each mile. I wondered what on earth had happened at 11572 Fountain Avenue, Apartment Five.

Chapter Four

The first thing I noticed as we cruised to a stop was the area. Its peacefulness did not reflect what we were about to see inside. The crime scene was in Hollywood; but it was far enough from a main drag to feel more like a neighborhood. The apartment was in an older brick building, with lots of trees surrounding it, and a landscaped courtyard. An older African-American woman was standing at the front door. In one hand she clutched a set of keys. With the other she waved us forward. Her black hair was tied back in a ponytail. Her face was grayish. I was worried she might fall over, so I gently took her arm. We sat together on the steps, which seemed to calm her. "Mrs. Bons?" I asked.

Instead of identifying herself, all she said was, "I don't know. I don't know." Perhaps she was in shock. I urged her to sit down. Even though the day was hot, the older woman shivered beside me.

"Ma'am, we're the police," Matt said. "We're here to help you. Can you tell us what's going on?"

Mrs. Bons took a shaky breath. "It's, it's her.

"Who?" Matt asked.

"It, it's Cassie."

"Alright," I replied, putting a calming hand on her shoulder. "Just take your time. Tell us what happened."

"Well, my husband and I own this building. We have for about ten years now. Nothing like this has ever…" She stopped again, taking deep breaths, trying to speak. "Cassie in Apartment Five. The neighbors complained of this awful smell and lots of flies coming into their units. So we went to investigate."

"We?" Matt asked.

"My husband and I. I saw that the flies were coming out of her unit. There were a lot of them. She's a clean person. It was unusual. I've never seen that many flies in one place. We knocked but got no answer. So I went and got the keys." She held out her hand with the keys. Matt gently took them from her. "I came back and opened the door. That's when the smell hit me. I don't even know how to describe it. Then I saw all this blood. I screamed and jumped back because clouds of flies came at me. The blood… there was so much. It was all over. So I ran out of the apartment. And that's when I called you."

10

"How did you know it was Cassie?" I wondered. "Did you see her body?"

"I couldn't go in past the front door. My goodness, there was so much blood. I saw enough to know that something really bad had happened in there. And you know what? That's all I needed to know." Mrs. Bons sighed heavily, forcing herself to continue. "Cassie Garrison lives in that unit; so I just assumed it must be her." A flicker of hope crossed her face. "Maybe it's not her. Maybe Cassie's okay. All I know is something really bad happened in there." She shuddered again.

Matt held out his arm to help her up. He told her to wait in her apartment, that we'd check everything out and come back to speak to her and her husband later.

As we climbed the stairs, the stench hit. We knew this smell all too well. There was no doubt about it. It was the unmistakable odor of death. "This can't be good," Matt said as we put on gloves and masks, along with booties over our shoes, then slowly stepped inside. As soon as we opened the door, clouds of flies swarmed onto and around us. We waved them away and shut the door.

"Mrs. Bons was right," I said. "Look at all the blood." It was all over the walls and the floor. The tiny apartment was covered in it. I'm no medical examiner, but it looked like the blood had dried into clumps and bright red streaks.

I drew my gun and held it in front of me. Matt did the same. "Hello! Police!" I called out. As expected, there was no answer.

We walked cautiously through the living room, checking to make sure it was clear. We passed a love seat, a coffee table, and a small TV. As soon as we entered the bedroom, we saw her. Her entire face was covered in blood. Right away we could see that her throat had been slit. I glanced around and saw a photo of a young blonde woman with two older people. She was beautiful, very photogenic. In the shot she had her arms around the older couple, and they her.

The body on the bed looked to be the same, but in a bloody and battered form now. The gaping, bloody wound on her neck and throat was deep. The flies were even worse here. "Oh!" I gasped, feeling a pain inside of me for the young woman sprawled across her own bed. It was obvious she was gone. Her blonde hair was matted in blood, as were her pajamas.

"Call it in," Matt commanded. I grabbed my cell and started dialing.

Chapter Five

Dr. Dave Locking, the Hollywood Medical Examiner, greeted us as he walked gingerly into the bedroom toward the victim. With all that blood, everyone had to step carefully to preserve every part of the awful scene. Together, we surveyed the room, and then the young woman on the bed. Dr. Locking was in his mid-fifties, with salt and pepper hair, and a kindly manner. Everyone in the Homicide Unit knew he showed great respect for the bodies of victims and compassion toward their loved ones. Looking Matt and me in the eyes, he asked, "Do we know who she is?"

"We haven't done a search of the apartment yet. According to the landlord, her name is Cassie Garrison," Matt replied. Putting a name to our victim made it personal for the three of us. For a brief moment, both Matt and Dr. Locking stood over the girl, hands folded, and lips silently moving. The moment was over as quickly as it had begun.

Dr. Locking spoke as he made notes. "It looks like her throat has been slit with-I would say-a 10-inch knife. Judging by these flies and the insect larvae, she's been dead awhile… maybe as long as three days." Matt and I nodded.

"She must have been strong. Look at these tracks." I pointed out footprints in blood on the floor. "If you follow them, they lead close to the door. She was trying to get away." Matt agreed.

"Yes, I thought that, too," Locking observed.

"We'll let you and your team get to work; and we'll figure out who she is," Matt said. He and I then left the room. As we walked into the combination living-kitchen area, I spotted a purse on the counter beside a pile of mail. As he flipped through the stack, Matt remarked, "These are all addressed to the same person." He pointed to the name: Cassie Garrison.

I nodded as I pulled a set of keys from the stylish bag. There weren't many on the ring: one car; two house; and a tiny mail box key. Next, I fished out a woman-sized wallet, opened it, and found $25 in cash, credit cards, a few store cards, and a driver's license belonging to Cassie. The photo matched the dead girl. I showed it to Matt and pointed to the one on the table of her and the two older people. Matt nodded. "No sign of robbery," I observed.

"Yeah. And I'm not sure how he got in," Matt said. "Nothing looks forced open. The windows are still locked. Mrs. Bons said she needed her keys to get in. So the door had to have been locked." He pointed to Cassie's keyring. She had her set, too. Light reflected off of them as they sat on the counter. They, like everything else, would be bagged and tagged as evidence.

"Hmm, did she let this person in?" I wondered. I saw Matt holding a cell phone. There was one voicemail. We listened together. The recording was from four nights prior. "Hi, it's Mom and Dad. We just wanted to say we miss you and love you. Call back soon, sweetheart." I had to blink back tears. How were we going to tell these poor parents their little girl was never coming back home?

Just then I heard a knock at the door and opened it for Jesse Smith and his crime scene team. "Hi, Blade." He gave me a quick nod.

"Hi, Smith" I replied.

"What do we have?" I told him the victim's name was Cassie Garrison, age 22, still pretty new to Los Angeles, from Kansas. Her throat was slit. And it appeared she'd been dead for about three days. "Who found her?" Smith asked.

"Her landlord opened the door. But once she saw the blood and flies, she quickly shut it and called us."

He nodded and looked down at the stained carpet under his plastic shoe covers.   "Judging by all the blood, it looks to me like she tried to get away."

Ben, another CSI, chimed in. "So if she ran out here trying to escape, how did she get back to her bedroom?"

Jesse responded, "The perp must have carried her back in there."

Bile rose in my throat as his answer hit me. "The killer must have waited until she was dead and carried her back in, since that's where we found her."

Jesse, who is normally quite calm and doesn't express much emotion, lamented, "What a monster!" Like the rest of us, this case was already getting to him. One thing I know for certain: our Crime Scene Unit is top of the line. They would spend the time necessary to sift through all the evidence, and would play a huge role in helping to solve this brutal murder. Jesse turned to his team and ordered, "Let's get started."

Chapter Six

Matt and I joined Mr. and Mrs. Bons in their apartment. She put out some cookies and coffee. The four of us sat around their kitchen table as we conducted the interview. Mrs. Bons looked less in shock than before. She had tied her hair in a neat braid and put on a sweatshirt over her blouse. As they talked, they clung to one another for support. Mrs. Bons told us Cassie had moved into her apartment ten months earlier and that she liked it because it seemed safe. She was an actress, who also waited tables at the Broadway, one of the local diners, which was about three miles away.

"She was a sweet girl," Mr. Bons added. He was a short, stocky man with graying black hair and large brown eyes. He took a bite of a cookie. "She was always smiling and seemed very happy here."

"How could anyone do this?" Mrs. Bons cried.

"That's what we're going to try to find out," Matt told her. "Did either of you see anything suspicious over the last couple of days?"

Both shook their heads. They told us they had been out of town and just got back home yesterday. "Was it a robbery? Should we change the locks?" Mr. Bons asked, as a look of alarm crossed his face.

"There was no indication of a burglar that we found. But if it would make you and your other tenants feel safer to change the locks, we would encourage that."

"You mean she knew the person who killed her? Is that what you're saying?" Mrs. Bons was nearly hysterical.

"We're not sure of anything just yet. Right now we are at the beginning of the investigation. Soon we hope to have more of an idea of what went on." Matt assured her, using a firm but calm voice. "We have detectives Cameron and Davis talking to other tenants in your building to see if they have any information that could be helpful."

"Could we have your file on Cassie, please?" I asked. "We are going to need to notify her parents. And we'll also use it to learn as much as we can about her."

"Mike and Cindy Garrison. They're from Kansas. We met them once. Such nice people. Our hearts just break for them. She was their only child." Mr. Bons bit his lip and fiercely blinked back tears as he spoke of Cassie's parents. He handed the file over.

Matt and I spent a little more time with the Bons, then thanked them for their time and left to go find a killer.

Chapter Seven

We drove back to the police station in silence, each of us deep in our own feelings, thinking our own thoughts. To say this work didn't affect us would be a lie.

"It never gets easier, does it?" Matt finally asked. I shook my head.

"No, it really doesn't." I engaged the turn signal and took a left into the station parking lot. Although this is a tough job, the compassion is what drives us.

"Cassie was somebody's daughter and friend. She didn't deserve to die like this," I agonized.

"No one does," Matt agreed.

I turned off the ignition; and we headed in to brief our Captain.

Captain George Mendoza was tough, but fair. He was a no-nonsense guy who followed the rules and police procedure to a T. Perhaps that was because one of his assignments after patrol had been working in Internal Affairs. He often said that had taught him about the ethics of what it meant to be a police officer. He wanted everything done by the book and demanded it be that way to protect his officers.

Captain Mendoza was sitting at his desk, feet propped up, looking over some reports. I am still a pretty new detective. I couldn't have asked for a better mentor and example. Even when I made little mistakes and he was hard on me, he somehow managed to be patient as well.

"Come in, guys," his voice boomed as he motioned for us to close the door and sit down.

"It's pretty bad," I said.

"By the looks on your faces, that's pretty clear to me. Who is she?"

"Her name was Cassie Garrison," Matt responded.

"She was from Kansas." I slid my phone to him so he could look at the picture I took of her driver's license.

"She can't be more than twenty-two," Captain Mendoza frowned as he spoke. "How long has she been here?" I started to summarize what we knew so far.

"According to the landlord, ten months."

"Time of death?"

"We're not sure yet - maybe three, possibly four, days ago. It looks like she came home, had a sandwich, and went to bed," Matt added.

"A voicemail from her parents had been heard on June fourteenth," I continued, "So we have to assume it was pretty recent." We all knew that for now that was just a guess—subject to change. When she died was what the ME would ascertain.

"Cause?"

"Her throat was slit, sir. That much was obvious. The ME thinks with a 10-inch blade." We all sat silently as the truth of her cruel death rushed at us. Finally, I said, "I know what you're thinking, Cap. That is a pretty personal way for someone to die."

"Yeah, and pretty messy, too." Matt added, "Lots of blood."

"Well, let's hope the killer's DNA is still at the scene. Have Smith and CSI gotten there?"   "Yes," I confirmed.

"Any leads or thoughts?" The Captain asked, a questioning expression on his face. "It's important to solve a homicide as soon as possible. The longer this goes unsolved, the harder it gets." We all knew that.

"No leads as of yet. As I said, I think it was personal. But why, I don't know."

"Our next step, of course, will be to notify the parents," Matt said aloud.

"Always the worst part," the Captain muttered. He was right. "After that, go to her job and anywhere else she was. See what we can learn about who would want to kill this poor girl."   "Yes, sir." We both agreed.

"Good work on this so far. Just keep me in the know."

.

Chapter Eight

Matt sat down, opened up his laptop, and scrolled to the note he made of the number for the parents of Cassie Garrison. With two hot cups of coffee in hand I sat beside him. He smiled at me as he noticed two creams and two sugars already in the mug, just how he liked it. "You're the best, Em. Not sure how you drink it black like that, though."

"Very funny, Matt." He put the phone on speaker as it rang and connected.

"Hello," he said. "May I speak with Mr. or Mrs. Garrison please?" A woman's bright voice came through the speaker.

"Yes, I'm Cindy Garrison. Who's calling, please?" For a moment, Matt was silent, his hands folded, lips quietly moving. Then, as if drawing strength to go on, he took a deep breath. "We're detectives Matt Parker and Emma Blade from the Los Angeles Police Department. We'd like to talk with you and your husband, please."

"Oh, no! What's happened? Is it our daughter, Cassie?" She was speaking so softly, we were almost unable to hear her.

"Ma'am, is your husband around as well?"

"Yes, just a moment…Mike, come quick. It's the Los Angeles Police Department."

"This is Mike Garrison. What's happened?" His was a deep questioning voice.

"Sir, this is Detectives Matt Parker and Emma Blade. We are from the Homicide Division of the Los Angeles Police Department. Mr. and Mrs. Garrison, we are so sorry to inform you that your daughter Cassie was found dead this morning at her apartment in Hollywood." The line went silent as the horrified couple tried to absorb what they had just heard. *But how can you?* I wondered as we waited.

"Nooooo. Nooo," Cassie's mother cried out in a loud moan. "No… no… no!!!" The cries grew louder. "It can't be her. We've been so worried. She hadn't called us back since we left her a voicemail a few days ago. Believe me when I tell you, that was not like our Cassie." Mr. Garrison was in a state of disbelief. His wife's sobs continued to fill the room. They were the wrenching cries only a mother could make.

It was just heartbreaking to notify loved ones. The ones 'left behind' is how I think about it. Left behind to pick up the pieces; left behind to mourn for a lifetime.

19

"I wish this wasn't true, but it is. I am so sorry for your loss. We are doing everything in our power to find out who did this to your daughter," Matt informed them. More sobbing, this time from both parents.

"When? How? How?" Mr. Garrison sobbed as he spoke.

"For now, the specific time is unclear."

"You are from homicide?"

"Yes, sir."

"So that means she was… she was murdered?" His wife put it together.

"Yes, ma'am." My partner spoke as gently as he could.

"Maybe it's not her. How do you know for sure it's our Cassie?" her mother asked.

"We made a preliminary identification from her driver's license photo. The mail in her apartment was addressed in her name, too. Plus, we heard the voicemail you left on her cell the other night. When you get here we will take you to the Medical Examiner's office to identify the body." I said that as gently as I could.

"How?" Mrs. Garrison wanted to know.

"Her throat was slit, ma'am." And then it really hit hard. The sounds made in grief no one wants to ever utter. Crying! Sobbing! Screaming! We waited for what seemed like an eternity as the couple let out their emotions.

Mr. Garrison finally was able to ask, "What can we do to help? We'll be on the first flight to Los Angeles and meet with you and whoever else you want us to."

"Come as soon as you can," I urged. "And yes, we would like to talk more about your daughter with you." Matt nodded for me to continue. "Before you go, I just need to ask you, was Cassie dating anyone?"

"No, she never mentioned anything about any boy."

"Was there anyone she was having problems with that you knew about?"

"No, no one she mentioned. But we're in Kansas. I'm sure the people at the diner where she worked will have more information on that."

"That's our next step. We're going to the diner to interview her co-workers," Matt informed them. "Email me your flight info. We'll pick you up at the airport and lead you through the process. Once again, we are so very sorry for your loss."

Chapter Nine

By the time we finished speaking with the Garrisons, it was time for dinner. Night was falling fast in the Golden State. The sun began to set. Matt and I headed out to grab a bite and conduct a few interviews at the diner where Cassie worked.

"Wow, it really does look Broadway in here," I observed. On the walls hung quotes from Broadway plays like Les Miserables and Wicked. Photos and framed autographs from the shows' stars hung from the walls. We took a brief moment to let our eyes wander from one to the other.

"Can I help you?" A young, pretty blonde with 'Tina' on her nametag asked as she looked down on us from her hostess stand. Matt pulled out his badge and asked to be seated. "Thank you for all you do to keep us safe," said Tina. "I'll find you a great table."

"Thank you," he said giving her his broad gorgeous smile.

Tina found a table for us in the corner.

"Besides the fact that we are starving, we have another reason for being here. Hi, I'm Detective Blade. This is my partner, Detective Parker," I said as I showed her my badge.

"Ha ha…Homicide? Who?"

"Please, Tina, sit down." Matt pulled out a chair and guided her to it. "We're investigating the homicide of one of your waitresses."

"Oh, no, not Cassie. Please don't tell me it's her."

"Why do you think this is about Cassie?" I asked. Her answer could help us with the timeline.

"Um, she hasn't shown up for work for the last three days. She's not answering her phone. We've all been worried sick."

I looked at her innocent face. I wished we didn't have to involve her in this. Her life was about to change forever. Matt slid a photo of Cassie in front of the hostess. She nodded that it was her; that's all she could do. Her face went white. She put her head in her hands and started to cry. Her body began to tremble. Gently, I put a reassuring hand on her shoulder. Tina looked from Matt to me. "How? I mean, who would do this?"

"That's what we're trying to find out. We know this is not the best time; but if you could answer some questions for us that would be very helpful," I said. She slowly nodded for me to continue. "How well did you know Cassie?"

"She moved here from Kansas City, I would say...ten months ago. She wanted to be an actress. She was always bringing in scripts and telling us about her class. She was so sweet and innocent, like. She worked really hard here. Like, Shelly was sick. Cassie not only worked her own shift but most of Shelly's, too."

Matt had left for a minute and returned with a glass of ice water in his hand. Tina smiled gratefully and took a big sip. "I guess you could say there's a lot of turnover here. People are always trying to leave early or call in sick. Those of us who stay have to work really hard. Way harder than we should have to." Tina spoke in a resentful tone.

"Did she have a boyfriend?" Matt asked.

"No, she was so focused on acting and just kind of getting out there. And what with working so hard... well, she always said she didn't have time for a guy."

"Was there anyone she was having problems with that you knew of?" Matt continued.

"I know she was not as happy in her acting class lately. But problems with anyone in particular? I don't know. She didn't really say. Everyone liked Cassie. She was just that kind of person, you know? I guess she did seem a little more jumpy lately."

"What do you mean?" Tina sighed and, for the first time, laughed a little.

"Oh, she was working on this scene for her class about a serial killer who slits her throat or something. She said it was making her feel uneasy." Matt and I exchanged glances.

"Did she say why?" I asked.

"No, she said it wasn't a big deal, that she just felt kind of creeped out by it. But she said sometimes you work on scenes that aren't always pleasant, and you just have to learn to deal with it."

"You're doing great, Tina. Thanks for your help," I said. She nodded for us to continue. "Did she have other friends who worked here at the diner?" I asked.

"Yes, there's Lisa, Nick, and Shelly. Lisa and Shelly are waitresses. Nick's a host like me." I told her we'd like to talk with them. "Yeah, ok. They're all here. Oh, my gosh, they don't know... Um, could they come by your table in an hour or so once things slow down here?" Tina cautiously asked.

"Sure, that's no problem. In the meantime, we'll get something to eat."

"How about your boss?" Matt asked.

"The owner is out of town and has been for the last three weeks. He should be back next week." She laughed. "He put me in charge while he's gone. Imagine that."

"Tina, one more thing. Where have you been the last three nights? We're asking everyone, just to clear people. It's nothing personal."

"That's easy. I've been here, since I'm in charge. So have Nick, Shelly and Lisa."

Matt handed her some business cards. "Please feel free to give these out to any of your regulars if you think they can add anything to our investigation."

"Yeah, whatever I can do to help." Tina got up. She motioned for menus to a passing waitress who put them on the table. We got her contact information. She offered to take our drink orders on the spot. We ordered coffee and water.

With our stomachs growling, we opened up our menus and began to read. "It all looks good," I said.

"I could eat anything right now," Matt said. I grinned mischievously at him. Just then, Tina came back and told us she was ready to take our order.

"He'll take the cardboard," I said joking. We all laughed.

"I did say I could eat anything." Matt decided on the corn beef on rye. I got the tuna salad. "I haven't been here in a long time; but I remember the food is really good," said Matt. I let him know I'd remember that.

"So what do you think so far?" he asked.

"That whole thing about her acting class and the scene was strange. I know it's just a scene. Still, it seems a pretty odd coincidence." Matt nodded. "Slit her throat or something," he said, bringing Tina's words back to mind. "I would be creeped out." Tina herself came back with our order.

"You're a great waitress, too," I said. She smiled shyly.

24

"In this place you have to wear a lot of hats sometimes," she said. Once things slow down, I'll send my crew over."

After that we dug into our meals. We've been partners long enough where we can let the silence be comfortable between us. I watched him eat and realized I even liked the way he eats. The thought was amusing to me. There was something I wanted to ask him, though.

"When you and Locking were at the scene, I noticed that for a second you both stood over the girl with your hands folded. I noticed it again tonight while you and I were talking to the parents." Truthfully, I'd noticed he did that a lot.

Matt smiled. "I was taking a moment to pray."

"Pray? What good does that do? Why would you do that right there?"

I hadn't been raised with religion. In our house we didn't pray. My parents didn't believe in God. They never had. I'd heard about God a little; but I was pretty skeptical, too. I wasn't sure I'd ever even been inside a church.

"Um, this concept of praying is kind of foreign to me," I said. "I don't get it."

Matt gently responded, "Emma, I know you've mentioned being raised without church or religion. Don't feel bad about asking. It makes sense that you would wonder. And I'm glad you asked. I pray because in those moments I need God desperately. Seeing her body like that, telling her parents their sweet daughter won't be coming home; those tasks are awful."

He was right. "I can kind of see what you mean. It is awful. I don't really know what to do in those moments."

"So that's why I take a second to pray. I am a human being. When God helps me, I'm a much better person, and I do a much better job. Without him, I would be lost and such a different person."

I nodded, not really understanding, not sure of what else I could say.

I knew Matt was raised in a large family of seven kids, with a Mom and Dad who made Christ the center of everything. Maybe that's why he was so different. As for me, I had no idea what I believed. I just felt confused about it all.

25

The time flew by as we ate. We talked easily about our lives and our interests, checked our messages, and made plans for tomorrow's agenda. Detectives keep long, often unconventional hours. Sometimes eating can be a luxury; other times it is not so much a meal, but a way to refuel. Tonight, I was glad it was the former. As we were finishing our meal, three young people in their diner uniforms approached our table. "Hi, are you the detectives?" A young woman about the same age as Cassie asked.

"Yes, who are you?"

"I'm Lisa. This is Shelly and Nick. Tina says you want to talk with us about Cassie?"

"Yes, please, have a seat. Nice to meet you."

"Is Tina okay?" Shelly asked, concerned. "She looked pretty sick or something over the last couple of hours."

Nick slid into a chair beside Matt. The girls sat across from them and on either side of me. Nick was stocky but well built. His hair was cut short. His eyes were piercing as he looked into mine. Lisa was petite, with bright red, curly hair and a broad smile. She frowned at us and wrung her hands nervously. Shelly, like Cassie, was blond, but with short hair and tiny green eyes. For the third time that day, we conveyed the terrible news.

Like Tina, they expressed profound grief. "We want to do whatever we can to help," Nick said. "We haven't known Cassie for that long - not a full year, I think. We loved her, though. She was awesome."

Lisa began to cry. I handed her some tissues. "Thanks." She took them and wiped her tears. "This is all too much. It sounds funny to say; but I didn't know people were actually murdered in real life." She continued to wipe the tears away.

"When did you last see her?" I asked.

"Three nights ago."

Nick nodded in agreement. "It was a zoo around here. I don't think we took a break until most of our shift was over."

"Yeah, that's right," Shelly remembered.

"Someone was having a large birthday party. It kept us busy all night. I don't usually help with serving. That night it was all hands on deck," Nick informed us.

"Where were you guys the last three nights?" Matt asked. Lisa's face went pale.

"You think…."

"We don't think anything yet. We're just trying to clear people and establish a timeline," Matt quickly explained. They all agreed they were at the diner those three nights, just like Tina said. Their interviews were similar to Tina's. Unfortunately, we didn't learn anything new.

"Here are some business cards. Please hand them out to any of your regulars who might be able to help us." They silently nodded and gave us info on how to reach them should we have more questions. Matt and I thanked them. He picked up the check.

"It's my turn to treat you", he said with a smile. I let him pay the bill.

As I drove home, I thought about all that had happened. Usually, a homicide makes things so busy we can't even think. Nevertheless, tonight I thought about what Matt had said. *He prayed.* He depended on God. He said that's where his strength came from. It was easy to see how strong he was as a person and as a leader. I pondered what that meant. To be honest, I didn't really understand it. I guess I always felt I was strong enough to handle anything. I haven't depended on anyone for a long time.

I wasn't really the life of the party. Some might even call me shy. Once I warmed up, though, I felt comfortable. I had a few friends. And I was fine with that. I had a good job and a place to live. I loved what I did. Solving a crime was like putting together a very large puzzle. Interviewing witnesses took skill and empathy. My job required lots of training and the ability to work both with a partner and independently. I never stopped to consider that there could be more to life than that. Now, for some unknown reason, I wondered if there was. What would it mean to be able to turn to someone, especially in the most challenging of times?

Matt was different. There was just something about him I couldn't put my finger on. Still, he was strong and confident and kind. He had this way about him. I envied him for that. My focus turned back to the road as I turned right onto my street and pulled into the parking lot. I got out of my car and walked through the lobby. My high heels clicked as I made my way up the four flights of stairs to my condo. I opened the door and walked straight to my bedroom. Before I knew it, I fell fast asleep.

Chapter Eleven

June 19th

Whenever there's a homicide, there's paperwork. Stacks and stacks of it. Matt and I spent the morning playing catch up and writing our reports on what we knew so far. This step-by-step record of our activities went into a red three-ring binder traditionally called "The Murder Book". That way, every officer or person looking at the case can track what we've been doing.   Captain Mendoza expected our paperwork to be on his desk as soon as we could get it there. He stayed on top of it, looking through the books every day, checking the progress of those in his command. Was it annoying sometimes? Yes. But his careful attention to detail meant ours as well. That made for good, solid police work.

Matt and I grabbed some lunch from a local taco truck. I munched on hard shell pork tacos, while he ate several with chicken. The day was sunny, the sky a brilliant blue. I was glad we'd made it just before the long line began to form. Matt noticed me looking at the busy lunch rush and smiled. "I know you hate waiting in lines. I'm glad we missed all that."

I laughed and nodded in agreement. We only took a half-hour for lunch. Sometimes not even that if we were swamped with several homicide cases. "Now that we're finished, shall we go see the Doc?" I asked. Matt agreed. We walked the two shorts blocks to his office.

Cassie's autopsy was scheduled for the afternoon. "Hi, Ruth," I said, smiling at Dr. Locking's receptionist. She was a pretty girl, about twenty-four, with long dark hair and a gentleness that made her perfect for dealing with grieving families. Even her voice was soothing. "Has he started the autopsy yet?"

"I was wondering when you guys would show up. Dr. Locking told me to send you right down as soon as you got here."

"Thank you, ma'am," Matt said, flashing that grin that made every woman's day. We rode the elevator down to the basement and entered through the steel doors into the exam room. It was a large room with a metal sink, several filing cabinets and very bright florescent lights. In the center on the exam table, Cassie Garrison's body lay beneath a white hospital sheet. With the blood and flies gone, the large wound on her throat was even more apparent. Blank eyes stared up at nothing. The Doc was just wrapping up the autopsy.

Dr. Locking was to one side of the body. He was using a magnifying glass to look more carefully at the dead girl's throat. We stood, quietly watching, until he noticed us. As soon as he heard the click of our shoes, he looked up. "I was a little ahead of schedule and wanted to get this done for you and her family as soon as I could." He explained, because normally we would see the whole autopsy.

I was fine coming in at the tail end. "It looks like she died three nights ago," Dr. Locking noted. He had pushed the button to stop the Dictaphone he was making official notes on, then continued off record: "Her last meal appears to have been a tuna sandwich."

The cause of death was what we thought. Her throat was slit with what looked to be a 10-inch blade. She bled out. While she was dying, she tried to crawl to the door of her apartment. "See these rug burns on her hands?" Dr. Locking turned one of her small slim hands palms up. Looking at the rug burns and realizing what this poor girl did to try to save herself, made me sick to my stomach. I couldn't help but turn away.

"So you're saying, as she was dying, she was trying to escape?"

"Yes, I'm afraid so. It looks like whoever did this must have carried her back to her room and put her on her bed."

"You have to be kidding me. Either this was personal, or our killer is one sick person." Matt was visibly upset.

"Not only that, the creep didn't just put her on the bed, she was tucked in." I couldn't keep my voice from rising as I spoke. Thinking about this poor girl's last moments was overwhelming. Matt sensed my emotions and put a calming hand on my shoulder. His gesture of kindness and understanding helped.

He pondered the theory and said, "That does make sense. I think the tucking in proves it was personal. If the killer didn't know her, he wouldn't have done that. I'm assuming it was a *he*."

Dr. Locking looked at us. "I did find that odd, too. There are no other surprises to report," he continued. "She looks pretty healthy; and from what I can tell, there were no drugs or alcohol in her system." He sighed. "I wish I had better news on the DNA front. I found no foreign DNA on her body. I realize that won't help you find the person who did this. With all that blood, it's pretty surprising there isn't anything foreign under her nails or left on her anywhere. Whoever did this was extremely cautious and obviously was wearing gloves," Locking observed. "Hopefully, the crime scene team can help you fill in more pieces to the puzzle. Fibers or hairs. Something."

As we were getting ready to leave, he asked, "When is the family coming in?" One of the most difficult jobs for a Medical Examiner is to show loved ones a body. It's a tough but necessary task in identifying the victim.

"We're on our way to pick them up from the airport now," Matt said.

"Good. I'll be here until six or so if you need me." We assured him we would call with a heads up on our arrival time, and thanked him, leaving him to finish his work, walking silently back down the hallway toward the elevator.

Chapter Twelve

Traffic was the same mess it always is during LA rush hour. We made our way back with the Garrisons from LAX at a snail's pace. Cassie's parents still appeared to be in shock, and were weary from lack of sleep and the flight from Kansas. Cassie's mother had the same blond hair as her daughter, although hers was sprinkled with grey. Cassie's smile was inherited from her father.

Despite losing their only child in such a horrific way, the Garrisons handled the procedural tasks with grace and dignity. They made it clear from the moment we met them that they were willing to do whatever they could to help. They were counting on us to find their daughter's killer.

"So what do we do?" Mrs. Garrison asked from the back seat.

Matt turned to look back at her from the front . "First, we'll go to the Medical Examiner's office and have you identify her body. Once that's complete, we can help you get settled into your hotel. If you want, we can have some dinner brought in. An officer will have your rental car brought to you, as well," Matt assured them.

"When can we go to her apartment and start…start…" Her mother tried to ask. We knew what she meant. The crime scene team had done their best to work quickly so Cassie's parents could have access as soon as possible. Matt and I had decided to conduct our interview on the hour-plus drive back from the airport. That wasn't everyone's method; however, we found from experience that, once a family identified a body, their emotional and physical energy quickly drained. In that state of mind, it would be hard for us to ask questions - and even harder for them to answer.

I turned on my blinker as I made a right turn onto the freeway ramp, while Matt began asking the hard questions. "What was Cassie like? We like to get to know the victims. It sometimes helps us solve the case."

"She was so sweet," Mrs. Garrison replied. "She was one of those kids, even from an early age, that you just knew had a tender heart. She was very popular. She had a lot of friends in Kansas. We were all so sad to see her move. My husband even tried to talk her out of it." Matt looked to Mr. Garrison.

"I did because, well, it's hard to let your little girl go off on her own, especially to a big city like Los Angeles. She didn't know anyone and was going to have to start over. I guess when you're twenty-two, that's not too big of a deal."

"Right," his wife continued. "The acting bug bit her early. She was always performing in dramas and plays. Her teachers said she was very talented." Mrs. Garrison laughed shakily. "And once she started going to the movies, that was it. It was like a switch was flipped. She told me, 'Mom, that's what I want to do someday… be in the movies.' At the time, we just smiled and nodded. We didn't realize how determined she would be. We were so proud of her. It took courage to pursue her dreams."

"That is admirable," Matt noted. "How often were you in contact with her?"

"At least once a week, often more than that. She really missed us and home, though. As a mother and daughter, we were close. She was close to her dad, too."

"That's nice to hear," I said as I glanced at her in the rearview mirror."

The traffic was down to one lane, due to an accident. I tried not to groan out loud. Instead, I concentrated on the road and continued to listen to the information Mike and Cindy were providing.

.   "What was her life like out here?"

Mrs. Garrison broke into a faint smile. "Even though she missed us, she did love it here. She had her friends from the diner, a cute apartment, and went to lots of auditions. She took some acting classes, too. I think the teacher's name was Marco. I don't know his last name."

"   "Did she say anything about Marco?"

"Oh, just that he was hard driving but gave out sincere praise when she deserved it." She paused in thought, before adding, "One thing that was odd, now that I think about it is she told us her teacher wrote a script he wanted her to star in. It was about a serial killer who commits the perfect murder. It sounds so ironic to say that now."

Matt nodded encouragingly.

"She was never into gory stuff. Scary movies really did scare her. So when he asked her to read some of the most frightening scenes, she had a tough time agreeing."

33

Mr. Garrison interrupted, "She was really uncomfortable doing that."

"So naturally as a mother, it made me uncomfortable as well. Cassie reassured us that's just how show business is. It really broke my heart".

"I can see why," I said.

We finally pulled up to the Medical Examiner's office and escorted the Garrisons into the real-life nightmare Matt and I knew they would never forget.

Chapter Thirteen

Cassie's body lay on the gurney. Her hair was brushed, the blood had been cleaned up, and the fatal wound was hidden by the sheet tucked tight under her chin. It almost looked as though she was sleeping. Her parents stood in the doorway, at first not wanting to look. Finally, they let their eyes turn toward their daughter. They clung tightly to each other. No words were spoken. There were just deep sobs of recognition and horror, sounds all too familiar to Matt and me—nevertheless, always heartbreaking to experience.

The dead girl's mother stepped forward and laid her palm on Cassie's cold cheek. Softly, she stroked her daughter's hair. She was shaking so badly, Matt stood behind her, ready to catch her if she fell. She took several deep breaths, trying to speak. No words came.

Her father simply moaned and put his head in his hands. Then he too stepped forward and knelt by the head of the gurney. He stroked his daughter's cheek and gently kissed her forehead. After some time had passed, the couple turned to one another and stepped away. Mrs. Garrison fell into her husband's embrace and sobbed uncontrollably.

Despite their deep grief, there were questions we had to ask for the record. Doing that felt like we were invading a very private moment. We waited for several more minutes to pass, giving the grieving parents as much space and time as they needed. We stood as far back as possible while they said their final words to their child. Matt folded his hands in prayer for a brief moment before he asked, "Can you tell us, for the record: is this your daughter?"

"Cassie, my sweet baby girl," her mother cooed.

All her father could say was, "Yes". Mr. Garrison turned his face from us and put his head in his hands once again.

"She was our only child," Mrs. Garrison wailed.

Then, the most surprising thing happened. They stepped forward again in unison and invited us and the doctors to stand with them. They laid their hands on their daughter and for about ten minutes prayed over her lifeless form. Matt and Dr. Locking joined in and prayed for her, and for the Garrisons as well. Never had I seen anything like it before. Even though I didn't know what to do, I can say it was both heartbreaking and powerful to witness. It was quite some time before any of us moved.

Ultimately, the Medical Examiner nodded for the attendant to roll the gurney away.

We all went into a comfortable room where everyone could sit down. Once settled, Cassie's mother wanted to know when they could take her home. The look of shock on her face told me that she still couldn't believe she was here or what she had just witnessed. Dr. Locking looked sympathetically at her.

"In the next day or so we can have her transported to a funeral home while you make arrangements."

"We will be taking her home to Kansas, to give her a proper Christian burial."

"We can help with that," he said. The doctor gave them several brochures for local funeral homes to look through.

Cassie's father spoke in a gruff voice, wracked with grief: "We would like to have a memorial service here before we go. Would all of you please come?"

"We would be honored," I replied.

Even the Medical Examiner was invited and agreed to attend if he could. He didn't normally do things like that, but this murder had become personal for all of us. It was standard for detectives to attend, out of consideration, respect—and observation. Maybe the killer would be there, and give himself away. It was more common than most people knew.

"Do you have any other questions for me?" Dr. Locking asked.

"No, sir. Thank you for taking such great care of our baby," Cassie's father said. Mrs. Garrison's voice broke into my thoughts.

"Please detectives," she begged before leaving, "Find the monster who did this. Please find him."

"We will do our very best," Matt said. "You can be sure of that."

Chapter Fourteen

Once the Garrisons were settled, Matt and I decided to have a planning session. The best way to do that was over food. Let's face it, a lot of things get accomplished over a good meal. My mouth was almost watering waiting in line at one of the best taco trucks in Los Angeles. We sat on a park bench. The crunchy tacos were fiery hot, just the way I liked them. Matt ate a huge burrito with everything in it. When I say everything, I mean it literally: everything but the kitchen sink.

"You can't mess up a burrito," Matt mumbled, mouth full of food, some of it dripping onto his chin. I laughed.

"Glad you're enjoying yourself, even if this is the second Mexican food truck we've been to today."

It was my turn to treat. I loved that. Generosity has always mattered to me. It's a core value I grew up with. I was lucky. I not only had a great partner but a great friend, too. We have always enjoyed being around one another and spending time together.

Matt's voice broke through my thoughts. "The first thing I want to do, Emma, is interview this acting teacher."

"Fine, but my question to you is - do you really think he is a person of interest?"

"Probably not; but over my five years being a cop, nothing surprises me. Remember that bird case from last year?"

I nodded. Last year exotic birds were being kidnapped from an animal sanctuary. The group who took the valuable animals claimed they should be set free and that certain species did not need to be protected. The situation grew more hostile by the day. After a while, the wildlife group had to bring in security. Sadly, one guard was killed during a kidnapping. The murderer ended up being a 68-year-old woman.

"We really we didn't see that one coming," Matt lamented before diving back into his burrito.

"Nobody did," I sighed. ""I'm hoping the crime report will come back tomorrow and that it will give us a starting point."

"Let's follow up on that tomorrow. Oh, yeah, and Captain Mendoza wants to meet with us to see where we are." I wished we had more to report. The info we had gathered was helpful as background only.

Once the conversation about the case dwindled down, I realized, to my surprise, that I wanted to ask Matt more about his faith. I still felt inadequate to discuss it. I wanted to know more, but I wasn't sure I wanted to embrace it. I'm doing just fine on my own, I thought. Still, I couldn't shake the feeling that it did matter.

"Matt…did you always believe in God?" I blurted. He turned to me with a surprised but pleasant look on his face. Then he picked up our trash and walked toward the large black dumpster. He slid his arm in mine and we began to walk.

"No," he answered. "For a while, I was just living my life on my own terms. I've always thought of myself as successful. I think, before I met Him, I attributed all of it to good parents and healthy self-esteem. I loved my life. Yet I always felt like there was something missing. I don't know how else to explain it. Until a certain moment happened, I honestly didn't give Him much thought."

I was surprised by his answer. In that moment, I felt understood. He didn't know it; but that's kind of how I had been feeling lately. I wanted to hear more, so I asked, "So… what changed your mind?"

We crossed the park. It was a big park - with a swing set, jungle gym, slides and a basketball court. There was also a walking trail, which is why we like it there. We began to stroll down the path toward the forest. Matt cleared his throat and proceeded.

"One day, we all found out my mom had breast cancer. Nothing like that had ever happened in our family. We were all healthy and happy. Then, one day, our lives changed forever. I think what it was for me was she always had such strong faith. That's what carried her through the treatments. Instead of feeling sorry for herself, she stayed joyful. My dad did, too. It was like their faith was their anchor in a storm of uncertainty. Both of them said they didn't blame God, because they knew he loved them and would never cause them unnecessary pain. They knew he would carry them through the tough journey. They were so certain of it."

Matt became reflective. "I thought, if anyone had the right to feel sorry for themselves, my mom did. It just made me stop and think about why she was reacting the way she was. Her great strength inspired me to seek more. One day while I was at chemo with her, she had this weak voice…"

He stopped, speaking now almost to himself. "…because she really didn't have the strength to talk. So I knew whatever she was trying to say was important. I leaned close to her bed; and she asked me to come to church with them. How could I say no to her? I guess I went more for her in the beginning."

The sun was setting, and it was starting to cool down. I took a deep breath, inhaling the fragrance of the trees. Matt continued.

"One Sunday, the sermon was on this verse in the Bible from the Book of Romans." He caught my look of irritation and embarrassment for not knowing what he was talking about. I had never opened a Bible in my life. I wasn't planning on it either.

"Romans V says we rejoice in our suffering, that suffering produces endurance, endurance produces character, and character produces hope. It was like that message was all about my mom. I realized that's what she was doing. That's what her great suffering was about. It gave it meaning for me. So when the pastor asked if anyone wanted to have that kind of help in the midst of their suffering, I realized I wanted that. Correction - I needed that. I mean, who wouldn't? So I went up to the front of the church and someone prayed with me. I asked the Lord to be my savior. I don't know what happened to be honest. But from that day forward my life was never the same." He stopped and looked around at the trees and then back at me.

"It's so crazy when you think about it. I mean who knew that one decision could make such a difference in a person's life. I certainly didn't."

I stood there in thought, reflecting on what he'd said. He gently tugged me along; and we kept walking. The ground was rough under our feet. We stopped to look at a mother pushing a stroller with two toddlers in tow as they passed by us. "What, Em?"

I sighed, not sure what to make of what had just happened. How could he be so sure it was faith that made him such a good person? Maybe he already was a good person. I didn't want to think about it anymore. So I changed the subject. "How's your mom now?"

"She's been in remission for two years. We're all so thankful. Emma, what do you think of that verse from Romans?"

"I don't really know. I'm really glad she's okay."

Matt smiled and nodded at me, accepting my non-answer. He didn't say anything more about it. He looked at me as he started to walk toward his car. "It's getting late. I'm ready to go home and begin again tomorrow. See you then, Em."

I was startled when I looked at my phone and realized how late it was. He was right. The time had flown by. As I drove home, I realized I hadn't wanted that evening to end. Matt was so sweet. What an amazing guy! Good-looking with an impressive personality, too… He would— *STOP it, Emma*, I told myself. I'd always been against dating someone you work with. That would be awkward.

Chapter Fifteen

June 20th

I hung up the phone and looked over at my partner. The day before, I had left a message for Marco Crane, Cassie's acting teacher. "Marco said we can come by around four p.m. and interview everyone. Class will be in session. That way, we'll have a chance to talk to Cassie's peers and see what they were working on."

I wondered if it was the same script Cassie had been working on. If they were acting out a murder scene, I sure wanted to know how the others felt about it. We had been working most of the morning at our desks on dreaded paperwork and write-ups. As I printed and signed the last page, I had to smile. I guess I could admit there was some value in all the paper, but not much. Writing down my observations and looking at the record helped me gain a mental picture of what we had already done and where we might be heading. For now, however, we had a meeting with Mendoza to attend.

Matt set down the report. I picked it up and scanned it. We were sitting in the Captain's office in a briefing with him looking at the write-up from the crime scene team.

"Not a lot there to work with," our boss observed. "No blood from the killer, no prints, no DNA. It's so ironic, because there was so much of her blood all over."

"Yes," Matt said. "It's pretty rare when you think about it. He must have been very careful. Maybe he wore gloves. That would explain the lack of fingerprints".

I looked up from the report. "What about his clothes? They had to be a mess."

Mendoza bit down hard on his pen in frustration. "Maybe he brought an extra set and changed into them? Oh, that reminds me, Davis and Cameron interviewed the neighbors and had good luck with one woman in the building across the street. She thinks she may have seen someone suspicious entering the Garrison building. They thought you guys might want to hear what she has to say."

Steve Davis and Mike Cameron were two detectives who work in our division. At times, especially at the beginning of a homicide investigation, it was helpful to have more people to divide up the work.

The Captain gave us the information. "How did the interviews go yesterday?"

"Good, but mostly background so far, what you might expect at this point," Matt replied. "Her parents came and identified the body. Gave us a sense of who she was. They seem like such nice people."

"Such a tragedy that this happened to them. She was their only child," I added.

Matt continued to explain. "From what everyone said, it doesn't look like she had any enemies."

I had to agree. "It's like someone committed the perfect murder. Even though that is pretty hard to do when you slit someone's throat."

"There really isn't a lot of evidence, is there?" the captain queried. "What's your plan for today, besides interviewing the person across the street?"

"Emma was able to get in touch with Cassie's acting teacher. Guy named Marco Crane. He's offered to let us come by today and interview everyone on site. He says he wants to be helpful. We have questions, especially since Cassie was working on a scene where a murder is committed. The scene pretty much matches what happened to Miss Garrison. That's quite a coincidence, don't you think? Maybe it won't lead anywhere; but we sure as heck need to check it out."

The captain raised his eyebrows and chimed, "That would be pretty ironic."

Chapter Sixteen

Ramona Grey opened the door to her apartment. I looked at the short woman with graying hair. She had pale skin and light blue eyes that looked our way in welcome. She smiled a tight smile. "Come on in," she offered.

"Thanks for seeing us, Mrs. Grey. I'm Emma Blade. This is my partner, Matt Parker."

The woman led us into a well-decorated living room. We sat on the couch, while she took the recliner across from us. "Can I get you something to drink? I have some coffee already made."

"If it's not any trouble and you're having some, too, that would be great," I said. Matt and I both accepted, grateful for the java pick-me-up.

A few minutes later, she brought three mugs and a hot pot of coffee. I picked up my cup and took a sip. "So much better than what we have at the station," Matt said. I laughed.

"He's right. Thank you." After taking another couple of sips, I asked how long she had lived across the street from Cassie.

"I've had this apartment for the past nine years. I love this place."

"Did you ever meet Cassie?"

"No, but I saw her a few times coming and going. We nodded and smiled 'hello' at each other whenever our paths crossed. You know, the neighborly thing to do. She seemed very nice. Always had a smile. What a tragedy."

"Can you tell us what you saw?"

"Several nights ago I couldn't sleep. I have a great view of Los Angeles from my window here." She stood up and walked over to a large window just beyond the television. The view was spectacular, even in the daytime.

I stared in wonder as I stood next to her. Sure enough, she had an unobstructed view of Cassie Garrison's front door and the courtyard beyond. Her apartment was high up, making her view panoramic and breathtaking.

Mrs. Grey continued. "It was around two a.m. I'm a writer and I was taking a break. I checked the clock; that's how I knew the time. A black car - I'm not sure what kind - pulled up and parked. Someone –

I'm pretty sure it was a man - walked to her apartment building. When he got to her apartment, he pulled out a key and let himself in."

"Was that unusual?" Matt asked.

"Well, he kept looking over his shoulder, like he was checking to see if anyone was watching. I guess that in itself doesn't matter all that much. It's just that, before he pulled out the key, I saw him slip on a pair of gloves of some kind. I thought at the time that was odd behavior. Of course, I had no idea what was to come."

That would explain why there were no fingerprints found on the door. He had a key, I thought.

Mrs. Grey continued, "That apartment building only has five units. I also saw something shiny sticking out of his pocket. I couldn't tell what it was, but it was silver in color. Now I wonder if it wasn't a knife. It was dark and too hard to tell for sure."

A questioning expression came over her. "It wasn't cold outside. I don't know… It just seemed suspicious, or at least unusual, to need gloves in this summer heat."

She crossed her arms with a thoughtful expression. "Don't you think so? That it was suspicious, I mean?"

We shrugged. Mrs. Grey was giving us a combination of facts mixed in with opinion based on what she had read and heard. It was important for us to sift through and stick to the facts. The killer would only be caught and convicted based on what we could prove—not what we thought.

"Could you identify the man if you saw him again?"

She shook her head regretfully. "I only saw his back. I never saw his face. He was average height and dressed all in black."

I set my empty cup on the coffee table. "Mrs. Grey, is there anything else you would like to tell us?"

She stopped to think for a moment and then said, "No, Detective. I just hope you catch whoever did this. I know I'll feel a whole lot safer once you do."

44

Chapter Seventeen

Lindsay Jones crossed the street. With a latte in hand she felt ready to continue with her day. To her it never seemed like there was enough time. If only there could be forty-eight hours in a day instead of twenty-four, she mused. Maybe that would be her superpower if she could choose one—that, and a whole lot more energy. She laughed to herself. Oh, to be so young and need so much caffeine just to get through the day. After class, she would be going back to her job. This was her toughest day of the week, because she worked a split shift, so there really wasn't a break.. Was it difficult? Yes, but rewarding.

"No wonder I need the caffeine," she muttered. "But that's living in Los Angeles for you." She worked hard and tried her best to afford everything she needed—and a little of what she wanted.

She walked into her acting class. Lindsay had worked on her scene, practicing it over and over again. She hoped she kept getting better. The class was like a community. She knew everyone; everyone knew her. As she took her seat, she glanced two seats down to where a chair sat empty. That was Cassie's spot. She'd always sat there. A lump formed in Lindsay's throat and tears filled her eyes. *How could this happen to someone so sweet?* she wondered. She'd never known anyone who had been murdered before. She wondered if she should have come back to class so soon after her friend was killed. Would she even be able to concentrate? Lindsay Jones wasn't sure, she was about to find out. The looks on the faces of her friends in the class revealed they were thinking the same thing.

Marco, their teacher, stood in front of them. "Thanks for coming, everyone," he said. "I know this is hard for you. I know, because it's hard for me, too. We will do our scenes as best we can, given the circumstances. I'm sure Cassie would want that, don't you think?" he asked the room. Nods from everyone gave him the answer he knew he would get.

"In the meantime, the police will be asking questions when you are not working on your scene. Please take time to talk with them. Cassie was important to our class. She had such talent. It's just a tragedy what happened." Everyone took a moment of silence in memory of their friend.

Marco looked in Lindsay's direction. "Lindsay, let's see what you have." She stood up and walked toward the front of the class onto the stage.

Matt and I sat in the back. We watched the scene unfold. Even though Crane's words were nice, the insincerity of them hit me. A pretty, young, blond woman slowly walked onstage. "What was her name again?" Matt nudged me, getting my attention.

"Lindsay Jones," I whispered, slightly irritated that he even needed to ask. Wasn't he paying attention when her teacher had just said it? I turned back to the stage as we both watched her. The scene played out. She walked inside her apartment. She put her keys and purse down on the counter. She made a tuna sandwich for dinner. After that, she sat down with a book. The narrator read: "... for about an hour or two. She grows tired and gets ready for bed. As soon as her head hits the pillow, she's out like a light. A little while later, there can be heard the sound of a door unlocking."

Marco continued narrating. "... but Lindsay doesn't hear it because she is sleeping so soundly."

All of a sudden Marco stood over Lindsay, holding a plastic knife. Her eyes flew open. A moment of shock hit her. As he pretended to act out wounding her, the actress let out a piercing scream.

"And cut." Marco's voice boomed through the theater. "Great job, Lindsay." He looked almost gleeful as he spoke. *What a sick guy*, I thought. "You really have improved."

Lindsay headed back to her seat. She was the first person we wanted to talk to. We made our way to her and motioned for her to follow us.

Chapter Eighteen

"Wow," Matt said. "You are talented."

The blonde-haired young woman who sat across from us smiled shyly. "Thank you. I work hard at it."

"It shows. I'm Detective Matt Parker. This is my partner, Detective Emma Blade. Thanks for talking with us."

"Whatever I can do to help."

I pulled out my iPad, ready to take notes.

"I can't believe Cassie is gone. It still isn't real for me."

"I can imagine," Matt said compassionately. "How did it feel to work on that scene, Lindsay?"

She shrugged. "I don't want to speak badly of Marco; but… it was kind of awkward. If you know what I mean." That was a nice way of putting it, I sarcastically thought.

My attention turned back to our interviewee when she said, "I felt almost like it was real. There was this look in his eyes when he stood over me with that fake knife, almost a look of pleasure. Maybe I'm imagining that. I guess what I'm saying is, it creeped me out."

"Understandable. Did Cassie ever act that same scene out?"

She nodded and replied. "We all did actually".

"Do you know how it made her or anyone else feel?" my partner asked gently.

"None of us ever talked about it; but you could see how uncomfortable it made Cassie just by the look on her face." Then it hit her. "Do you thinkkkkk?" she stammered, nearly jumping out of her seat.

Matt put a firm hand on her shoulder. "I don't think anything, because I don't know anything yet. I'm not jumping to any conclusions right now. We're just trying to get a sense of things. Marco is someone we will talk to later."

Lindsay began to cry. "After what happened to Cassie, I don't think I can come back here anymore. I'm not even sure why I did today."

"Other than the specific scene, was there anything else about Marco that made you feel uncomfortable?"

"Sometimes I caught him staring at me. I just thought it was harmless, maybe a little weird. He never acted on it or hit on me during class."

"Where are you from, Ms. Jones.?"

"I was born and raised in Southern California. My family is still here. I work as a waitress at a diner close by. Truthfully, I have to work hard and hope for good tips to afford this class."

"How much is it?" She sighed.

"About $150 a month for one class a week." We exchanged glances. With twenty students, Marco is doing pretty well for himself.

As if reading our minds, Lindsay said, "He teaches several classes, I think. He really is a talented teacher. He's one of the best in Hollywood."

Matt glanced at me, silently asking if I had anything to add. I shook my head.

Suddenly a look of fear and concern came over Lindsay. "Um," she said. "Do you think I'm safe?" '

'Why would you ask that?" Matt said.

"No reason. I just feel scared, I guess."

"We have no reason to think anyone is in danger. But be watchful and alert. Feel free to contact us anytime if you have any concerns," he said. "One last question: do you know anyone who would want to hurt Cassie? What I mean is, did she have any enemies that you knew of, or did she mention anything to you that might help us?" The frightened young woman gave a helpless shrug.

"No one I can think of. Everyone loved her. We were in class together for six months. Her parents posted on her Facebook page that they would hold a memorial service here in LA for her friends and coworkers tomorrow. It will be tough; but I'm glad to go."

"Then we'll see you there, Lindsay. Thanks so much for your time and help."

We all stood. She shook our hands. As with all the others we'd interviewed, we gave her our cards. "If you think of or need anything, day or night, give us a call, okay?" I said. I wanted her to feel safe.

Chapter Nineteen

The rest of the afternoon and evening went by quickly. We interviewed several more of Cassie's peers: one Scott Hall, a Lisa Brooks, and other actors in the studio. No one had anything else to add. Cassie was very well-liked. And clearly everyone was shaken by her murder. We had interviewed a total of eleven fellow students. Our brains were fried. We needed a break. At the moment we were taking a mini one.

Matt paced the small room. So far, we had nothing. "Emma, did anyone or anything jump out at you from those interviews that seemed suspicious?"

"Nothing, Matt. And that's so frustrating. I thought we would get more info than what we got. We still have one more interview left, though. Marco Crane."

I stood up and stretched, took several sips of water, and sat back down. I reviewed my notes, just in case we had missed something.

"This is a world I don't know much about," Matt observed.

"Yeah, like who knew everyone would do the same scene," I said.

"And don't people usually do scenes from movies or shows or plays or something like that?" I shrugged and then laughed out loud.

"As if I would know."

"Ok, let's say my guess is right. What does that tell us about this teacher?" We were about to find out.

.

Chapter Twenty

Marco Crane stood at six feet tall. His shoulder-length brown hair was tied back in a ponytail, revealing a long face. His hazel eyes were piercing as he stared directly into mine. "Detectives, nice to meet you in person. Tragic under these circumstances, though."

Matt nodded for me to take the lead as he took out his iPad to take notes. More often than not, he did the questioning; however, we decided that Marco might give more away if a woman did the asking.

"Yes, it is very tragic. Thanks for meeting with us," I said in a flat, expressionless tone. I thought he was one of those interviewees who could gauge reactions. I wanted to give him nothing. "What can you tell us about Cassie?"

"She was a very talented, very pretty girl. She was like everyone else who moved to LA with big dreams and a long road to get there."

"How long had she been taking classes from you?"

"Hmm, about six months. I do these free workshops as a way to let actors know who I am and how I teach. Cassie signed up."

"How many classes do you teach a week?" I asked.

"Three per week, with up to twenty students in each."

"Where did Cassie move from?"

"Kansas." He said this in a condescending tone. "Surely you must know that?"

His sarcasm wasn't lost on me. It was like watching someone change on a dime. The condescension dripped off of him.

"If you don't know that, then… I hate to say it… but you're probably not very good at your job.

Let's be honest, he didn't "hate to say it" at all. I'd always had a temper. I had to count to ten and take a sip from my bottle of water before I went on. And still, my tone turned a little sharp.

"Yes, we notified her parents yesterday." I was done being nice. "Mr. Crane, when was the last time you saw Cassie Garrison?"

He turned to Matt. "I don't want to deal with *her*. Clearly you have an incompetent partner. Am I a suspect or something? Why would I need to answer that question? Isn't it obvious when the last time I saw her was? At our last class."

Matt was always so calm. His steadiness helped in this case. "Sir", he said in a professional manner. "We are doing the best we can. I can assure you that both detective Blade and I are competent officers. If you have a complaint about something, I'll be happy to give you our Captain's number. If not, let's go on, shall we?"

Marco stared hard at Matt and my partner stared right back. Marco blinked first. In a confident voice Matt said, "This is just the beginning of the investigation. Everyone is a person of interest at this stage."

Marco turned toward me, looking embarrassed. "Oh. Sorry," he murmured. "This has all just been so difficult on everyone. Cassie is the fourth student to die in the last couple of years in our community. So naturally, I'm on edge."

Did he just say the fourth to die? Matt and I were on the same page and exchanged startled glances. This was the first we had heard of it. I looked into Marco's eyes, trying to read him, and continued with the interview. "It's fine, Mr. Crane. I understand. What do you mean when you say Cassie was the fourth person to die in your community?"

"Well, first there was Sally Haze. She was murdered three years ago. Come to think of it, her throat was slit like Cassie's. The police never solved the case; it went cold. The second was CC Garden. She died about nine months after that. Police said she died of a suicide. She hung herself. But I think, if I remember correctly, it looked suspicious. I can't remember. The third was Mini Loash. She was poisoned."

Why, I wondered angrily, *hadn't anyone connected the dots until now?* Matt's confused expression mirrored my own. I knew that he was wondering the same thing. I went on. "This is very helpful, Mr. Crane. Do you know if there were any similarities in the girls who died?" He paused in thought.

"I guess one thing was weird. They all had blonde hair. They all looked like Barbie dolls. They were so beautiful."

"Were they all in your classes?"

"Oh, no, ma'am, only CC and Cassie. I just heard about the other stories on the news; and just now something clicked in my head. That's why I'm telling you, I guess. I never met Sally or Mini."

I turned to look at Matt, who pointed down at the iPad indicating a question. I read it and continued. "We've heard from several of your students that you are writing a screenplay about the perfect murder. What's that all about?"

Marco looked surprised and a little flustered. "Who told you that?" he demanded. We didn't answer and just let him thunder on. "It's not relevant to this case. I can assure you of that."

This guy was hard to figure out. One minute, he was kind and funny, the next, he was angry and hostile. "Maybe not, sir, but we'd like to read it as soon as possible," I said in a calm voice.

Before I was finished asking, he was already shaking his head. "Sorry, that's not an option. No-one can read my work before it's ready. I can't let you do that."

"Why not?" I persisted.

"Because it's not finished yet. I don't want to just hand it over before it becomes something."

I gave an exasperated sigh. "Mr. Crane. First, we're not proofreading it. Second, we're not interested in stealing your work or revealing the contents. Third, and most importantly, this is a murder investigation. It might be helpful. We would appreciate your help in solving this murder."

"No, sorry. No way," he repeated, this time more forcefully." At that, he abruptly stood up.

"If you have more questions, here's my lawyer's business card. And since I'm not under arrest, I'm leaving. I suggest you do the same. I have been more than accommodating. And this is what I get in return? Nice meeting you." Then he strode out of his own office.

For a few tense seconds, Matt and I just sat there in shock. Then, I stood and started packing up our things.

"Well, there's someone with nothing to hide," Matt said sarcastically. I laughed and picked up the business card in front of me.

"He has a good lawyer from an expensive firm. I'm not sure we'll get access to that script," I said with a sigh.

Matt stood up. It was after nine p.m. by then. And now we had more questions than answers. One thing was certain: Marco Crane was someone we would be looking into very thoroughly. "There was something really spooky about how fast he changed. Know what I mean?" I queried, as we walked out the front door.

"My guess is, he's a good actor," Matt said dryly. I laughed again.

As we got into the squad car and prepared to leave, I glanced back at the front doors of the acting school and saw Marco Crane peering at us. When he noticed me, he darted away. *Spooky indeed*, I thought as we headed back to the station.

Chapter Twenty-One

Once they got back to the station, Matt and Emma went their separate ways. He made sure she got into her car and watched her drive away before climbing into his and starting the engine. He thought about all that had happened in such a short amount of time. Four young women had been murdered in Hollywood over the past few years. Could it be that they were just beginning to connect the dots now? He couldn't help but wonder if there was anything to connect, though. Sadly, murders happened every day. So did suicides. It was a leap he was not ready to make. There was so much work that needed to be done. *Connection?*, he thought as he drove. He was glad he had a top-notch boss and team to work with. They would need the help of everyone in the homicide division.

The night was muggy and only slowly cooling down. He flipped the switch and turned on his air conditioner. The cool air finally hit his face. He needed a new car. His was one of those where it took time to get the AC to a working temperature. He tried to keep his thoughts focused on the case, but they kept straying to Emma. In the two years he had known her; she had never asked him about his faith before. If he said something in passing, she would politely listen before changing the subject. Right away he knew it was something he had to slowly ease into with her. It wasn't a comfortable subject for her. That much was obvious. So it had taken him by surprise when she questioned him when they were at dinner, and then again in the park. He had wanted to mention it but wasn't sure the time was right. Emma was cautious, not easily convinced of things. He knew how much the Father loved her and how he wanted a relationship with her. He knew how much she needed more than just her human strength. Sometimes, the weight of the job shone through her eyes. He worried about that.

Emma was beautiful inside and out. No-one at the station understood why or how she was still single. Matt liked her very much. He wondered how else he could reach her. He did pray for her regularly, mostly to ask God to keep them safe and for help solving cases. He knew for certain that his job was to be there for her, to be present in her moments of need. The gospel said to go and proclaim the kingdom. *I guess there are different ways to proclaim it*, he thought. It was his job to share the message of Christ with those around him in ways they would receive it, without making them feel uncomfortable. That wasn't always easy. He was sure he made some mistakes. Who hadn't, though? At least he was trying.

As he entered his condo, exhaustion fell upon him. Tomorrow would come soon enough. Right now, sleep was calling his name.

Chapter Twenty-Two

June 21st

At approximately midnight, Lindsay Jones drove home after a long day of work at the diner. She was beat. She was normally a hostess; but tonight they'd been short, so she'd pulled double duty as both hostess and server. That was a lot of running around and taking customers' food and drink orders. She felt her eyes drooping slightly. She shook her head to wake herself up. The last thing she wanted to do was fall asleep while driving. At least she didn't have a long way to go.

The worship songs that filled her car brought a feeling she couldn't describe. They were an anchor for her. She thought about the detectives working Cassie's case. A pretty blonde like herself and a tall good-looking guy. It was nice they told her to call if she needed anything. She wasn't sure if she had anything to add, but she'd think about it. Who would want to hurt her friend? Tears filled her eyes. She blinked them back so she could see the road ahead.

God," she prayed aloud. "I am so thankful for you. You give me great peace. I couldn't have survived this horror without you. No matter what, I know who you are and who I am in you." That simple prayer gave her such security in the face of everything that had happened. Cassie's horrible death, long hours, and pursuing her dreams. It wasn't easy. She didn't know how she managed. But with Him she could handle anything. Little did she know how true that statement was.

Chapter Twenty-Three

The killer put the vial back in his pocket. He looked around the small kitchen. A toaster, coffee maker and microwave sat on the countertop. Just a drop of it would be enough. He opened her fridge and took out the jug of water. As he unscrewed the cap, he thought of her. His plan was almost complete. He was so good. No one even suspected. The police were so clueless. He should give himself credit, he thought. He laughed as he thought about detectives Blade and Parker. They would never catch on. "Stupid cops," he muttered, smiling wickedly.

It was time to go. He closed her fridge. As he did, a bunch of menus, along with the magnets that held them, fell from the stainless-steel surface. That was not in his plan. He had no time left. He grabbed a few of the menus and quickly put them under some magnets left on the fridge. Perhaps she wouldn't notice. To him, it looked like they just fell accidentally. It was too bad he couldn't watch, he thought. Oh, how he wanted to. Too risky, he decided. He opened her door and slipped out. His job here was done.

Chapter Twenty-Four

Lindsay turned off her car and got out. She was smiling and singing as she walked into her apartment. *Home sweet home*, she thought. It was small, but it was hers. She was proud of that. She plugged her phone into the charger, right next to the toaster, microwave and coffee maker on the kitchen counter. She straightened and walked to the fridge. Suddenly her foot crunched something. She looked down. Several menus and magnets were on the floor. *How did that happen?* she wondered. She was such a neat person. She wouldn't just leave it like that. Maybe she forgot. Her mind recalled how she had left so early yesterday. Her paranoia made her laugh. She wondered what was spooking her.. No matter. She was too tired to deal with it tonight. Being careful not to step on the debris, she leaned forward and opened the fridge. Then she pulled out the half-full, gallon-sized bottle of water that was left from yesterday morning and grabbed a glass from the cabinet. She disliked wasting food or water and was glad to have a cold drink on a hot evening.

The large bottle felt cool in her hand. She put it against her cheek and then poured some into her glass. She didn't want to step on the menus still littering the ground, so she put the bottle on the counter. She turned and walked to her living room. She plopped down on her couch. It had been a very long day. Despite that, she was not ready for bed just yet. She took her bible from the end table and began where she had last left off: "For I know the plans I have for you, says the Lord, plans not to harm you, but to give you a future full of hope." Yes, it was a verse she heard often at church. Somehow, the words of Jeremiah brought her even more comfort in the midst of murder and the roller coaster of her emotions. She put the glass to her lips.

STOP!

Her head jerked to the right. *What was that?* she wondered. It sounded like a voice. But no one was there except for her. A chill came over her. The air was hot, yet she felt cold. She looked at the glass in her hand. She put it to her lips again, ready to take a drink on this hot summer night.

STOP! DON'T DRINK THAT.

The voice sounded so real. She knew Jesus. She knew his guiding voice. It caused her to pause and look again at the glass in her hands. That's when she saw it - tiny bits of powder dissolving at the bottom. What was that? Her heart started hammering in her chest. She wanted to throw the cup across the room or in the trash. She wanted whatever it was away from her NOW. Instead, she slowly placed it on the coffee table. Something told her to keep everything. Without knowing why, she decided to listen. For a long moment, she just stared at the water, unsure of what to do. After a little time had passed, she got her answer. She stood on shaking legs and made her way to the kitchen, picked up her cell phone, and dialed. A sense of dread filled her.

"911. How may I help you?" A woman's calm voice came over the line.

"I… I…It's an emergency."

"What's the emergency, please?" Lindsay almost hung up her phone. How could she explain this?

"Hello, sweetheart, please let me help you." Somehow, the dispatcher's kindness eased her fear. She started to cry. She thought about the police she had met that afternoon. They would understand.

"There's something in my water. I think someone's been in my apartment. I need detectives Parker and Blade."

"What do you mean something is in your water? What's in it? Did you drink any of it?"

"I'm not sure. Wait. No, I didn't drink any of it. I was going to… I…". Her voice cracked as Lindsay realized how serious the situation was. Hot tears slid down her face.

"They're not here right now, but I can send a car by." The dispatcher spoke evenly.

"No, I want them. Please. I met them this afternoon. They said I could call. Please…" she begged. Then she took a deep breath and continued to explain. "My friend Cassie Garrison was murdered a few days ago. That's why they were talking to me," she said, her voice rising with a mixture of fear and hysteria.

"Just calm down if you can. I'm right here. We will page them and send officers to you immediately. Just stay on the line with me until they get there."

"I'm scared," Lindsay cried.

Chapter Twenty-Five

She felt the blade of the knife against her throat. She couldn't move. Her arms and legs felt like weights. Her breath caught. She heard a shrill sound but didn't know what it was. She wished it would stop. "Help!" she screamed. She grabbed at the bloody knife; her hands were sticky and of no use. The burning made her feel sick as the blade went through her skin...

I woke up with a start. I had to hold my blanket against my mouth to keep from screaming. *Oh, it was only a nightmare. I'm safe now*, I told myself. *Thump, thump, thump,* drummed my heart. I took a few breaths before what I heard registered through the fog of sleep. The phone was ringing. That was the shrill sound from the nightmare. Normally, calls in the middle of the night meant only one thing - an emergency.

Ring...ring...ring...ring...ring... It wouldn't stop. I was in no mood to talk to anyone. I finally leaned over and in a groggy voice, said, "Hello, Blade here."

"Emma, it's Matt. Are you okay? Your phone has been ringing and ringing. Why didn't you answer? You sound, I don't know..." I nodded, but then realized he couldn't see me over the phone. Tears slid down my face. A sob caught in my throat. Just hearing his voice made me feel safe. "Emma, what's going on?"

Taking a deep breath, I answered, "I'm fine. Sorry, just waking up. What's up, Matt?"

"We have an emergency."

I thought, *Emergency... what kind*? My heart started beating fast again. "What's happened?"

"Remember Lindsay Jones, one of the girls we interviewed at the acting studio?"

I had to clear my mind. Meeting Lindsay came back to me quickly. "I do."

"Well she came home about an hour ago. She thought someone had been in her apartment. Then, she opened a bottle of water and found something in it. She called the police. Officers on the scene said it looked like a suspicious substance. Some kind of powder that could have harmed her."

60

I jumped out of bed. "I'll be ready in twenty. Meet you out front." With that, I got off the phone and started getting ready. I pulled on some clothes quickly and slid my toothbrush around in my mouth. I practically pulled out my hair as I raced to get out the tangles from my thick waves. My interrupted and restless sleep had made it resemble a Brillo pad. I glanced at the clock. It read one-thirty a.m. I thought about the girls Marco had mentioned. Didn't he say one was poisoned? A chill ran through me. What if Lindsay was the next victim? I grabbed my keys and ran out the door, taking the steps two at a time. Matt was already there waiting for me.

We sped all the way to Lindsay's address. Matt didn't have more details for me. We drove in silence for a while, drinking the coffee he had purchased at an all-night café. Then Matt turned to me, a worried look on his face. "I really hope," he said, "this is a false alarm."

"That makes two of us. Matt, do you think—?" He cut me off.

"Let's not jump to any conclusions until we get results back from the lab, okay?" I nodded. He was right. Assumptions can lead to poor police work. We pulled up to Lindsay's apartment building.

Ironically, it was five blocks from Cassie's. An officer stood out front waiting to let us in. He let us know he wasn't sure what we had here, if anything. We understood his hesitation but kept walking at a fast clip. The building was a modern high rise. As we walked into the lobby, we could see across to the pool and courtyard. We were led to the elevator and rode it up to the third floor. That short ride felt so long. *?* I thought. I wondered if we could have somehow prevented this. The hammering was loud in my chest. *What would we find inside?*

When we entered her condo, we found Lindsay Jones huddled on her couch. She looked so small and scared. Her eyes were red from crying. "Thanks for coming," she sniffled.

I sat on the couch beside her and placed my hand on her shoulder. "Of course. How are you doing now? Do you need to go to the hospital?" All she could do was shake her head 'no'. The tears came fast. The words she wanted to speak were stuck in her throat.

In situations like that, the best thing to do is just be present. We sat with her for a while in compassionate silence. Matt reached into his bag and took out a bottle of soda, extending it to her. "Even with everything that happened, I figured you were thirsty. Here, take this."

He unscrewed the cap and handed it to her. She drank quickly. The cold drink refreshed her. I looked at the scared young woman beside me.

"Lindsay, where did you go after we interviewed you?" The question took her by surprise. She thought we would just jump right into tonight. We needed to track her movements. Her answers would help create a timeline. Matt took a chair from the dining room and pulled it over to sit near us. "I had to work after class. I think I mentioned I work at a diner not too far from here. It's one of those fifties-style type places. It's a pretty fun place."

"How long have you worked there?"

"About a year, Detective Blade."

"What shift did you work tonight?"

"I got there…" She thought about it as she tried to give us a specific time. "Normally, I work from five to close. I got there around 5:30 and worked until we locked up at midnight."

Matt jumped in. "Was there anything out of the ordinary? Maybe something unusual that happened during your shift? Anything that set off alarm bells in your head?"

"No, I was thinking about that, and I can't think of a thing. Everyone was really nice and gave good tips. I'm a hostess, not a server. Tonight we were short, so I had to do both. I don't think I'm the best server, but it went pretty well."

I had done a little waitressing in college and remembered how hard it was. "Been there; done that. It's not easy. What time did you get home?"

"Around twelve fifteen."

"Was there anything unusual about your drive?"

"No, but I did think someone had been here. In my condo."

"What makes you say that?" Matt asked.

"See those two magnets?" She pointed to two Minnie and Mickey Mouse magnets that held papers on the fridge. "I like to put menus from restaurants clipped under them, since I have so many. When I got home, that's how I found them. They were scattered on the floor just like that." She pointed to the several menus and a couple of magnets on the kitchen floor. "That was the first inkling I had that something was wrong. I'm like a neat freak. I wouldn't do that. Normally I would have cleaned that up, picked up the menus, that sort of thing. I was just so tired when I got home. I thought I would wait until tomorrow." She looked thoughtfully at the mess. "At first, to be honest, I didn't want to listen to that feeling. So I tried not to think too much about it, until I saw some of the other menus hanging crooked on the fridge. That's really not my way."

She was right. We could tell just by looking that Lindsay Jones kept a clean apartment. Nothing else on her fridge was crooked. There was an order and organization to her things. I nodded for her to continue.

Lindsay continued : "So I plugged in my phone like I always do, right by the appliances. I grabbed a half full jug of water from the fridge, poured it into a glass and went over to the couch. The bottle was opened, because I drank half before I left for work and wanted to save the rest for when I got back home. I was just about to take a drink."

The young rookie officer held up the glass for us to see with a gloved hand. Right away we saw the bits of powder at the bottom. The scary thing was, unless you really looked at the water, it wasn't that visible.

"We brought the portable lab over and tested it," he informed us. "We don't know what kind, but it looks like it was tainted with some kind of poison. We're putting a rush on it and will know later today or tomorrow. We'll also be taking the menus and magnets to dust for prints. We did a work-up on, in and around the fridge. If you guys got a good look, I'm going to take this away to the lab. Is that alright?" Matt looked to me for confirmation. I nodded in agreement.

I continued questioning Lindsay. "So Lindsay, *you didn't drink any of it? How come?*" I just blurted it out. I couldn't help it. Matt shot me a sharp look. Point taken, I thought. He was right. These interviews had to be done slowly and with great care.

Just by looking at her, it was clear Lindsay was traumatized. As if reading my mind, she said. "I just realized I could have died. What if...?" She started sobbing, unable to speak. Matt waited patiently, giving her time to breathe and collect herself enough to continue. "I'm sure it was terrifying."

"I can't even imagine. Hopefully, it was just a bad gallon and nothing too serious," I said, attempting to reassure her. "We'll know more soon." I put my arm around her and felt her relax. Her breathing slowed and the tears subsided. She looked at Matt, prepared to answer more of his questions.

"How come you didn't drink it, Lindsay?' he asked.
"This is going to sound really weird to you, I'm sure... But *I know Jesus.* I'm a believer. I was going to drink it. Just as I picked it up and put it near my lips, I heard a voice say, 'Stop'."

"Is there any place you can stay for a while?" Matt asked.

"I can go to my sister Amy's house. I already called her. She said I can stay as long as I need to."

"That's good, Lindsay. It may take a day or two. It just depends on what we find out. Please wait for our call before you come back here," I told her. She agreed. "Just one more thing: do you know anyone by the name of Sally Haze, CC Garden or Mini Loash?" She stopped to think.

"No, should I?"

"Not at all. Just curious."

Once Lindsay was packed, she left with the officer to go to her sister's, and the evidence team began doing their work. They paid close attention to the fallen menus as they looked for fingerprints, and then put them in clear plastic evidence bags.

Chapter Twenty-Six

"You've got to be kidding me!" Captain Mendoza practically shouted, after we'd briefed him on everything we had learned over the last very long day and night. It was mid-morning. After arriving late, the first thing on our plate was a meeting with the whole squad. We all sat crowded into a conference room. The Captain sat at the head, with Matt and me on either side. On Matt's left sat Detectives John Shields and Tamara Case. The veterans in the unit, Detectives Mike Cameron and Steve Davis, sat taking notes beside me. Then there were the newest rookies, Officers Kelsey Jones and Ross Caplin, who sat at the end of the table, taking it all in and eager to help. Our team was like a family. Even outside of work, we hung out. There were Happy Hours, BBQs, watching and playing sports.

"How did we not make this connection before? How did we not know about these other girls? Why is the killer striking again?" Our boss asked. These were all questions we wanted to find the answers to.

"Sir," I said. "We don't actually know what was in Lindsay's drink from yesterday."

"Oh, yes we do. The lab report just came back. The powder in her drink was tested and was confirmed to be strychnine." We all groaned.

"Who would do something like that?"

"Obviously someone very sick," Caplin observed.

"Thank God she didn't drink it," Matt said. "What a miracle."

It was then that I noticed Jesse Smith, the head of CSI, standing at the white board. "One drop, and it would have ended her life. She would have felt her stomach start to tighten. Her airway would have closed. The fumes from the poisonous gas would have been lethal."

Jesse Smith was a skilled profiler. He'd attended the FBI Academy and was top in his class. He'd stayed with the LAPD, heading up the Crime Scene Unit, because, he said, it was a way he could use his skills in both evidence collecting and profiling. He was a valuable asset to everyone in the Police Department. He was often called on to testify, consult, and collect evidence. To say that he was busy was an understatement. He continued, "The amount was so small, we barely saw it. What I want to know is, how did she not drink it? You would have to be very lucky not to take a sip."

I looked to Matt to explain. He cleared his throat and began. "Well, Miss Jones got home from work about twelve-fifteen in the morning. Right away she noticed something was off. Several take-out menus and some magnets that held them up were scattered on the floor. She was irritated and puzzled but didn't think anything of it at first. Then she noticed some other menus haphazardly hung on her fridge. Trust me, this girl is clean and organized. Not the type to just leave things laying around or hung crooked. She said she was so tired she just left it like that. We did see it. It looked strange."

I nodded in agreement. Matt continued. "Lindsay told us she got a glass and poured water from an open bottle in the fridge. She sat down on the couch and was about to take a drink. She put the glass to her lips. Then she heard a voice that told her to stop. At first, she wondered if she was hearing things, so she again tried to take a sip, only to hear the voice again. It sounded so loud to her ears that she put the glass down immediately, startled. She is a Christian and believed that it was a warning from God telling her not to drink. She thought she saw something in the bottom of her glass and called the police. We had just met her earlier in the day at the acting studio that Cassie Garrison attended. We did a full interview with her. That's why she asked for Emma and me."

No one spoke for a minute. They all needed time to process what Matt had just told them.

Even though I had heard it last night from Lindsay herself, hearing it again today made me wonder: *Did* God warn her? Could He do that? What did it all mean?

"Jesse, is there anything new to report on the Garrison murder?" Matt asked.

Jesse shook his head regretfully. "Official time of death was during the middle of the night on June fifteenth."

"That squares with what her neighbor said. She saw a man wearing gloves entering Cassie's apartment building around one a.m."

Detective Case asked, "Do we have anyone we would put at the top of the list for the murder and attempted murder of Lindsay Jones?"

I rolled my eyes in irritation thinking about Marco Crane. Everyone turned to me. "Yesterday we interviewed Marco Crane. He wrote - or is in the process of writing - a script about a guy who commits perfect murders. When we asked to read it, he wouldn't let us. He said he wanted to help, but obviously didn't. He did, however, tell us about three other murders. It's hard to say if they're connected; but he must think they are. He abruptly ended the questioning and gave us his lawyer's business card. He said he wouldn't speak with anyone without his attorney present."

Audible groans could be heard around the table. Certainly, it was a person's right to have a lawyer present during an interview. But that would probably mean we wouldn't get much from the question-and-answer session.

I took a sip from the cup of coffee that was in front of me. "The lawyer is a good one from an expensive firm. I'm not sure we have enough to bring Crane in. What do you guys think?"
Everyone agreed. "I don't even think we could get a search warrant without more," said Captain Mendoza. "All we have is speculation. No physical evidence."

Jesse spoke up. "If he *is* committing the perfect murders, he's not going to let you read the playbook for it."

Matt looked at him. "So how do we catch the perfect murderer, since we have no evidence and can't talk with him?"

Jesse thought about it, but it was our supervisor who answered. "I think the key is to figure out if those three murders and Cassie's are, in fact, connected. Let's interview the other victims and their families. Matt, Emma, you take CC Garden. Cameron and Davis, you focus on Sally Haze. And Case, you and Shields take the Loash girl. And bring our newest rookies with you so they can learn. Jesse, could your team look at the evidence from those cases, see if our man, or woman, wasn't always mistake-free?" Jesse nodded. "Fine, fine. Let's meet back here tomorrow morning and see what everyone has. Maybe once we've done these interviews, we'll know more. Good work everyone. This'll be a tough case. But we'll solve it."

We were then dismissed to begin our tasks.

Chapter Twenty-Seven

CC Garden was such a sad case. We weren't even sure it was murder. Before conducting any interviews, we decided to do some online research to see what, if anything, had been posted about her. Surprisingly, there wasn't much; just one article from the local newspaper, Hollywood Together:

Suicide or Murder? That is the Question.

"Christina Chala (CC) Garden was found in her Hollywood home. Her death is suspicious. Detective Jed Flagger of the Hollywood Homicide Division reported, 'At first, we thought it was suicide.' Students from the local acting studio CC attended wondered if she'd been murdered or had committed suicide.

The twenty-three-year-old appeared to have had a larger=than life-personality. She was a California native who moved from Bakersfield to Los Angeles to pursue her dreams of becoming an actress. In just nine short months, she had booked two commercials. 'Her talent was evident,' Marco Crane, a local film star, recalled.

On the night of March 12ᵗʰ, police received a 911 call from the girl's mother. Worried about her daughter, Chala Garden asked for the police to perform a welfare check. That's when they found the body of CC Garden hanging from a rod in her closet. Friends Brit and Joel Clark told police they had been out partying with the deceased the night before. The Medical Examiner reported she was well above the legal limit. Other friends who were at the party reported Ms. Garden had been too intoxicated to walk home. There is much speculation about how she would have been able to take her own life when she was so under the influence. Garden was starring in Hamlet at the time. Those who knew her say she had no reason to end her life. So which is it, suicide or homicide?"

Matt turned from the computer screen and looked at me. "I thought Marco Crane said he didn't know CC?"

I remembered that as well. When a person lied to the police, it changed their status to suspect very quickly. Why would he deny knowing CC? For now, we had no new evidence, just speculation== and the lie.

"Even if he knew her and didn't tell us, it doesn't mean he, or anyone, for that matter, killed her. I highly doubt it was murder," Matt continued.

"Yeah," I interjected, "but I think we should interview her family and friends anyway. Let's see what else we can find out about Ms. Garden."

Chapter Twenty-Eight

Bronson and Chala Garden lived in Bakersfield. Matt and I made the hour-long drive to their home. Once you get out of LA, the environment becomes more laidback. There's a lot less traffic. Life takes on a slower pace. There's a strong sense of community. As we drove into Bakersfield, we noticed several parks and restaurants. The air was cooler, which was a nice break from the stifling summer heat in LA. Matt breathed deeply. Definitely more of a small-town guy then a city dweller, I thought.

The Gardens lived in the Northeast part of Bakersfield. Their house was large and sat on several acres of land. As Matt and I got out of the car, they came out to greet us. Mrs. Garden was stunning, about six feet tall, with a slim figure. Blonde hair framed her defined features. She looked to be in her mid-fifties. Mr. Garden reached out and shook our hands. "I'm Bronson. This is my wife, Chala. Thanks for coming all the way out here."

"Of course, sir. I'm Detective Matt Parker. This is my partner Emma Blade."

"Nice to meet you both. Let's sit outside on the porch and talk. It's such a nice afternoon," Mrs. Garden said in a welcoming tone.

The couple led us up the stairs to a closed-in porch. It was cozy, with large lounge chairs and a clear glass-topped table.

"This must be a wonderful place to read or just sit when it gets too hot," I said.

Mrs. Garden nodded, then pointed to a plate of cookies and pot of coffee on the table. "Oh, we do love it. Have a seat. Please help yourselves to the cookies. Can I pour you some coffee?"

We thanked her and sat down. The scent of fresh-baked cookies and fresh coffee filled the air. The cookies were as good as they looked. They were still warm from the oven. The coffee was some of the best I've ever tasted. I drank it to the point of becoming jittery.

Mrs. Garden grinned widely when she saw how much we were enjoying ourselves. "My husband is a pastry chef and works at a local restaurant. The cookies are homemade."

Matt, whose mouth was full of cookie dipped in coffee, tried to speak. All that came out was, 'Mmmmmm!'

"What do you do, Mrs. Garden?" I asked.

"Please call me Chala. And my husband, Bronson. I'm an interior decorator."

I looked around. That was obvious just by the stunning porch. I told her so. They were open, friendly, and easy-going. I took out my iPad to take notes as Matt began. "We know this is difficult for you."

Mrs. Garden's face turned grim. With determination she said. "It was *not* suicide. My daughter *did not* take her own life."

Matt sighed. "The Medical Examiner's report lists cause of death as suicide, but did make a note that the circumstances were suspicious."

"Why are you even asking us about CC's death?" Mr. Garden asked. "We told the detective everything after she died." His voice caught, the pain evident.

"Three other young women around your daughter's age have died before and since then. We're interviewing everyone who knew and loved them to give us a sense of who they were and to help us solve the cases. We're not even sure where this will all go. We just need to start somewhere. What makes you think she didn't commit suicide?"

Chala tightly wrapped her hands around her hot mug of coffee. "Because CC was very happy. She loved life. She wasn't depressed. We had just talked with her the afternoon before… " She couldn't go on.

We sat in silence for a moment. The breeze blew around us. The lemon trees in the yard were bursting with fruit. Bronson picked up where his wife left off. "We knew she was going out with some friends that night. She went out with them every Friday. They lived in the same building. It was her day off. She didn't have many, working in a restaurant. So when she did, she took advantage of the time off and had some fun."

"Do you have her friends' contact information?" I asked.

It was always good to ask that question. The department files were not always up to date. CC's parents might have more current information. "Of course. We'll get that to you. They saw her right before she died. Please talk with them. CC moved to LA and was successful in a very short amount of time. So taking her own life doesn't make sense. It never did."

CC's mother took out a photo album and slid it across the table to us. "*Please*, open it and look at pictures of our daughter. Get to know her."

Matt opened the album. A headshot of a beautiful blonde-haired young woman jumped off the page. The royal blue blouse she wore brought out the blue in her eyes. Her hair was swept up in a bun on top of her head. This was a girl who was photogenic. He flipped the page. A young Bronson was holding a tiny baby in pink. Even in that picture, she had thin wisps of light-colored hair. The love in his eyes and the protective way he held her spoke volumes. "That," he said, "was taken the day she was born."

We took our time as we looked through the rest of the album. Shots of dance recitals, birthday parties, and school dances and plays were captured in those pages. Matt closed the book and gently handed it back.

"Could we borrow one of her head shots?" I asked. "It would be great to hang up while we're working on the case." Chala handed us one.

"I don't have many, so please return it once you're done." We nodded.

Matt turned back to the couple. "I just have one more subject to bring up with you. A guy named Marco Crane was quoted in an article we read about your daughter's death. How well did she know him?" Uncertain looks crossed their faces.

"I'm really not sure who that is. Is he important? Did he kill her?" Matt put his hand on top of Chala's.

"We don't know anything yet. But I can promise you we will do our best to find out everything we can about your daughter's case. If she didn't take her own life, be assured we will seek justice for her. And if by chance she did… Please know either way you have our deepest sympathies." His words reassured them.

As I listened to him, I couldn't help but admire how loving and caring he was to these people. He always seemed to know the right thing to say and just how to say it. They nodded in agreement often as he spoke.

Interviews like these were so hard. Hope filled the air. They wanted answers. I hoped we could give them some. What if everyone thought someone I loved took their own life and I knew it wasn't true? How hard must that be for them? A sadness filled me, followed by firm resolve.

The couple must have seen it on my face. Mrs. Garden took my hands in hers. "Thank you for caring. Thank you for coming out here. Please help us find justice for our baby."

We stood and thanked them as we ended the interview. I gingerly slid the photo of CC Garden in my shoulder bag as I got into the driver's seat, ready to make the long drive back in rush hour traffic.

Chapter Twenty-Nine

As I drove, Matt placed a call on speaker to Joel and Britt Clark. They sounded puzzled but were cautiously cooperative. It was important to hear their story, since the Clarks were the last people to have seen CC Garden alive. Matt was able to set up a meeting with them for the following morning. In contrast to the Garden family, the Clarks lived twenty minutes from the station, so it would be a quick trip, which was a relief. We were both hungry and stopped at a local food truck. This one sold sushi.

We sat at the red outside tables on hard chairs. I was enjoying a variety of rolls, while my partner ate rice and tuna topped with a sweet sauce. The rolls were good enough; but I was eyeing Matt's dish, wishing I had ordered what he had.

Knowingly, he slid his plate over and gave me a bite. "I'll have to remember how good this is next time. Thanks." The flavors were like firecrackers in my mouth. "Matt, you're the best." He grinned.

"That's what friends are for."

I don't know what it was in that moment. It felt like our relationship changed. I felt an attraction to him I didn't know I had, or maybe that I'd been avoiding. He put his hand on mine just for a second.

Ok, if I'm being honest, I knew how I felt about Matt. I was just trying hard to ignore it.

As if he was reading my thoughts, he spoke. "Emma, you're an incredible woman...beautiful, bright, sweet, caring, compassionate. I was thinking about what Marco said. I know you know this - you are a great detective. I was really upset when he questioned your competence. I know he was just being a jerk and trying to throw you off your game. It didn't work. I'm really proud of you."

What a quote. Just knowing he was proud of me made such a difference. My face grew red for a moment. I sheepishly thought it was too bad my skin was so pale and it was so noticeable. As I listened, his words and taking them in made me smile. In the eighteen months we had worked together, he had never said anything close to that to me before. And just like that, the moment was gone. We turned back to the business at hand.

"Maybe we could also get the old reports on the Garden case and find out from Mendoza where that detective is now. I'm hoping we can get in touch." Matt was always a planner, always had an agenda.

"Sure, Matt, that sounds good." That was all I could say. For a second I thought he was going to ask me out. Although I didn't want to admit it, that's what I had been hoping for.

Chapter Thirty

Detectives Steve Davis and Mike Cameron drove to the former apartment of murder victim number one, Sally Haze. What struck them most was how similar her murder was to that of Cassie Garrison. Both girls were twenty-two. Both were from Hollywood. Each had blonde hair and was an aspiring actress. Lastly, the method seemed to be the same. However, unless there was some connecting evidence, it would be hard to know if it was the same person. Cold cases were harder than others. The fact that this one hadn't been solved yet didn't bode well. Still, both men had a passion for advocating for victims and getting their loved ones the justice they deserved.

Steve drove while Mike navigated. The victim's apartment was in a more secluded part of Hollywood, up in the hills. There were lots of winding trails. It was common for the GPS to get a little confused. For the millionth time, they heard, "Recalculating…". Mike sighed in frustration. "Let's try this again," he said, as he closed his maps app and restarted it.

They took a sharp left onto a narrow road that was almost too small for a larger car to navigate. "Parking? See any, Mike?"

"Try that spot along the curb. It's a tight fit, but I think we got it."

The car was nudged in as tight to the curb as Steve could get it. His partner barely had enough room to open his door and get out.

Luckily, the manager was still the same as when Sally lived there. They were hoping he could shed some more light on this cold case and their victim. The two detectives headed toward a very modern-looking apartment building.

A compact man with green eyes stood on the other side of the glass doors, peering out at them. Mike pulled out his badge. Once he carefully read it, the manager opened the door and motioned the detectives inside. 'Hello, Detectives. I'm Gram Bellington, the manager here at Hollywood Estates." He held out his hand to shake.

Taking the man's hand, Steve said, "I'm Detective Steve Davis. This is my partner, Detective Mike Cameron, the one you spoke to on the phone."

"Did you find it okay? I know the GPS isn't the best out here."

That was an understatement, Steve thought as they looked about. The leasing office was beautiful, with big picture windows showcasing spectacular views. "Wow, this must be a great place to work and live," Steve observed.

"You'd better believe it. These are top-of-the-line apartments. Luxury everything. Would you like a brochure?" The answer was obvious.

They each took one and looked at the rental prices. Mike whistled. "Way out of our price range."

"I understand. At $6000 a month they are out of most people's." He offered coffee, which they took. "So what would you like to know about Sally—I mean, Miss Haze?"

Just like with Matt and Emma, one detective was the lead interviewer, while the other took notes and occasionally chimed in with helpful information or questions. Mike took out his iPad and started to type. Steve Davis began. "Let's start with you telling us what you know about Sally. I can tell you knew her, and that she was important to you."

Gram dropped his head. "You're right. Both my late wife and I loved that girl. She was a lovely young woman, and a very talented actress." Gram held out a playbill. "This was the last play she was in. I've saved it all these years. It might be the last thing I have of hers. I made you a copy. You may already have one in your files. I can't remember if I gave that other detective one," he stammered. "

"Thank you, sir. This is helpful."

"Please, call me Gram. Just weeks before she died, Sally had starred in the play, 'Alice in Wonderland.' Naturally, we saw it. My wife and I got to know her quite well while she lived here." He smiled as memories of the play came back to him. "She was one of those girls who you knew had something special to share with the world. It was a privilege to know her and support her." He blinked back tears as he continued. "She had a twelve-hundred square foot, one-bedroom plus den."

"Did she live alone or with roommates?"

"She lived alone."

"Did she have a boyfriend, or was she seeing anyone?" the detective asked. Gram stopped to think.

78

"It was a long time ago. Towards the end of her life she was seeing someone. It wasn't serious or anything. Sally often wondered if maybe he was more impressed with her money than with her."

"Why do you say that?"

"Because she told us he always wanted to know how much this or that cost. Sally tried to be discreet when it came to finances. She was almost embarrassed by her affluence, although she had no reason to be." Gram took a sip of his coffee. "She was a very low-key person, even though she was on stage. She wasn't a party girl. I never met a single close friend of hers." Steve wondered why a pretty, talented young woman like that seemed to keep to herself and have no friends she was close to.

"What about family?"

Gram took a deep, slow breath and let it out. "Unfortunately, she had no living family. Her parents died in a car accident. Well, more accurately, they were killed by a drunk driver. It was all very sudden and tragic. I think that's why she kept to herself so much. There was a lot of pain behind those beautiful eyes. And you know what, why wouldn't there be?" he said, empathizing with her plight. "Anyway, her late parents left her a large inheritance which enabled her to pursue her dreams and never work again if she didn't want to. That's why she was able to afford this place. But you know, the funny thing was, you wouldn't know she was from money unless you knew her. She was a very down-to-earth, hard-working young woman. She had a lot of discipline and focus."

"How long did she live in your building?" Steve asked.

"About two years. Her parents were killed six months into her time here. As far as I knew, she had no other family. Just to make sure I was accurate, I checked her file. My wife instantly liked her and made a point of reaching out. We had her over for dinner at least once a month, if not more. We all got along great." He sighed and smiled. "Sadly, now they're both gone." Gram paused to compose himself. "A detective did come after Sally was murdered. He asked questions," he added helpfully.

"We saw a call box as we came in. I'm assuming that's how residents opened the door to guests."

As if reading the detective's mind, Gram replied, "I always wondered how the killer got in. She and I were the only ones who had

79

keys. The detectives nodded. "The electronic lock box I store all keys in is automated, and keeps track of whether I need to access one and for how long. I gave those records to the police back then."

Steve and Mike exchanged glances, both remembering that part in the report. What was strange was there was no sign of a break in. Maybe she'd given someone a key. But who?

"Just to double check the timeline, where were you the night Sally was murdered?" Both Cameron and Davis watched him carefully for his reaction.

"My wife and I were at a board meeting that night. It went late and after, we went out for drinks. I don't have the receipts anymore, but if you need, I can give you the numbers for other board members to confirm with." He said in an even tone.

The detectives tended toward believing him. The sincerity in his eyes was evident. In the old file, his alibi had been verified. That added to his credibility.

Steve continued. "You found her?"

"I did. Her air conditioner had been leaking. I knocked on the door to check it out. The stench coming from her apartment was so strong. There was also a buzzing sound from inside her place. I knocked several times but got no answer. She had filled out one of those cards giving me permission to enter if necessary. So I opened the door just a crack. Once I saw the flies and smelled that odor, I knew something bad had happened. I didn't even go in any further. Instead, I called the police."

Steve looked at the man's face. Watching the pain that consumed him reminded him of just how difficult reliving trauma could be. "I can't imagine. I'm so sorry we are having to ask you these questions. I'm sure it brings up the murder all over again. We wish we didn't have to. I know you understand that your information will really help us. It was very smart of you not to go in any further."

"How come you are, I mean, um, bringing all this up again? Truth be told, I would rather just leave it in the past. This might sound terrible; but I don't think Sally will ever get justice." With that, he put his head in his hands.

"To answer your question, Gram, the reason we are dredging all this up again is because another young woman was murdered. There are some similarities between the cases. We want to know if it's a coincidence or they are somehow linked." Steve stopped and took a sip of coffee, then continued. "Since Sally's case was never solved, we thought we would start there…"

Gram interrupted. "Do you think the same person killed both girls?"

Steve shook his head. "I'm a straight shooter; right now it's too soon to tell."

"My wife and I cared for that girl. She didn't deserve to die like that." Gram's throat was tight and his emotions were evident. "My wife died last year of terrible stomach cancer. Like I said before, she was the one who took Sally under her wing after her parents died. I think Sally's murder sped up her death, if you know what I mean. Please solve this for both of them." A single tear slid down his cheek. He grabbed a tissue from the box on his desk and quickly wiped it away.

"We will do our very best," Steve said, as he looked him straight in the eye. "I'm glad she had the two of you. I'm sure you were a blessing to her."

Gram quickly added, "And she to us. We never had any children. She was like our daughter."

"When we have news, we'll get in touch. In the meantime, here are our cards. If you need anything or think of anything else you would like to tell us, please don't hesitate to call, day or night." With a shake of his head, Gram watched them walk out the door.

Chapter Thirty-One

Back at the station Detectives Davis and Cameron studied the old case file on Sally Haze once again. It really was such a sad story, Steve thought. Hearing about the loss of her parents and then her life coming to an abrupt end was gut wrenching. "Sometimes I wish I knew why things happen the way they do," Davis said. His partner couldn't help but agree.

"It says here Sally Haze died three years ago right around this time—June tenth."

The interview with Mr. Bellingham was similar to the one they had just finished. Mike rested his cheek on his arm in thought. "I found a very short obituary for her." They read it together:

> *"Sally Haze, age twenty-two, of Los Angeles, California left this earth on June tenth. She was the daughter of Susan and Samuel Haze, who were killed in a drunk driving accident. An alumnus of the distinguished Forest Hills School for Girls, she graduated with honors. She received her Theater Arts Associate Degree from Sanford Community College. Members of the Los Angeles theater scene noted how lively and talented she was. One member said her life was cut way too short. Services will be held at Peaceful Waters Funeral Home on June 20th. In lieu of flowers, please make donations to the Forest Hills School for Girls Theater Arts Program."*

Having learned nothing new from the obit, the detectives moved on. "Mike, look what I found in the case notes!" Steve said in surprise. He held it out for his partner to see. "It looks like the Bellinghams offered a reward of $50,000 for anyone who could help solve this case. Fifty grand! So far no one has claimed it yet. Let's bring this to the task force meeting tomorrow."

When a reward was offered, tips came in from everywhere. Finding helpful information was like looking for a needle in a haystack. Mike groaned aloud, "You know that's a double-edged sword. But if it helps us solve this case and maybe the others, I'm all for it," he continued. "Let's ask the Medical Examiner's office to compare the fatal injuries of Cassie and Sally." His partner nodded in agreement. "We also don't know how the killer got into her unit. Time of death was late night.

Would she let him in? If so she had to know him. The report said her throat was slit with a twelve-inch blade. One motion; one fatal wound. Just like the Garrison girl. Okay, enough." He paused.

"You know this boyfriend angle is intriguing. What if the guy truly was only dating her for her money? Say he wanted it. I wonder what lengths our mystery man would go to get his hands on it." Mike sighed. "I wish we had more on that. Let's look into it. From what her landlord said, he hadn't seen a steady boyfriend, just a new and infrequent visitor. He also said he didn't see people coming to her house much. And that she didn't talk about friends that often. We still don't know who she was close to. Let's check out the theater scene. Maybe that will give us a clue."

Using the program Gram gave them, the partners were able to locate the theater where Sally Haze had last performed. They were put in touch with the stage manager who, thankfully, still worked there. Considering the usual high turnover, that was a big break. Solving cold cases was difficult enough. People moved, died or couldn't remember details as time went by. The interview was set up for the next afternoon.

Chapter Thirty-Two

Driving back from Bakersfield was exhausting. When I got home, I tried to relax. I opened a bottle of red wine and poured myself a glass. The wine felt good as it slid down my palate. Unfortunately, it wasn't enough to ward off the effects of the three cups of coffee I consumed at the Gardens' home. I breathed slowly and deeply, trying to shake off the burden I was feeling. A friend of mine taught some relaxation classes. Maybe was something I should look into. I'd never been good at letting anything go. I knew it could be a flaw at times. How do you master it? The popular saying is, things should just roll off your back. Yeah. Right.

I leafed through some magazines, but didn't really read the words on the page. I was wound up, and couldn't stop thinking about the cases, and then about Matt. It was tough turning it off. Even as the night got later, sleep didn't come. My legs felt heavy. My brain was tired. Still, I couldn't rest. Whenever I was in the middle of a case, it consumed me. It ate at me until we got it solved. That made me both a good cop, and a complicated one. Sometimes, your biggest strength can be your biggest weakness. When I got a case, I was like a pitbull, wanting to chase down every lead and leave no stone unturned. Not only was I fierce, quickness and efficiency mattered to me. I picked up the notepad on my bedside table and began to write. At first, I played the free association game. I jotted down all the words that came to my mind about the case:

Actors
Entertainment
Screenplay
Perfect murders

Blondes, women, maybe *stalking…* I sat and thought for a moment. The list went on and on. To anyone looking at it, it would appear to be just a jumble of words that didn't make sense. It didn't to me, either, at this stage. But writing it all out like that helped. We really needed to get a hold of Marco Crane's screenplay. It was the one piece of the puzzle that was elusive. He held it so protectively—but why? How, I wondered, could we get him to show it to us. I thought hard, to no avail. What if we just asked really nicely? I laughed. It was getting late. I bit down on the pen in my mouth. There weren't any new spaces my teeth could sink into. I took it out and twirled it in my hand.

As I did my eyes began to blink rapidly. I yawned several times. I wondered if we could somehow find the bartender who had served CC drinks that night. It seemed like a long shot. Still, I was eager to get his impressions if we could. What would her friends tell us? I sleepily wondered. Just how impaired was she? Was it possible that she was too intoxicated to hang herself? Maybe her agent or manager would be of some help as well. What was her state of mind around the time she died? If this was a suicide, that would be important to understand. I was especially curious as to why Marco Crane lied about knowing her. Let's just say that only put him on my radar even more. There was something off about that guy. Despite that, my reasonable mind knew it was one thing to lie to the police, but a whole other thing to kill. I wondered if he was capable. I didn't have the answer to that, but I wanted to find out. Satisfied, I put the pad of paper back on my nightstand and turned out the light. The clock read two a.m. There was still time to get some sleep before the morning came.

Chapter Thirty-Three

June 22nd

The next morning, we all sat around the conference table with coffee and rolls. Our Captain had thoughtfully brought in breakfast. Matt took a bite of a huge caramel roll. "If I went to this bakery, I would buy a dozen of these and finish them off in one sitting."

"I think that goes without saying," Ross Caplin teased. We were all constantly amazed at how much Matt could eat without gaining a pound.

Mendoza sat at the head of the table as he made small talk with everyone. Rapport has always been important to him. He cares about each of us and is sometimes scarily attentive and observant. "Emma, you need some sleep. Are you alright?" he asked with a concerned glance.

"Fine, sir, thanks. I guess this case is keeping me up. You know how I am." Everyone around the table chuckled.

"Well then, Madam Detective, why don't you start." I laughed and walked to the front of the room to the white board. I grabbed a red marker and playfully held it in front of me like a mic, then got down to business.

"Matt and I interviewed CC's parents in Bakersfield yesterday. We spent a long time with the Gardens. They told us their daughter wasn't depressed. Her death took them by surprise and, of course, devastated them. She was their only child. She had success in her acting career and was a rising star. So suicide didn't make sense to them."

"With all due respect, what parent wants to think that about their own kid?" Tamara Case asked.

"You make a good point, Tamara. We're going to talk with her friends, Joel and Britt Clark, today and see what help they can give us."

I turned to look at Matt. "So much about her death doesn't add up. Let's talk to the bartender, if we can find him or her."

"I was thinking that last night as well. Great minds," he quipped with a wink.

"Here's an interesting thing, though," I continued. "We looked at anything we could find publicly online about the case. Sadly, we only found one thing, although sometimes little things add up. It turns out Marco Crane was quoted in a news article as one of her peers. When we interviewed him about Cassie Garrison, he said he didn't know her. Mini either."

Case spoke up. "Can I just say it? It could have slipped his mind."

She was right, of course. I knew she was debating our theory to push us. Still, it seemed unlikely to me. I reluctantly nodded. "Yes, Tamara. It's one thing to lie to the police, but murder? I'm not sure either."

"What do you think, Parker?" Steve Davis asked.

"This is a frustrating case. There's no real evidence against anyone. All we have is a lot of theory and speculation. I would say we are still at the gathering information stage. We need to move beyond that. It's too soon to make any conclusions." I was done and indicated as much as I walked back to my seat.

"John, Tamara, what do you have to report?" our Captain asked.

"Sorry, Cap, not a lot yet. We haven't been able to get hold of anyone related to the Loash case. We spent time reading the file, though," John said, as his long-time partner got up and walked to the white board.

"What did the case file say?" Matt asked. He wanted to compare that death to the attempted murder of Lindsay Jones. Everyone knew it wasn't always like the movies or those one-hour cop shows where every meeting or interview falls seamlessly into place.

"It does look similar to the Jones case," Tamara observed. "The police found that someone had crawled through an open window. CSI found an unknown print on the outside of the frame. That's a good sign - our first piece of physical evidence. Poison was found in a water jug and in a glass she was drinking out of. The tox screen showed high levels of it in her blood stream as well." She took a breath. "One thing that Caplin caught was that most of the water in the one-gallon jug had been drunk. So it made us all wonder if she died after one glass or if it took several?"

We all gave one of our newest rookies, Ross Caplin, a thumbs up. "That was a good catch, rook," Mendoza said. "Obviously, getting in touch with anyone who knew her would be helpful. Maybe it'll shed some light on that."

Chapter Thirty-Four

Just then the door opened and Jesse Smith walked in. "Greetings all." He grabbed a cup of coffee and a huge caramel roll, pulled another chair up to the table and sat down beside Tamara. We all welcomed him warmly. "Perfect timing, Jess. Why don't you go next?" Cameron suggested.

Confidently, Jess walked to the front of the room. We watched him take a minute to read what had already been written. "Davis and Cameron asked both the crime scene unit and the ME's office to run some comparisons and tests. I went back over the reports. I also spoke with the ME's office and told them I was going to brief you and would pass along their message. It looks like the same type of knife was used on both young women. It could be the same one. We won't know that unless or until we have the weapon in evidence. To answer your question, Davis, there was no unknown DNA at the Garden crime scene. However, there was an unknown fingerprint just under the doorknob. That was a lead. That being said - unless it was followed with some other form of evidence, it wouldn't hold up in a court of law. It was impossible to say whose fingerprint it was or when it came to be on her door." We all groaned, thinking the same thing.

"Alright, let me ask another question. Would there be a way to compare the poison from the Jones and Loash cases?" Matt inquired.

"I think the best we could do is compare and contrast the types of chemicals used. I know, again, not hard evidence. The only way we can know for sure if it was the same is if you find me the bottle."

"Yeah," Matt nodded at our friend. "Please do what you can for now. Every bit of info will help." Solving a crime was like solving a puzzle, so many pieces to put together. With that, we'd gotten another one. .

Jesse sat down. Steve took his place. "This is where our first victim, Sally Haze, lived," he began. Jaws dropped as we looked at the image of the very nice apartments he flashed on the screen.

"Can I live there?" Kelsey joked. "How did she afford that?" She looked again at the astronomical price tag on the captions under the photos.

"She had a very large inheritance. Her parents were killed in a drunk driving accident just a few years before her death. So she had no living family. The landlord remembered her well, though. Apparently, he and his late wife took her under their wing after her folks died. He even saved a program from a play she was in that they attended."

Our captain interrupted. "This is a pretty nice place. High security, I imagine. Did he know how the killer got in?"

"No, he didn't. He said only he and the victim had keys. We're going to interview the stage manager this afternoon to see if she can shed some more light on Sally's life and career. One thing he did tell us was she was seeing someone. It sounded like a new thing. The landlord didn't know him well at all, but our victim told him that she was bothered by his intrusive interest in her finances."

"Wait, back up. What?" I said, feeling a prick of excitement.

"Gram Bellingham told us she said he always wanted to know how much things cost. She wondered if he was more impressed with her or her things.

I know what you're thinking, Em. We want to know more about this guy, too. We'll be looking into it." Steve paused, started to take his seat, and then stood up straight. "I almost forgot, Gram and his late wife offered a $50,000 reward. No one has claimed it yet. I'm wondering if we might want to consider having a press conference and mention that detail?"

It was such a tricky decision to make. The second we put that a reward is being offered out there was the second we would begin hearing from everyone with a "tip" in hopes of getting a little richer. Some were sincere, of course. Most were trails to nowhere.

"The media could get their hands on the story of the attempted murder of Lindsay Jones at any moment. Right now, we have the upper hand with details and our theories. Maybe that will bring more information without mentioning a reward. Let's wait on it and see what happens in the next couple of days," our Captain interjected.

As the meeting came to a close we had one more task in front of us. One of Kelsey's gifts was organization. The way she connected the dots helped us all put things together. She stood up and walked to the white board.

"So what do we know so far?" Matt asked. "What similarities are there?"

Kelsey began making a timeline. "We have four girls, all in their early twenties, all with blonde hair, and all in the acting business."

"How many did Crane know?" Matt asked.

"So far three, but only two he admitted to. Not sure on the fourth," I added. Kelsey wrote that down. "Two had their throats slit with a similar type blade. One was poisoned. If it hadn't been for a miracle, Lindsay Jones would have been the fourth."

Kelsey turned to Jesse. "Would you run the unknown fingerprint? I wonder if it's in our system." He agreed and jotted it down.

"Finally," I added, "correct me if I'm wrong - but it looked like they were all killed late at night." Kelsey added that to the summary notes.

"I'm wondering how many practiced Marco's perfect murder scenario?" Ross wondered aloud. Kelsey put a question mark by the phrase: perfect murder plot?

"Hey, one more thing guys," Steve added. "I'm wondering who Detective Flagger is? I noticed in a couple of the cases he was the lead investigator. Where is he? And how can we get in touch with him?"

Shields informed us he had known Detective Flagger before he'd retired and moved away. He would get in touch with him and see what he remembered, or if anything new occurred to him.

As we wrapped up, Captain Mendoza encouraged us to keep working hard. "You are all doing a great job. The city is lucky to have you to protect and serve them. I know everyone has a different piece of the puzzle. We're a team. Let's keep at it and keep one another in the loop." We nodded in agreement as he ended the long and informative meeting.

As the chatter about life began, I found myself staring at the board. A depressing thought occurred to me. Was it three murders or four? We didn't even know if CC Garden fit into his picture or not. Was her death a homicide or a suicide?

Chapter Thirty-Five

He was enraged. The killer threw the remote at his television, missing the glass by inches. The perky blonde delivering the news smiled broadly at him. He could tell she was pleased to have such a nice feel-good story to report on. "And so today the victim is safe. We can all be glad for that. Back to you, Jim." The pretty woman concluded.

For now, a tragedy averted. The killer had to admit he was not only annoyed with the reporter but with himself too. He. Didn't. Make. Mistakes. *I'll change that!* Yes, the plans were changing slightly, but desperate times called for desperate measures. He wanted to scream, and was angry at his own stupidity. How could Lindsay still be alive? He had done his job. All she had to do was cooperate by drinking the poisoned water. The newswoman reported Lindsay had heard a voice that told her not to drink it. *How could that be*? he raged. In a panic, he briefly wondered if anyone else knew what he was up to. Impossible. Couldn't be. He was always careful. No one had seen him come or go. At least he didn't think so. He pounded his fist. He was not about to give himself up by making some sloppy mistake. That was just irresponsible.

He almost wished he had killed her in another way. He guessed it would have been more successful. He could have slit her throat like the others. Or better yet, she could have died in an inconclusive manner, maybe by hanging like another girl from just a few years ago. He smirked at the thought. What do these police officers know anyway? That night he had watched those detectives pull up quickly to her house, with urgent and alarmed looks on their faces. He kept waiting for the Medical Examiner to come. He kept waiting for her body to be covered and brought out on a gurney. It didn't happen. That's when he knew something had gone terribly wrong. He wondered what it could have been. The poison wasn't visible to the naked eye. She would have had to look very carefully to see it. And he didn't think Lindsay was that smart. *Was she?* he now wondered. He knew one thing. He flipped off the television and stood up. She had to die! It was part of the script. He went to his desk and opened his laptop. He set about making plans as to how that should happen.

Chapter Thirty-Six

Detective John Shields found the number for his former colleague, Jerry Flagger, with no trouble. He wasn't sure if he still had it, so he was pleased when he found it right away. He remembered Jerry as being a conscientious detective. He was determined and had a good rate of closure on his cases. He wondered if those attributes had stuck with him. The phone rang. The old cop picked up.

"Hello."

"Jerry, this is John Shields with Hollywood Homicide. How are you?"

There was a slight pause, and then : "John, how the heck are ya? It's been awhile."

"I'm doing pretty well."

"How are Julie and the kids?"

"I'm happy to say everything's good. The kids keep growing. I'm still here working away." John Shields smiled when he thought of his wife and four kids. They were the light of his life. "How's your family? How is retirement?" John asked.

Jerry and his wife of forty years had moved to Florida to be closer to their children and grandchildren. The older couple was loving it. "I tell you what, John, Florida is the best place to spend retirement."

John thought of his wife and the four teenagers who regularly ate them out of house and home. Secretly, he admitted, he wouldn't mind if they never grew up.

"So how can I help you, old friend?"

"Well, we are looking at some cold cases that we think might be connected to a recent murder. The cases we are looking at are CC Garden, Mini Loash and Sally Haze. Do you recall them?"

"Hmmm, let me think… all three were mine. I regret I was never able to solve them. All three of those poor girls were only in their early twenties, young women pursuing acting, if I remember correctly. Sally's parents were killed in a car accident. She lived in a very nice building by herself. Her throat was slit, right?"

"Yes, that's correct." John was impressed by the former cop's memory for detail even years later.

"A couple of other cops re-interviewed the landlord. Apparently, it's a really nice building. High security and all that. Did you have any theories about how the killer got in?"

He listened as Jerry recounted: "If memory serves, we did find a fingerprint under her doorknob. That's not conclusive evidence or anything, but that's all we had. We never were able to match it to anyone." Jerry paused and John heard him popping a top off some kind of drink. He took a long sip and continued. "Otherwise, he could have gotten in by invitation. I think she had a sketchy new boyfriend. I vaguely remember that. That was a dead end. I tried to find more info on him but never had any luck."

John felt for the old detective. It was frustrating to work so hard and hit dead ends. He had experienced that a time or two himself. The retired detective continued. "There were no defensive wounds; he must have surprised her. The guy used a ten-inch blade, right? I remember wondering if he was a doctor or something, because the cut was just one fatal wound. I'm sorry to say, my partner and I never found who did it. We looked hard, though. At the time I thought it was just a random sad murder." The former detective paused in thought. "You mentioned a couple of my old cases. Are you telling me they're connected, and we missed that?" Dread filled his voice.

John avoided answering the question and went on. "What can you tell me about Mini Loash?"

"Now that one was strange. Who would want to poison her? How many homicides have you seen where the victim dies like that?"

John thought about it. That was a good observation. It was, in a word, rare.

Jerry continued. "We talked to her friends and family at the time. She didn't have any enemies. She did have a boyfriend. He had a verifiable alibi . . . He was out of the country, overseas somewhere. I can't remember where. I'm certain it's in the case file. Heck, he even took a polygraph and passed. He was nothing but cooperative, and devastated by her murder." His voice became reflective.

"That case has always stuck with me because it was so complex. She had a close family, several siblings. All were heartbroken by her murder. We also knew we had an intruder, because the lock was picked and broken. The killer must have worn gloves. No fingerprints. No physical evidence of any kind. We knew she was murdered. Just how and why eluded us."

John asked about the final victim. "How about CC Garden, Jerry?"

"That one wasn't a murder to my knowledge. I thought that was a suicide. Did I miss something?"

John answered. "So far that is the ruling and cause of death listed on the certificate. So it could have been. I'm not even saying it wasn't— except, a potential suspect mentioned her name. We thought we would take another look at it."

"Oh… I get it now. That's why you think they're connected. Makes sense," John continued.

"So you thought she took her own life?"

"No, actually, we didn't. I didn't say that. Nevertheless, that's what the ME went with. I thought it was suspicious at best. The girl was so intoxicated she couldn't even walk according to her friends. Almost couldn't stand up straight. So how did she hang herself? It was always an open question. Sadly, like with the others, we didn't solve it. I thought it wasn't what it appeared to be. Still, there's this thing called evidence; and we didn't have any," he went on. "What made it suspicious was, she wasn't depressed. No-one close to her thought she would take her own life. No history of that. She was also having real success in acting. So I wondered, why would this girl do that? We never found a note either."

John knew that sometimes victims of suicide left notes and other times they didn't. No note was not an indicator of suicide. He asked his next question. "Did you ever think these three cases were connected?"

"Not at all. Different methods of murder, several months and years apart. It didn't seem like they knew each other."

"Does the name Marco Crane mean anything to you?"

There was a pause. "Marco Crane? The name does ring a bell. I'm not sure why. What do you have on him?"

"He is a potential person of interest. Admittedly, we don't have much; but it's a start. We found out he wasn't being completely truthful. In fact, he was writing a screenplay that was about someone who committed a series of perfect murders. When detectives asked to read it, he wouldn't let them."

"It is strange that he brought up those cases to you. Why do you think he did that?"

"You're right, Jerry. It does put Crane in the hot seat."

"It's strange that he won't let you read it. How does he know them?"

"The latest victim who was murdered days ago had her throat slit like Sally. She and another girl took acting classes from him."

There was a long silence on the line. Jerry took a breath. "Come to think of it, that's why the name sounds familiar. I remember now. He was in a commercial with the Garden woman. I can't put my finger on what it was. There was something off about him."

"Did he tell you that?"

"It sounds like you have a couple of hot cases," Jerry mused. "To answer your question, Marco didn't. One of the detectives read it in an online article."

John thanked Jerry for his time and help. The theories he had were invaluable. He'd worked on those cases firsthand. He wished his old friend felt better about the call. He could tell Jerry felt as dejected as he sounded.

"I hope you solve them. Please keep me updated. I want to know."

John agreed and hung up.

He thought about Jerry some more. He didn't want him to feel guilty for not connecting the dots. It was an easy thing to miss. Hadn't they missed it, too? It wasn't obvious. None of them had made the connections until Marco Crane let them in on it.

Chapter Thirty-Seven

Detectives Cameron and Davis went to a small coffee shop near the theater where Sally Haze last performed. They scanned the tables in the crowded cafe. Students on their laptops and business people on their phones made for a busy place. A family of four crowded around a big table in the center. It wasn't a chain store. Davis and Cameron liked that. It had a kind of small town feel. They could tell by the way everyone said "hello" and "goodbye" that most knew each other.

Then they saw her. A petite young woman was sitting by herself. She noticed them and waved them over.

"Hi, I'm Juliet Hall." She had the features of a porcelain doll. Right away they could tell she was anything but fragile. She was a young woman who was determined, with an abundance of energy. Mike extended his hand and they introduced themselves. He could tell she was eager to get this done with.

"I thought about Sally a lot," Juliet began. "She was so nice. No one could ever figure out who would want to murder her. I'm glad you are looking into this... again."

Steve nodded to Mike, who asked his first question. "How did you meet Sally?"

A sad smile crossed her face. "My husband, Scott, was in an acting class with her. They practiced scenes together. They had a real on-screen chemistry. She was his favorite person to work with, because she was smart, professional and always prepared."

Steve wondered if Scott Hall was someone Matt and Emma had interviewed yesterday. He made a mental note to ask them. Juliet brushed a lock of strawberry-colored hair out of her eyes. "Like my husband, Sally took acting very seriously. He thought she would enjoy being in a play; so he introduced us. I, in turn, introduced her to the director. She easily got the part of Alice in a children's show. She was so good at it. The kids and grown-ups in the audience loved her. She got standing ovations after every performance."

"How long after the play ended was she murdered?" Juliet sighed and took a small sip of her latte.

"I would say a month later. I hadn't talked to her or anything since. Not because we were upset with each other or anything. Just because, well, you know how life here can get." She said it more as a statement than a question, then took a second sip of her foaming drink and continued.

"Both Scott and I were so upset about her death. It really put life into perspective for me. I still stage manage, although I've always wanted to be a court reporter. So I went back to school. I admire what you officers do. I don't know you, but I can tell you care about your cases."

"Thank you so much. You're right, we do. So: now you work in a courtroom?" Mike asked.

"Yes, that's what I do for a living now. Acting isn't really my thing."

"Did Sally have any enemies that you knew of?"

"No, not at all."

"How about a boyfriend?"

Juliet stopped and almost dropped her drink. "Come to think of it, she was dating someone at the time."

Why she had such a look of surprise on her face as they asked the question startled the detectives. She continued in a more timid manner. "I remember she mentioned he might come to the show. But I'm not sure if he did. I never met him. It didn't sound too serious, though."

"Do you remember if you mentioned this to the detectives when she was first murdered?"
She looked sheepishly at them. "I don't think so. Like I said, it wasn't serious. I didn't think much of it until right now. I'm so sorry."
She'd said all of this without looking at them. Was she lying? Mike wondered if maybe her lack of forthcomingness was less about her not wanting to get involved than he had previously thought.
He let it go. The young woman looked distraught. "It's alright, Juliet," Mike proceeded. "What can you tell us about him now?"

"That's the worst part about it. Nothing. I never saw a picture of him or met him. Wait... I remember she said something about wondering if he wanted to date her for who she was or for her money. Sally said she couldn't tell." Then Juliet broke down.

Steve gently laid a hand on her arm in comfort. They had more questions they could ask, but the poor woman was so upset they cut the interview short.

"Thank you so much for the information. You've been very helpful. Sometimes people remember something later, and that's how a case is solved. If you could give us your husband's info, that would be great. We'll need to talk with him, too."

Juliet dictated her husband Scott's work and cell numbers to them. They thanked her. As they left, the detectives realized they had confirmation of a clue in an old case.

Chapter Thirty-Eight

As Steve drove back to the office, Mike called Gram. He picked up on the first ring.

"Hello, Mr. Bellingham, this is Detective Mike Cameron. I just have a couple more questions for you about Ms. Garden."

"Of course, ask away." Gram responded cheerfully.

"What bank did CC Garden use? Do you have a copy of one of her rent checks or anything else with the banking information on it?"

"Don't you need some kind of court order for that?" Gram wanted to know.

"If we were looking at a suspect's info, yes; but since CC is no longer alive, this may help us solve her case."

"I saved her file. I can fax it to you if you like."

"That would be great." Mike rattled off the office fax number.

"I'm just wondering, Detective, why you need it?"

"We interviewed someone else who, like you, said she had been casually dating someone, someone she had recently met. She mentioned Sally's concerns about his interest in her finances."

"Oh, I see. She was pretty tight-lipped about her life. I'm surprised anyone else knew that. It seemed out of character for her to have revealed that. Anyway, I'll fax you the info."

Mike thanked Gram and got off the phone. He said, "I wonder who this mystery guy is. He would have to know the others somehow."

Steve interjected. "Right, let's start looking through her bank records. Perhaps there's a clue in them. Maybe there's something Flagger and his partner may have missed, or not known about at the time. After all, one of the big motives for murder is often money."

It seemed sad to Steve that so many murders were triggered by the almighty dollar. He was always happy for the next person if they were successful. Still, was there anything worth killing over? He didn't think so. As soon as they returned, Davis and Cameron went to their Captain's office and updated him.

"Your landlord is on top of things. I just got the fax. I was wondering what this was all about. Here it is." He slid the fax to them from across his desk. Like his detectives, he was excited about this new lead.

"How was the interview with Juliet Hall?" the Captain inquired.

"Okay. I think she's lying or holding back information about knowing Sally's mystery boyfriend, though. Our questions on that score surprised and scared her. After that, she wouldn't look at us." The captain nodded. "She became so distraught we cut the interview short. Even if she was holding back, we weren't going to get any more from her at that moment."

Mendoza looked at them through steepled hands. "Hall, that name sounds familiar. Why do I know that name?"

Cap didn't miss a beat, that was for sure, Steve thought. "I think Matt and Emma might have interviewed her husband, Scott . He takes acting classes from Crane, but I could be wrong on that count. We'll ask them the next time we see them."

"Sounds good to me," the captain concluded.

There was a lot of paperwork to fill out when requesting records. It would take a little time. At least they had a starting point. Everyone in the squad wanted to solve these cases. Steve checked his watch. It was getting late in the day. He wasn't sure if a judge would be around by the time they were done.

As they passed by Matt and Emma's cubicle, they gave them a quick update. Like the captain, Matt and Emma were curious about what Sally's finances would uncover. "Say, guys, we just finished interviewing a Juliet Hall. She was the stage manager at the time of Sally's performance of "Alice in Wonderland" right before she died. She's the wife of Scott Hall. Did you interview him at the acting studio?" Steve asked.

"Yes, we did." Matt responded.

I jumped in. "Wait, you're saying his wife knew the first victim?"

"Such a bright woman you are," Steve smiled at me. I smiled back. "We just got done telling the captain we thought perhaps she knew Sally's boyfriend."

"Interesting. How about we all pay them a visit together?" Matt suggested.

They agreed and wished us farewell for the evening. Once back at their desks, the two detectives began the process of subpoenaing Sally's bank records.

Chapter Thirty-Nine

It was nice to feel like the case was moving in some direction. Hearing from Cameron and Davis made my heart beat a little quicker. Maybe everyone was connected, I thought. We were much more eager to hear what Britt and Joel Clark had to tell us. We decided that the first order of business was to make a final determination on cause of death. But how to do that?

"Matt, I think we should exhume her body." Since my eyes were on the road, I couldn't see his expression. I just waited through his silence until he spoke.

"We don't have enough evidence for that just yet. Besides, I don't want to put her family through unnecessary heartache unless we have no other choice."

"I think you might be right."

"Let's go interview Joel and Britt and see where that takes us. Maybe we can find the bartender somehow, too. If it still seems suspicious to us, then let's clear it with Mendoza and her family and have it done."

"Sounds like a great idea, Matt. That's what I like about you. I guess I'm impulsive and impatient sometimes. You think things through and always have a plan. How lucky am I to have you as a partner?" I glanced at him just in time to see a light blush color his face.

"I'm pretty lucky myself. Being your partner has been really great."

Then he took a breath and slowly, deliberately came out with it. "Emma, I really like you. I wanted to say it last night when we were having sushi, but I didn't. I'm wondering if we could get to know each other a little more. I mean, get to know each other outside of work. Be more than just friends." He laughed. "Ugh, this is all coming out clumsy. What I mean is, I would love to have the pleasure of dating—courting you. In the world of Christianity, that's sometimes what they call it."

I almost laughed out loud at the term. Then I remembered how seriously he took his faith and clamped my mouth shut as I waited for him to continue. "It's like dating, just a little more intentional," he clarified.

It struck me as a sweet gesture. Most guys I had been with were only interested in one thing. They would do or say whatever they could to make me feel like they cared. Once they got what they wanted, they didn't stay interested for long. I definitely had some regrets in that department.

So even though this courting thing made me nervous, I played it cool. "Sure, Matt. I'd like to get to know you better, too. I don't know what courting is exactly. It sounds kind of sweet, maybe old-world."

Matt laughed. "It's a little old-fashioned, I guess. It's sort of a more foundational type of dating. It has intention behind it. Not dating just to date, if that makes sense." He smiled. "I do think you're beautiful."

I have to admit, I almost ran into the Honda ahead of us. Now, it was my turn to blush.. Matt chuckled and gently touched my cheek. "Your facial expressions sometimes…" he said with a grin.

We pulled up to a small house. Not exactly what I expected. One of those tiny houses that is popular today. "How do people fit all their stuff in such a small space," I wondered aloud.

"Ha, ha, I guess we're about to find out," Matt said.

We rang the doorbell. A tall, athletic-looking man of about twenty-six answered the door.

"Hi, I'm Joel. Come on in."

He led us into a tiny living room. Even though it was small, the house was tastefully decorated. Everything was organized and had a place. Shelves and bins lined the ledges. The walls were a cream with tiny yellow and blue flowers along the edges. A tan couch with two matching chairs sat near one wall. Small tables surrounded the furniture. A large TV was mounted above a fireplace.

"Wow, this is lovely. I've never seen one of these tiny houses before. You've done a great job with your space." Yes, we were there to do an interview, but I've found that sometimes starting with the personal goes a long way.

"Why, thank you," a sweet, very pregnant young woman said from behind me. I turned to shake her hand. I would guess she was around nine months along.

"Hi, I'm Detective Emma Blade. This is my partner, Detective Matt Parker. Nice to meet you. You must be Britt?" She smiled.

"Yes, I am; and this," she said, putting her hand on her stomach, "is Lacy Kay."

"When are you due?" Matt asked.

"In about four weeks. She's our first." Both parents beamed with pride. "I just made some coffee. Would you like some?"

"Yes, please," I answered. Her husband went to the kitchen and brought out mugs, cream and sugar, and a large pot of coffee with a small plate of croissants. "What a treat. Thank you both so much."

We sat on chairs that faced the couple on the couch. Matt took out his iPad as I started the interview. "Thanks for meeting with us. What can you tell us about CC? How did you guys meet?"

"She was one of our neighbors. She lived right below us. We met one day and just became fast friends. She was smart, sweet, gorgeous, and very talented. We knew her for two years. Every Friday night we would go out to the same bar."

Joel looked a little embarrassed. "At the time, we were all into partying. We drank too much. We didn't live the best life. Maybe if we hadn't always gotten so wasted, CC wouldn't have died."

"We should have taken better care of her," Britt said, as a single tear slid down her cheek.

"You can't blame yourself, no matter what," I said, doing my best to comfort. "Do either of you remember how impaired CC was?"

It was a tough question, given what Britt had just said. Still, it was one that needed to be asked.

"I had to carry her to the cab we took home," Joel lamented. "We even helped her into bed. She didn't always get that intoxicated."

"But that night she went a little overboard," Britt admitted.

A mix of embarrassment and devastation crossed their faces.

"You said she may have drunk more than usual. Why is that?"

Joel shook his head in puzzlement. "I honestly think she lost track of how much she had. I just don't see how she would have been able to get up and hang herself. Her balance and coordination were pretty much non-existent. Let alone her judgment." He took the thought right out of my head.

I glanced at Matt, who nodded in agreement and understanding. "You found her?" I asked gently.

They joined hands as he spoke. "Some Saturdays we would go to the Farmer's Market. We got home the night before around midnight. The next morning we all slept in—or so we assumed. We went to her place around noon and knocked on the door."

Britt continued the story. "When we didn't get an answer, we used the key she had given us. We had keys to one another's apartments just as a backup and for things like watering each other's plants and picking up the mail if we were out of town or if she was… that sort of thing. We called her first but got no answer. So we got our key and went in."

Joel took a shaky breath. "She was hanging in her bedroom from the high rod in her closet. Just dangling there. Her neck was swollen. Her entire body and face were all bloated. Her skin was blue and purple. And her eyes were wide open. She didn't look human."

"If she hadn't been wearing the same dress from the night before, I don't know that I would have initially recognized her," Britt added.

"We got out of there and called 911 immediately," Joel finished, as his wife rested her head on his shoulder.

We gave them some time to be in their grief, then I asked, "Since you were regulars at this bar, we're wondering if you know the bartender?"

"Actually," Britt said, "We do. He's been a friend of ours since college. We told him we were meeting with you. He gave us permission to share his information."

Bingo! What a break we'd just gotten. I wasn't sure how we would find him. It had just gotten easier.

"Did CC have a boyfriend—or any enemies?" Joel shook his head vehemently.

"Absolutely no enemies that we knew of. She didn't have a boyfriend either. Believe me, she would have told us."

"Can you tell us about the acting class she took with Marco Crane?"

"Marco Crane?" Britt blurted out the name.

"That's a blast from the past," Joel inserted. Both he and his wife sat up straighter and exuded great interest. "She loved acting. She was doing really well. And she enjoyed her class… until… "

I didn't want to lead or suggest anything. I just waited, letting the silence make a point.

"It's just that, even though she loved it, there was this scene she had to do about some guy committing the perfect murders. It was spooky how true to life that became."

"How do you mean?" Matt asked.

"In the scene, this girl had been stalked. The killer hung her but made it look like she did it herself. That was his way of avoiding being caught, I guess." Joel said. "What I remember is that CC was really creeped out by it. Her teacher was Marco Crane. She liked him but wished she could work on something else. Right, Honey?" Britt nodded to her husband.

"Yeah, and when she told her teacher about her feelings, he just told her to keep working on that same scene. She was upset, because she felt he minimized her feelings."

Matt looked at them and agreed. "I can understand that. Do you remember when this was?" A look of realization crossed both their faces.

"Oh, my gosh," Britt blurted. "Right before she died— like a week before."

Neither of us wanted to continue the interview. We decided to end there. Britt Clark was pregnant and already deeply upset. Any more would not be good for her or the baby.

"Thank you both so much. We're taking a second look at the case. If we have other questions, we'll call. Is that alright?"

Joel spoke for both of them. "Of course. We want to help. Her death was tragic. We'll never forget her." With that, Britt burst into tears. She fell into her husband's comforting embrace. We quietly left them and headed back to the car.

Chapter Forty

According to our directions from the Clarks, the bartender didn't live too far from their tiny house. We decided to stop in and see if he could talk with us. We got to his apartment and went to the call box on the wall. We buzzed his apartment number and waited. Once we explained who we were, he let us in immediately. We walked to an elevator and took it to the second floor. The open air felt good as we walked down the maze of hallways until we stopped at apartment number 216. Matt knocked on the door.

The door opened halfway to reveal a man in his mid-thirties. He smiled cautiously as he looked out at us. He wore an apron over a blue shirt and jeans. His apartment smelled like pasta.

"Hi, I'm Jason Castro. Come on in. Hope you don't mind the smell." Jason closed the door and released the security chain before motioning us inside. The delicious aroma got even stronger. "I'm cooking dinner for the next couple of nights. Sometimes bringing food to work is the only way I can avoid eating my paycheck."

I inhaled the wonderful aroma deeply. "What is it? It smells delicious."

"Spaghetti Carbonara," he said proudly.
I nodded. "Thanks for letting us come by. This shouldn't take too long. I'm Detective Emma Blade. This is my partner, as you already know."

Jason led us into a cozy living room where we took seats on the large leather sectional. "How can I help?" he asked earnestly.

"The Clarks said you've known each other since college. How long did you know CC Garden?"
'

"They brought CC into the bar for the first time about four and a half years ago. She was a neighbor they had just met. They came by every Friday after that."

"They told us that, too. How well did you know her?" I asked.

"Pretty well, I would say. She was the life of the party - very energetic. One thing I remember about her was she always wanted to try new drinks I made. It was one thing that stood out about her. Most regulars are particular and order the same or similar drinks every time, but not her. CC liked to experiment."

Jason sat silently for a minute. I could tell he was debating if he should say what he was thinking. I nodded encouragingly. He paused. "It's maybe not my place to say this, but she probably drank too much. She was intoxicated to the point of not being able to walk out on her own that night. I don't want to speak ill of the dead. Still, sometimes I worried about her. I knew she was in good hands with Britt and Joel. Still, too much alcohol can be a bad thing for the body."

"Was there any trouble with her at the bar, or with her and anyone else?" I asked. I wanted to find out more about her. I got my wish.

"Actually, no. She was wonderful, a kind person, and a good tipper. She did mention there was someone she thought might be watching her. One time she came into the bar alone, and I saw this guy looking at her, just staring. When I brought it to her attention, she freaked out. She really looked scared and told me she was being watched, or at least that's how she felt." He cleared his throat and got up to stir the pasta. Once he sat back down, he continued. "She wanted to get out of there fast that night." He rubbed his arms like he was cold, then went on, "I only saw her again one other time—the night she died."

Matt looked him straight in the eye. "Could you identify the guy if you saw him again?"

"Yeah, I think so. He stayed and finished his drink. Then, all casual-like, he asked me what I knew about CC. That really made me mad. So I told him nothing. I watched him carefully and wrote out his license plate, because I wanted to give it to CC or Joel when they came in again."

Say what ? Matt and I were both surprised. It's rare to find someone who is that smart and proactive.

"Your actions are commendable," Matt said. "Do you still have the license plate number, or remember anything about what the guy looked like?"

"Hmm, maybe six feet, brown hair. That's what I remember. He didn't really stand out or strike me as a killer or anything."

They never do. "As for the license plate, he drove a Chevy. I remember the first three letters of his plate spelled ACT, like the word actor. I'm not sure if I still have the number. I moved last year, so maybe I do. I'll look around and let you know."

"Thanks, we'd appreciate it if you would," Matt said.

"How about," I asked, "the night she died. How many drinks do you think she had?"

"That is something I do have an answer for. Once I learned of her death, I made a copy of her bar tab, only because we were all so upset. I wasn't convinced it was suicide. I don't know; maybe it was. I just thought if anyone asked I would have it." He pulled out a slip of paper and handed it to us.

Matt and I read through the list: six shots; three glasses of wine; and one orange juice mixed with vodka. "That's a lot for one person," Matt said.

"I know. I thought about it later. Maybe I should have been more responsible and served her less. That night the bar was so busy. I wasn't keeping track of how many drinks she had. They were in the bar for a few hours, though, so maybe she drank them slowly. I really don't remember. Do you see why we don't think she killed herself? How could she with that many drinks in her system?"

"Do you mind if we take this for evidence?" I asked. Jason nodded.

"I'm sort of glad to give it to you. It's kind of weird having it around."

I pulled out a tiny clear plastic evidence bag from my purse and held it open. With tweezers, Matt slid the bar tab into the bag. Jason looked relieved to get rid of it. "One more thing. We may need to call you for a lineup once we find that car and its owner. Is that alright with you?"

"Sure, anything I can do to help." We thanked him and left.

Chapter Forty-One

Matt and I wanted to follow up with the leads we had, but it would have to wait. We had a memorial service to attend that evening. One of the hardest parts of the job, besides notifying loved ones, was attending funerals. It was a way to support a victim's family while checking out who attended.

We stopped off at my house briefly so I could change into something somber. Matt patiently sat in my living room with a soda in hand and waited for me. Our interviews had run later than we thought. I had to be quick, quicker than I would have liked. I wondered who we would see at the service. I poked my head into my closet. The black dress I chose was fitted and accented my curves. The white pearls popped and were eye catching. *What must her parents be going through,* I wondered. I didn't pray, but I was pretty sure Matt could handle that for both of us. I slid my blonde hair into a high clip on top of my head. As I snapped it into place, several thin strands of hair fell loosely on their own, framing my face. The high heels? Well, let's just say they made me even taller. After I applied some lipstick and blush, I was ready to go.

For a moment I just stood in the doorway watching Matt. He sat completely still. I was right about the praying thing. For once, I was glad to see it, although it made me feel a little guilty for dressing, not just for the service, but so he would notice me. My guilt vanished when he turned his head toward me and broke into a wide smile. He stood up, walked slowly my way, and reached for my hand.

"Wow, you look amazing! Can I say that? I mean, we *are* going to a memorial service."
I laughed. "Why, thank you." He took my keys, locked my door, and escorted me down the steps. My heels were high. I held on tight to his arm, hoping I didn't fall, and glad for the excuse to cling closely to him.

Chapter Forty-Two

The chapel where the memorial service was held was meant for an intimate setting. About 100 people showed up to pay their last respects. Services like this were so hard, because the death had been so sudden and unexpected. Most of the crowd looked in shock, just at having to be there. Flowers lined the closed casket. Pictures of Cassie were displayed on easels and tables: Cassie as a newborn wrapped in a pink blanket with lace on the edges, with a sign that read "baby girl" in the background; little Cassie in a Brownie uniform with a smile that revealed a gap where her front baby tooth had been; Cassie in a volleyball uniform; a cheerleading costume. The biggest photo was her headshot. Her blonde hair was wind-blown, casting a halo around her face. Her eyes jumped out at us. The plaque on top of the casket next to the flowers read, "In loving memory of Cassie Marie Garrison - March 20 1995 - June 14, 2017 - A long life in a short span of time."

That phrase caught my attention. She had lived a lot of life in twenty-two years. I wondered how much longer it would have, could have, and should have been. How much more could she have accomplished had she had the time, had someone not cut her life short? Matt took a shaky breath as he observed the memorials and photos. A lump grew in my throat. I grabbed Matt's hand. The sorrow on the faces of the mourners made it clear that this young woman had been loved. Even in her short time in Los Angeles, she had made a difference.

There were several familiar faces in attendance. Scott Hall was there with someone who looked like his wife. Then there were John, Lisa, Lindsay, and others from her acting class, her landlord, and those from work at The Broadway. At the front of the room, her parents greeted those who came to remember their daughter. And tucked in a corner stood Marco Crane. I couldn't help but wonder if he was a killer.

"Matt, look." I tried not to be too obvious as I cocked my head toward Marco.

"I just saw him, too. He looks sad, but disconnected. Know what I mean?" I had to agree.
There was an odd air about that man; he was there but not there.

We walked toward Lindsay, who was talking with a group of students from her acting class. As soon as she saw us, she excused herself and rushed over.

"Hi, Lindsay," I said, "How are you doing?" She reached out and gave me a hug.

"I'm doing really well. Thanks so much, Detective Blade. You guys were amazing. I can't thank you enough. I've been staying with my sister. It sounds weird; but we've actually grown closer after this."

Lindsay waved to her sister. "Amy, come over here and meet the detectives."

A young woman who looked a little older than Lindsay walked over. Like her sister, she was blonde. Her eyes were a dark brown. Her mouth curved into a smile as she saw us. Lindsay made the introductions and then asked, "Do you have an update on my case?"

Matt stepped forward and took her hand. "We're still working on it, of course. That was poison in your water jug. I'm glad you didn't drink it. *Thank God for that.* As for any leads on who might have put it there, I wish I had better news to report." She nodded and gripped his hand tightly.

"Thank you, too. Please keep me updated and let me know what else I can do. I got a security alarm, so that should help. I'm planning on going back to my apartment now that it's more secure. I know I sound paranoid. I'm still pretty scared, though."

Matt stepped back. "I get it, Lindsay. I would be feeling that way, too, if I was in your shoes. To be honest, though, if you could stay with Amy until this is wrapped up, that would be best. That way, we know you're safe. Okay? Hopefully, it won't be for too much longer." Both girls nodded their agreement.

"One more thing, Detectives: Amy and I will be praying for you as you solve the case." Matt's smile was so broad. The appreciation in his face didn't have to be spoken aloud.

"Thank you," I mumbled, feeling uncomfortable, but grateful. For good measure we gave them both business cards. "If you need anything or think of something please let us know, I urged. They agreed.

Next, we made our way to Mr. And Mrs. Garrison. Taking her hand in mine, I leaned in and quietly said, "We just wanted to offer our deepest condolences on your loss from both myself and Detective Parker, and from the entire Police Department. We're all working hard on your daughter's case, and will do everything in our power to get you some answers."

Matt added, "And I'm personally praying for you. You're in our hearts and our prayers today."

"Thank you both so much for coming," Mike said. "We're glad you're on the case. Cassie didn't deserve to die like that. We need answers. I don't know if I could live the rest of my life without knowing what happened to my baby." And then his words failed him.

We both nodded and shook their hands one last time, before we stepped back as they began to talk with others in line behind us.

Chapter Forty-Three

We walked to the closed casket. I stood on one side, while Matt knelt down and said a prayer. He looked so sad. I watched him staring at a cross that hung above. It seemed to give him strength somehow. Then he stood and took my hand as we moved away.

The announcement was made asking everyone to take their seats so the service could begin. We sat in the very back row, in a place where we could see everyone and everything without being intrusive. There was a short prayer given by the pastor.

"Father, we thank you for the life of our dear sister, Cassie. Her life was cut short by violence. We pray for an end to all violence, hatred and murder. Be with her family and all those gathered here today. You promised to comfort those who mourn. To weep with those who weep. We ask you to be here with us now. We ask that justice be served quickly, in Jesus name."

Everyone chorused, "Amen." As I listened to the popular hymn, *Amazing Grace*, I thought about the pastor's prayer. Would justice be served? Would we be able to find the killer? Lord, I hoped so. That thought surprised me. Normally, I didn't pray. Was that a prayer? I really didn't know. If it was, I'm not sure why I prayed it. Why would God take time to listen to me, when I hadn't paid much attention to Him? Somehow that seemed like a big ask on my part.

The hymn ended. A girl stood and read a passage about how one day there would be no more tears, no more sorrow. It was touching, but what did it all mean? Then Cassie's mom, Cindy Garrison, stood up and made her way to the front of the room. She took a sip of water and a deep breath before she began to speak.

"Just a few short days ago, our lives changed forever. Our baby, our only child, was taken from us. I ask why, but find no answer. I would be lying to you if I told you I knew. She did not deserve a fate like this." Anger filled her voice. "I pray for justice to be served for my daughter and others who have had their lives cut short through the devastation of murder. It changed our lives in ways we never thought possible." The look of pain on her face was so deep, I almost felt it myself. Even so, she continued. "And I must confess: I never thought this would be us. How could this be us? Our hearts are broken, and our family is devastated." Then her voice softened. "In Romans, Chapter

VIII, it says that all things work together for good for those who love God. I really don't know how, but I believe that is true, and somehow it will. Murder is evil. God is not. Both my husband and I know we need to forgive. Forgive even this. How do we do that? I don't yet know the answer to that question. I'm trusting we will find it. Until then, we will work on it. We will forgive. We will not stay stuck in the past or let this bitterness consume us. Instead, we will rise up. We will remember her, our Cassie, our angel that God gave us for a short time."

By now, many congregants were crying. With dignity and an incredible inner strength, her mother continued. "That time was precious. No, we will never be able to see her walk down the aisle on her wedding day or have babies of her own. But we know she is in the best place possible. The best place we, as her parents, would want her to be in. She is now face to face with the God who loved her more than anyone. She is now in the arms of Jesus." With that, she took her seat.

Believe me when I say there was not a dry eye in the room, including my own. Her words, her dignity made me want to know more about this Jesus whom the Garrisons, Lindsay, Matt and Dr. Locking knew. In truth, I had always felt bitter toward anything having to do with faith. I couldn't understand it. I think I had been so resistant because I always thought religion was about rules. I didn't want to be told all the things I couldn't do. But now, what I realized, as I sat there absorbing her beautiful words, was that maybe I was the one who had it all wrong. There was something strong and brave and secure about this Jesus they knew. A kind of happiness and confidence that those that knew him exuded.

I felt a tug on my hand. Matt's gentle touch caused me to look up. I realized everyone was standing. I stood, too, and with tears still coming down, put my head on his broad shoulder. Cindy's words had affected me in ways I didn't yet understand. In response, he wrapped his arms around me and just held me. It was such a kind gesture, just what was needed in that moment. As we stood, the words of the final hymn encompassed us: *"Now the Lord is raising her up on wings like eagles. He is holding her in the palm of His hand."*

Matt stepped back from our embrace and held my hand tightly. "That's a very popular funeral song. It's from Psalm 91. You should look it up sometime."

I smiled. I didn't have a Bible but was too embarrassed to admit it.

We stayed for a while after the service ended, watching, listening, observing. Nothing seemed suspicious or out of the ordinary. Once most had left, we gathered our things and headed out. As we neared our car, we saw Marco Crane standing beside it, leaning on the hood. He cleared his throat.

"Detectives I have something I would like to say. Truthfully, the words that Mrs. Garrison said touched me. They changed my mind on something. I would like to let you read my screenplay. I want you to find the killer. It was not me. I can assure you of that. Could we talk tomorrow?" We were stunned. Moments like this didn't ordinarily happen in a case.

Cindy Garrison had helped us with her daughter's case; and she didn't even know it yet. After we picked our jaws up off the floor, Matt managed to get out, "Thank you. That would be helpful. Why don't you come by the station around ten and bring us a copy. We would like to talk with you as well, if that works for you." Marco agreed. The appointment was set.

We got in the car and drove off, still stunned. As Matt stared at the road, I zoned out. Our ride was completely silent. Each of us wanted to respect the others need to process and grieve. The car stopped. I looked up to see a local soup and sandwich cafe. I wasn't sure I could eat a thing.

As if he read my mind, Matt said, "Food will do us both some good. I know you are not hungry. But once the food's in front of you, I bet you'll change your mind."

He was half right. My body was hungry. Truthfully, I always had a hard time doing anything after someone dies. Even things like eating or going out with friends can be tough. Once inside, a steaming bowl of creamy tomato soup and a grilled cheese sandwich were set before me. Matt had a turkey bacon club with a bowl of wild rice soup.

I took a bite and began, "I was so impressed by Cindy Garrison's words. Her dignity, grace and courage in that moment were inspiring to me. How do you think she did that?"

A long silence ensued between us before he spoke. I could tell he wanted to give me a thoughtful answer, not just something off the top of his head. That was one of the many things I appreciated about him. "No person is that strong on their own; we just aren't. Finding words like that in the midst of the circumstances would be impossible for anyone, don't you think?"

I gave that some thought. "I don't think I could have done it."

Matt stared at me thoughtfully, then said, "The only way she could do it is with the help of Jesus. He makes up for what we lack. I've found in my own life, He stands in the gap for me and is there when I need him. Plus, I could tell she was relying on him to lead her."

"What did that verse in Romans she mentioned mean?" I was puzzled by that. "I mean, how could good, any good, come out of this?" My voice sounded angry, even to my own ears.

"It sounds illogical, I know," Matt explained in a calm voice. "What it means is that even in our deepest suffering, God has not left us. It means that despite the circumstances, any circumstances, evil does not win out. It does not prevail. Martin Luther King Jr. once said, 'Darkness cannot drive out darkness; only light can do that. Hate cannot drive out hate; only love can do that.'"

I remembered reading that once myself. The old quote touched me in a new way. "So that's why they talked about forgiveness?"

"Exactly, Jesus teaches that we must forgive. I've found sometimes it means the most in the hardest situations. It sets us free. That's why he commands us to do that. It will take them time, but they'll get there."

Something occurred to me in that moment. "And that's why Marco Crane decided to let us read his screenplay, because her words of goodness affected him deeply. I think it changed his mind and heart."

"You could be right. I thought that too, Emma."

We got back in the car. Matt got behind the wheel and started to drive to my house. It took about twenty minutes from the cafe where we had dinner. I was in no mood to keep working. The day had been long. It was almost ten p.m. Morning would come soon enough. We were both emotionally drained and exhausted. I was silent on our way back from dinner. I had a lot on my mind. And most of it wasn't about the case.

Chapter Forty-Four

After he dropped Emma off, Matt drove the twenty minutes to his condo. He thought about his partner as he opened a coke and sat down on his couch. He knew that they needed to be *equally yoked* before he could have a relationship with her, although he desperately wanted one. He knew it was important that they share the same values if they were going to take this into the future. Until that happened, he was unsure about how to date/court her. Still, he felt like she was who he wanted to marry one day. He had realized that from the moment they met. It was difficult being assigned her partner and having that sense. Until now, Emma had been almost bitter about matters of faith. He hadn't known how to proceed, since God was such a big part of his life. Something was changing in her. He could see it. Mostly, she had avoided the subject. She respected his faith, sure, but was not interested in learning more. Now, he remembered that he had prayed for a whole year, asking the Lord to soften her heart and to give him opportunities to share. He was disappointed when none came. He wondered if maybe his sense about her and their future was off. Then along came this case. There was something about it that made her want to know more. That gave him space and time to share, or to answer her questions. He could tell she was thinking deeply about some very complicated life issues.

Emma came from a good family. That was something to be grateful for. Still, she didn't come from one that knew the Lord. So all of this was pretty new for her. Respecting where she was at was a big deal to him. He didn't want to push or pressure her in any way. If she was going to know Jesus, that had to be her decision, one she made on her own, not because he wanted her to. So Matt knew for now he needed to be patient, even though he didn't feel like it. Patient and available. Willing to be her friend while getting to know her better.

"Aaah," he moaned aloud in frustration. All this was very complicated. He would have to be careful as he walked this line. He took the last sip of his coke and said a prayer. "Lord, help me to help her, to love her well and be the best example of you that I can be." He meant it.

As he got ready for bed, he prayed aloud for the Garrison, Garden, Haze, and Loash families and all who knew and loved these victims. He asked for help and guidance to solve these cases. He knew they would all need it.

Chapter Forty-Five

June 23rd

Matt and I both stared at the clock. It seemed to take forever to get to ten that morning. The two of us would take the lead on our meeting with Crane, while our colleagues watched behind the one-way mirror. Everyone felt the anticipation in the air. What a break this could be. Matt must have had three cups of coffee already. The door opened, and in walked Marco Crane. Accompanying him was a white-haired man in an expensive-looking suit.

"Hello, Mr. Crane. Thanks for coming down," Matt said as we all shook hands.

"Detectives, this is my lawyer, Burt Morris."

We led them through the room full of police desks and down a hallway to the interview room. "Have a seat, folks. Would you care for anything to drink; water, soda or coffee?" I asked. They both shook their heads, pulled out chairs, and sat down.

"For the record: Mr. Crane," the lawyer began, "has come in of his own accord. He did this for two reasons. First, because of that stirring eulogy last night. It touched his heart. Second, because he wants you to know he is not guilty of these horrible crimes. You must know that. We are here to clear the air."

"Oh, good," Matt said, "Let's start."

We turned on the video camera. Matt, who was the primary interviewer, stated the necessary identifying information for the video: name, date, who was in the room, and what time it was. "First, do you have the screenplay for us?" Matt asked.

"Yes, of course I brought it. I'm a man of my word."

Marco slid the briefcase to the center of the table. I took it and opened the latch. Inside was a large stack of typed pages. Two hundred was not a far-off estimate. Marco saw my surprise at how big it was.

"It looks big now; and it is. But it will be edited later," he reassured.

"Thank you for bringing this in," I said.

I kept my focus on him, when what I wanted to do was run from the room and start reading. He smiled at me, then turned his attention back to Matt and the camera on the wall.

"Some of this will be repetitive to you. Just hang in there and answer our questions to the best of your ability, alright?" Matt was detailed and thorough. He wanted Crane in his own way to know what to expect when it came to procedure. Crane affirmed he understood. Matt continued. "How long was Cassie in your class?"

"About six months."

"How did she hear about you?"

"I give a free seminar, and she came to it. She signed up right away and was eager to work."

"How well did you know her?"

"Teacher-student, that sort of thing. Nothing funny going on if that's what you're thinking." His lip started to curl as his tone became just a tiny bit irritated.

With genuine patience, Matt responded, "Actually, I wasn't thinking anything. This interview is to find out more about you."

Bravo, Matt, I thought, working hard to keep my face a blank mask. He went on. "Do you know if she had a boyfriend?"

"Not to my knowledge."

"Was she having problems with anyone you knew of?"

"No one that I know of."

Matt switched subjects. "Could you tell us about the last scene the two of you were working on?"

"I think you already know that."

The lawyer put a hand on Marco's shoulder in a calming gesture. "Marco, just tell them what they want to know." He took a deep breath.

"It was similar to the scene you saw with the Jones girl. Girl walks into her house. Gets ready for bed. Goes to sleep and never wakes up again. The main difference in the scene you saw with Ms. Jones and the one with Cassie was... her throat was slit."

"Kind of ironic, don't you think?" Matt looked straight at the teacher when he spoke.

"I don't know. I guess so. I never really thought about it like that."

"Ok, then think about it now," Matt challenged. "You do this scene about a girl whose throat is slit, a young blonde actress. And that night, it actually happens. See, what I can't figure out, Marco, is why that didn't cross your mind."

Marco turned to his lawyer. "Do I have to answer that?" he asked defensively.

"No, you don't, because it wasn't a question. More of a statement," Morris responded. The lawyer continued, "He didn't know the future. And he already told you he did not give it much thought."

Matt was unfazed. "You're a smart guy. All I want to know is why that didn't cross your mind."

"Why should it have? I don't have some crystal ball," Marco interrupted in anger. His face grew red.

It was my turn to play good cop. "Ok, yes, I can understand that. Let's move on. Tell me again where you were the night that Cassie died." I spoke in my sweetest voice.

Marco Crane looked a little panicked and turned toward his lawyer. "I was… I was… let me think. Class was over around two p.m. I went to do some private coaching and consulting on set until around midnight. I can give you that number to verify. I then went out with some friends until three a.m."

The lawyer pulled out a receipt and two signed documents. "This is the receipt from the bar Mr. Crane went to. And these are statements from the bartender and the valet who saw him there. He got his car and drove home around three thirty a.m."

We found such an organized alibi suspicious. "Obviously, we will need to verify this. Still, it is helpful," I said. "We don't have an exact time of death for Cassie—so that doesn't mean you didn't do it."

"Tell me something, Mr. Crane, do you always have a ready alibi?" Matt asked roughly.

Marco searched for his own self-control before continuing, "I got home around four a.m. and went to bed."

Even though Matt had said that we knew something that might clear him, Marco and his lawyer didn't. Mrs. Gray, the neighbor from across the street, said she saw someone around one a.m. If his alibi could be verified, it couldn't have been Marco. On the other hand just because she saw someone suspicious didn't mean it was the killer, either.

Matt switched gears instantly, changing his demeanor. "How long were you working on this scene with Cassie?"

"About three weeks. It's pretty normal to practice something several times so the actor can improve. I find the best way to see progress is to work at something for several weeks in a row."

"Did Cassie ever express her discomfort in acting out this particular scene?"

Marco smirked. "Come to think of it, yes. I told her that was what we were working on and she would have a chance to improve. Every one of my actors was doing this scene. Looking at different interpretations of it is an effective teaching and learning technique."

His know-it-all manner was grating. I challenged, "If she was uncomfortable and expressed that to you, didn't that matter?"

"Quite frankly, it didn't. Sometimes you have to do things you don't like. Surely you know that, Detective."

Neither of us responded. Instead, Matt plowed ahead. "Ok, tell us more about the screenplay."

"Can't you just read it?" Marco said with a deep sigh. "Five women are murdered in a couple different ways. The killer is brilliant. He is quick-thinking on his feet and is cool under pressure. He decides who lives and who dies. No one suspects him. He commits the perfect murders."

Maybe it's just me, but I wasn't interested in reading about some guy who gets away with murder after murder. Brilliant is not the term I would use. I mean, think about it. In this day and age, it would be hard to commit the perfect crime. Not a question. Just my opinion. I kept it to myself.

Marco went on. "It's an intriguing story when you think about it."

"You told us you only knew Cassie and Mini. They were in your class right?"

"Um, yes, that's correct."

"But what about CC Garden and Sally Haze. Did you know them?"

"No, I told you that."

Matt took out the article we had read about the death of CC Garden and showed it to Crane. He and his lawyer read it together. Matt pointed. "Right there, Marco, is a quote from you about her talent. I thought you said you didn't know her?"

The lawyer slid the article in front of him, reading it again carefully. "My client—" but before he could finish his thought, Marco jumped in. "I lied." Matt, his lawyer and I all stared hard at him.

"You lied to the police? Why would you do that, Marco?" his lawyer asked. His blunt response was strange. Most suspects don't admit they lied just like that. Matt glanced at me with a deep frown. "Why did you lie?"

"Because I didn't want you to suspect me. I wrote the screenplay. And these girls started dying. If I said I knew all four, surely you would think I did it."

My turn to be blunt. "Not your best move, Marco. You knew Sally Haze and CC Garden, too?"

"I did, Ms. Blade."

Now that we had new information, it felt like we needed to dig deeper and start again. "Tell us again about Cassie?" For the second time, we listened to his story about Cassie and how he knew her and where he was that night.

Matt switched subjects again. "How well did you know CC Garden?"

"We worked together on a few projects. She was lovely and talented… and a party animal. She was fun to be around."

It was my turn to look exasperated. "If you had told us you knew CC, that might have helped." He just shrugged in a casual sort of way.

"You're lucky I even told you about the other murders; otherwise, you incompetent fools probably wouldn't even have known about them." A smug look crossed his face.

And there we were, sitting across from this arrogant, strange man - speechless. Matt took a deep breath. "From what you know about CC Garden, do you think she took her own life?"

"I don't think she did. She was going places. She was talented and very photogenic. She was not depressed at all. In fact, she was going to audition for an insurance commercial in the next couple of weeks, which, obviously, she didn't get around to doing." A look of genuine pain and sorrow crossed Marco's face. "I was even thinking about asking her on a date. It never happened. I never got the chance."

Marco's ability to change his personality and emotions on a dime was telling and a little scary. Was it just the actor in him? I wondered. It was hard to read him. When was he lying—and when was he telling the truth?

"How about Sally Haze? You said you knew her as well."

"I met Sally through one of my other students and friends, Scott, and his wife, Juliet Hall. She was and is the stage manager at a local theater. Sally was in one of her plays. Scott was, too."

"What did you know about her money?"

Marco looked puzzled. "What are you talking about? Wait, she had money? You've got to be kidding me, right? So did the first girl in my screenplay whose throat was slit. I swear, I had no idea she had money." Strangely, I believed him.

A knock sounded at the door. Matt glanced at me, my cue to see who it was and what helpful info they might have to offer. "Excuse me," I said as I walked toward the door and stepped outside.

Mike Cameron stood outside the door, hands on hips and a scowl on his face. I took a few steps away from the door. "What is it, Mike?"

"Remember yesterday how we told you we'd just interviewed Juliet Hall? Well, she never mentioned she and her husband knew Crane very well… not to mention that he knew CC. From what this character says, it sounds like they all knew each other. I don't get it."

"I agree. Something strange is going on here. And I intend to find out what it is." I turned to go back in and thought of something else. "Mike, can you check what kind of cars both Marco and his lawyer are driving and run them?"

"Already on it. We'll talk after the interview. If I have more to add, I'll send you a text." I reached out and gave him a quick hug of thanks and watched him walk back to continue to observe.

I opened the door and stepped back into the interview room. Marco was in the middle of an intriguing statement. "The ironic thing is that my screenplay seems to be mirroring what's going on. At first, I didn't think so. Now, it is disturbingly accurate." I raised my eyebrows.

"What's that, Marco?" The goal was for him to repeat himself to see how well his two similar statements matched.

"In the beginning, Sally died; and it was tragic. But after CC died, I started to become suspicious. I wrote about someone who committed suicide, or so the police thought. Right after that, about two weeks later, CC died. Time passed. I just ignored my gut feeling. Then, I wrote about a girl being poisoned. Mini died a month later."

"Why on earth didn't you not report your suspicions?" I asked angrily. I thought that maybe Cassie could have been saved. Maybe

Lindsay wouldn't have almost died. I didn't say anything, just let the question hang in the air.

"I didn't murder them, Detective Blade. Surely you know that. And I can't be blamed for future deaths."

Of course not, I thought, feeling disgusted. A popular quote by Edmund Burke came to mind: "The only thing necessary for evil to triumph is for good men to do nothing." We might not be discussing political theory right now. But somehow, that message, spoken so long ago, applied in this situation.

"You think I should have done something, don't you?"

I looked Marco straight in the eye, and very calmly, in a low voice, said, "in my opinion, yes! You may or may not have committed these murders. Nevertheless, you are just as responsible. And don't you forget it." Probably the wrong thing to say as a detective. But it was the right thing to say as a woman and human being who felt deep compassion and sorrow for those young dead women and their families.

The lawyer cleared his throat. "Is there anything else, detectives?"

"How did you know Mini Loash?" Marco looked pained but found his voice.

"She was in my class. She wasn't the best actress; but she worked hard. She didn't mind as much portraying the murder scene from my screenplay. Only, in her scene, the girl is poisoned. As I said, it's not meant to be real or taken literally, folks. Don't you see that?"

Matt looked at him. "But obviously, someone did take it literally. Who, Marco, do you know that would have access to your screenplay and then act it out in real life?"

"No one I know is a murderer!" he shouted.

Abruptly, the lawyer stood up. "This interview is over. Mr. Crane has done everything in his power to help you. And look where it has gotten him. If you have any more legitimate questions, call me. Perhaps we will find the time to come in for another interview." He and his client quickly walked out the door.

Chapter Forty-Six

As we neared our desks, Matt and I were confronted by the familiar face of our captain. His look of frustration and anger mirrored our own. " Who does that guy think he is?" he bellowed. "There is something really off about him." We were all frustrated with the arrogance and indifference Marco Crane often displayed.

"Well, Cap, that interview went about as well as our last one with him did," I quipped. Everyone chuckled.

"And… I think that might be our last one," Matt conceded. Captain Mendoza glared and crossed his arms.

"You're probably right. Although you both did an excellent job. I mean, what kind of person brings us a ready alibi for the night of a murder? Jones, Caplin, run down his alibi. Maybe there are some security tapes you can take a look at."

He then turned to Cameron and Davis. "Get on that interview with Scott Hall. While you're at it, ask his wife why she didn't clue us in to all these connections. Talk to them separately. See if their stories gel."

Matt and I were next. "I know you want to go with Cameron and Davis to interview the Halls. And that's fine. Until then, get busy reading and analyzing that screenplay." We nodded.

Then Matt cleared his throat and said something surprising. "I know it might be a little premature; still, I'd like to call the ME and get what we need to exhume the body of CC Garden."

When our boss shook his head no, Matt continued. "Captain, with all due respect, all indications are that her death was not a suicide. Another examination couldn't hurt. I think her parents would be willing."

None of us really wanted to exhume CC's body. Nevertheless, at this point, we had few options. Captain Mendoza knew it and relented. "Alright. I trust your instincts. I know you wouldn't ask without a good reason. Your first step is to talk to Locking. See what he says. I'm going to let you run with that angle for now. But if the ME finds no new evidence, we are done investigating her case. We move on to cases we can actually solve. Got it?"

Before we had time to respond, he turned to the newest members of the squad. "Caplin. Jones. You guys take the car identification assignment from Cameron and Davis. I want to know what cars the people connected to this case drive. Maybe we can start to solve it that way, or at least gain some traction."

Facing the veterans, the Captain continued. "Case, Shields, what about Mini Loash?"

"We know nothing about her so far," John Shields sighed. "No one has called us back to date. We'll keep at it, of course."

"One thing that bothers me, sir," I interjected, "Marco Crane said five women died in his screenplay. Lindsay didn't. I'm thinking about the next victim, worried about who that might be. What do you think?"

"I've been thinking about that, too. Just more incentive for us to move quickly and solve this case."

He wanted to put twenty-four-hour protection on Lindsay. Unfortunately, it was not in the budget. Everyone knew that. His words echoed in my mind. Solve this case quickly. That was just what we intended to do.

Chapter Forty-Seven

The first thing we did was walk over to the medical examiner's office. Ruth sat at her desk. She had just popped a life saver in her mouth when we walked in. "Hi guys. Want one?" She cheerfully held out the rainbow roll. Matt and I each took one. We were hungry. On days like this, there was no time for lunch.

"Dr. Locking is in his office. He told me to have you go down as soon as you got here." The large metal doors opened. We took the elevator down to the morgue level and the office of our friend and colleague.

Spread out on Dr. Locking's desk was the report and full color pictures of the autopsy of CC Garden. The doctor was in deep thought when we walked in.

Matt cleared his throat to announce our presence. "Hey, Doc, thanks for seeing us."

He led us to the two chairs facing his desk and motioned for us to sit, then turned the report and photos around so we could study them. CC Garden's once-pretty face was swollen. Her skin was blotchy. The rope burns around her neck were clearly visible.

"Britt and Joel Clark said when they found her she was almost unrecognizable. I can see what they meant now. That's a brutal picture. I forgot how horrific hangings can be. Haven't had one in a while," Matt said.

The doctor glanced up at us. "I've been sitting here going over these photos and report with a fine-toothed comb. I didn't do the initial workup—Dr. Crass did—so it took a while; but look at this." He took a pen and pointed to a tiny bruise on the inside of her left wrist.

I took a closer look. "What's that? Where did it come from?"

"I wasn't sure myself, so I had it enlarged." He put the enlargement on top of the other photos. "What does that look like to you?" he asked.

I took in a sharp breath. "Is that a needle mark?"

"I think so. Sure looks like it."

A long silence fell as we thought about the late Dr. Crass. He had been one of Doc's best assistants, a kind, young, knowledgeable doctor whose life ended way too soon in a freak boating accident while he was fishing last year. His unexpected death rocked our world.

Dr. Locking continued. "It's tough to say what that is for sure or how it got there. Closer examination is necessary. Do I think it's something to be alarmed over? The answer is yes." He went on. "Given that and the high alcohol content I think further examination is warranted." He took in a breath and looked down at the photos.

"While you were on your way here, Mendoza called. He already got permission from the girl's family to exhume her body so we will take a closer look."

Sometimes our Captain surprised us. Earlier, he seemed less than excited about taking a second look. I had to give him credit. We appreciated that not only did he trust our judgment, he helped us make it happen even sooner than we thought. He was always on top of things. He would rather be out in the field, but often had to focus his time and attention on meetings, paperwork and general administration.

"We should bring that man his favorite latte when we get back," I noted. Matt and the Doc agreed. Getting permission from CC's parents was huge.

The ME continued. "So I talked with the cemetery where she's buried. If we leave now, we can be there while they're still in the process of digging her up."

We were amazed at how fast and how favorably the wheels were turning for us. Usually, these things take a bit of time to arrange. We immediately agreed and got ready to leave. Dr. Locking tucked folders into his briefcase and grabbed his medical bag. "I'm going to take the ME van and a couple attendants. I'll meet you there." He slid a slip of paper into my hand. "Here's the address. See you in about thirty minutes."

Chapter Forty-Eight

When we entered Captain Mendoza's office, Matt extended his hand to our boss. In his other hand was his favorite latte. "Thanks for your help, Cap. That was a major break, you getting the parents' permission."

"No big deal. What's this? My favorite? Thanks, guys." The captain grinned. "My day just got way better." He took a long sip and said, "I take it you are off to the exhumation?"

"You got it, sir. The ME found an unexplained bruise on her body that he wants to take a closer look at. We may not be back tonight. We have the screenplay with us. We'll read it while we wait," I told him.

"One of the other errands we ran was getting four additional copies of the manuscript made so others could read it as well." Mendoza looked surprised and delighted when I produced the stacks and put them on his desk. "We figured the more eyes the better."

Mendoza beamed. "Thanks. See you in the AM." We left him happily sipping his latte.

"Matt, have you ever been to an exhumation?" I asked. The air was humid and muggy as we pulled out of the parking lot.

"No, but we've both been to the scene of lots of homicides. I assume it's similar." He thought for a moment. "What troubled me about this morning's interview, besides Crane's condescending attitude, was that he mentioned that every time he would write another portion of the screenplay, another girl would die… weeks or months later. I can't figure out how that could happen. I don't think we can assume someone stole it, because it has been ever-changing and updated. I mean, say his alibi checks out. He is still involved somehow. Maybe… maybe he has… a partner?"

I caught up to the Medical Examiner's van and followed their lead. Matt's phone chimed and he looked down. He explained that the text was from Ross Caplin who checked into Marco's whereabouts on the night of the Garrison murder. When I glanced over at Matt, his eyes asked me to consider his theory. I thought about it for a moment and finally said, "I see Marco as an abrasive, know-it-all type personality. But I'm not sure I think he murdered anyone. Or not Cassie that night since his alibi checks out. Maybe he is the mastermind behind it. I just don't know, Matt. One thing is for sure, him being the killer would make things a lot easier."

Neither of us liked Marco Crane. Still, we had to treat everyone, no matter our personal feelings, as innocent until proven guilty. We wanted to avoid tunnel vision. A long silence stretched between us as we considered this oddity in our case. The blinker flipped on as I pressed the button to signal a left turn onto the freeway.

"Maybe he knows who is behind this. Maybe he gave them the screenplay. Or maybe…" It hit me then. It was one of those light bulb moments that just felt right. "Maybe it's someone who has been in his classes." I paused as I thought it through. "Say he keeps sharing his work with the groups of students he teaches. Maybe he doesn't present it as new material—just something new for them to perform. They keep practicing the scenes. Someone would know the story and be able to put it together."

Matt finished my thought. "And act it out in real life."

I nodded and went on. "If it's not Marco, it would have to be someone who worked on the same scenes as our victims or who Marco let read the screenplay."

Matt kept pace with my theory. "I agree with your first thought. I think he knows the person or they know him and want to do him harm, make us think he killed those girls. He's been holding something back, that much is obvious. Maybe protecting the person? That would make sense, because he comes across as unwilling to help us and odd. Of course, we would suspect him."

There was so much for us to think about, just not at that moment. We pulled into the parking lot of the Grace For All Cemetery and parked next to the ME's van.

Chapter Forty-Nine

Dr. Locking was flanked by two morgue attendants. They wheeled a gurney with an empty body bag on top that would soon be full. We were all somber in that moment. The weight of what we were about to do was a burden unlike any other. After a half-mile of walking our ears led us the rest of the way. The loud machine hummed along. As we approached, two men dressed in black were using machine-like shovels to dig into the ground. The dirt came up in large piles that were tossed by the machine to the sides of the large opening that was exposed. With every pile of dirt that was thrown, the hole grew deeper and wider.

The grave marker sat next to the open space. On it read: CC Garden - our child - our heart - the fruit of all that was good in us. Under that were the standard dates of birth to death. A large bundle of fresh flowers was carefully placed on top of the stone. I gazed in awe at the site and wondered how many times these cemetery workers had to do the reverse, unbury a body. A lump formed in my heart as they kept digging. All the men around me wore the same expression of deep sadness. Hopefully, this would be worth it. *Please, let it be worth it*, I thought. The sun hid behind the clouds as they dug. What was once humid air was now almost cold.

Matt and Dr. Locking prayed silently as they stared at the hole that continued to expand with every dig. Finally, we heard it. The shovel banged against something solid. A small square of white could be seen as the dirt was removed and flung to the side. Once the dirt was cleared, the full casket was revealed. The casket was hoisted slowly out of the ground. Carefully, the lid was unlatched. With every sound, I wondered what I would see. Instinctively, I reached out and grasped my partner's hand. Just his touch calmed my nerves.

"Ok, folks, we should be able to take the lid off," an attendant announced. He handed Dr. Locking the tool. He grasped it in his large hands, leaned down, and slowly moved it from side to side until the lid creaked open.

The first thing we saw was a lot of long blonde hair. I was struck by how similar her hair was to Cassie's and Lindsay's. It was a reminder that she was human, as her body was badly decomposed. I watched Matt as he sucked in his breath. He never took his eyes off CC. Gingerly, Dr. Locking and the crew slid her into the bag so nothing would break. With gloved hands, his   assistants gently held her legs. Matt and I stood on either side, carefully placing our hands under the arms. Dr. Locking cradled the head. It had to be done very slowly. First one leg, then the other. After that, with coordination, her torso. Then, one arm and the other. And finally, her head. Once that task was completed, they zipped up the body bag and turned the stretcher toward the van. Now, the cemetery workers would lower the casket back into the ground and cover up the gaping hole until her remains were returned. Dr. Locking extended his hand to the men who had dug up the grave and who would later place her back in it.

"Thank you for your help. You did good work." All they could do was nod in answer. Then the esteemed doctor turned and walked slowly toward the van.

Matt and I watched them drive away with CC's remains. We thanked the cemetery workers and made our way back to the car. At that point, I just needed to drive. Matt knew that and patiently sat in his seat lost in his own thoughts. I was in such a somber mood. I mean, who wouldn't be after that. As I drove, I thought about how short life was. What did it all mean anyway? What was the purpose? I was lost in my own world and jumped when I heard Matt ask, "What, Emma?"

He took my hand in his. Tears blurred my vision. I had to blink a few times. Matt's thumb traced the tears that slowly fell. I was unable to speak. There was plenty to say; but no words came out.

Sometimes I wondered if I was tough enough for this job. My emotions could just bubble over. That's what I appreciate about my partner. The silence was fine. Even my emotions were okay with him. And they wouldn't be with everyone. Instead of going off into his own thoughts, he stayed focused to comfort me. The whole experience was draining.

We decided we needed to look at the screenplay later. Right now our hearts and heads were not in it.

"Would you mind if we stopped somewhere?" Matt suddenly asked. I nodded. He gave directions.

We found ourselves in front of a large church. We got out and walked in. For about half an hour, we just sat. The large room had traces of the smell of incense. That brought me peace. The church was comfortable and quiet. A place of peace for us to go and be alone, Matt with his God, me with my thoughts. As I sat silently, Matt prayed beside me. I could tell he was gathering strength just by coming here. As he leaned in, a calm look crossed his face. He saw me watching him.

"What you're seeing on my face is the peace that surpasses all understanding. We might not have most or all the answers right now, but being with Jesus like this makes me feel at peace." For a brief second, I could almost understand that. To be honest, for a moment, I wanted that. I didn't voice it, though.

As we walked back to the car, I noticed I had more energy and strength to keep going. Just being in silence with myself for the last hour really helped. I felt more centered, more balanced. Just then, Matt's phone rang. He grabbed it and put it on speaker so we both could hear. I started the car and made a 180-degree turn to make our way out of the large lot.

"Parker," Matt answered the phone crisply, back to business. He, too, sounded like he was ready for what came next.

"Matt, Emma, this is Ruth." There was an urgency in the voice of the usually careful ME receptionist.

"Hi, Ruth, what is it?" Matt asked.

"Dr. Locking asked me to call you to see if you guys can come right away. He has something to show you in the Garden case."

We were only thirty minutes away. We agreed and hung up the phone. I hit the buttons for lights and sirens and we sped off. Fortunately, I found a parking spot close to the building. That was rare. We jumped out of the car like we were shot out of a cannon.

"Hi, Ruth," we said in unison, as we practically ran past her desk. We had been tired. A lead changed everything.

Dr. Locking was just as fired up when he met us at his office door. "Come with me to the morgue," he said. He walked so fast I almost couldn't keep up. Like Matt, he had long strides. Luckily, I knew the way. He led us to the familiar large autopsy room.

Laid out on a long table were the remains of CC Garden. Her body was spread out on a clean white sheet. I noticed he had cleaned up any dirt from her body being buried. Without the dirt, it was easier to see the outline of her body. Dr. Locking walked over and used his pen to point to an area on her wrist. The unusual mysterious bruise came to mind as we looked over his shoulder. He was pointing to that exact spot.

"What is it?" Matt asked.

The doctor pointed. "Well, I just saw traces of it on her autopsy photo. It was too faint to tell then, as you know. That's why we dug her up. Although it is bittersweet, it's a good thing we did. Have a look."

On the wall was a large screen. From his laptop, he projected the image of the bruise. I stared, too shocked to speak. Now you could almost see the mark even though the color was not the same as a bruise. Like a marking that went deep into her bone. In examining it closer under that much magnification, it looked to be an injection mark.

"You mean she was given a shot?" I asked.

"Of what?" Matt wanted to know.

The Medical Examiner continued. "I thought when I saw the earlier photos that was what it might be; so earlier today I found a sample of her blood we took at the time of death and had the lab run specific tests for drugs in her system. Nothing was found before because we were not looking. At that time, everyone thought it was most likely a suicide. Luckily, it was still able to be tested. Jesse doesn't have all the results back. So this is off the record. He said it looks like she was injected with some form of a paralyzing drug. In other words, she could not move her arms and legs or any part of her body. She was already very drunk. That, plus the drug, made it impossible for her to defend herself. She wouldn't have been able to stand up on her own, let alone hang herself."

"I'm certainly not blaming you, Doc. But how do you think we missed this?" Matt asked.

"You've got to remember that at the time of death her body was bloated. And that injection mark is tiny. She had several bruises due to the hanging. It was easy to miss. We thought it was a suicide. So we didn't look too deeply. On the surface, that's what it looked like. I'm sorry guys. We screwed up." The look of regret and sadness that he wore made my heart hurt. I touched his arm.

"No, I can understand that. The police missed it, too. We all mess up. Your assistant did the best he could given what everyone thought the circumstances were at the time." It was true. No one is perfect and everyone tries to do their best. Matt nodded.

I was just glad we caught it now. The more we had learned about CC, the less I thought suicide. Now, our instincts were proven true. The cause of death for CC Garden would be changed to homicide.

"Thank you for doing all this so quickly. You are so busy; and a million other cases need your attention. We know that." I said sincerely. It was a kind act on his part, dropping everything to help us.

"It was the least I could do."

Now CC could finally rest in peace. Her family would now know the truth. An investigation would begin.

"What will happen to her body now?" I wanted to know.

"Tomorrow we'll transport her remains back to the cemetery. They'll bury her again. I'm glad we caught it, too. And I'm thankful we could exhume her quickly and put her back in the resting place her family has for her. I've already faxed your captain the report and the magnified photos, so he is up to speed. He also said he would call the Gardens."

"Thank you again for responding and working so quickly," Matt said with gratitude. Not every medical examiner would go above and beyond like Dr. Locking did. It certainly made our job easier and spoke volumes about his ethics and character.

Like zombies, we walked out of the ME's office. The news shocked us. It was one thing to suspect, but another to have proof. It changed everything. Matt said, "I'm thankful for the answers. But now I have so many more questions. The first being: who wanted CC Garden dead?"

Chapter Fifty

The inviting smells wafting from one of our favorite coffee shops was a welcome distraction. Matt and I entered prepared to read. The same question still nagged at me, however: I wondered if the script would become a lead or a dead end. There was only one way to find out. The place was always busy. Comfortable seating was abundant. Students sat with their laptops; businessmen and women held meetings. There was even a play space for moms to bring their energetic kids. We found two leather chairs with a little table between us. Matt grabbed our lattes. We settled in, ready for whatever awaited us on those pages. The iced mocha was just what I needed on a day like today. I took a sip.

"Mmm!" I smiled at Matt, who was preparing to read over my shoulder. We had decided that, even though we each could have had our own copies, it would be best to stay on the same page. The screenplay began:

INT : KRISTA'S APT. - DAY
KRISTA, blond, mid 20's, sits on her couch, the phone to her ear. She's talking to her new boyfriend, SAM, dark hair, rough around the edges, mid 20's.

KRISTA
Hello, Baby.

SAM
Whatcha doin'?

KRISTA
Oh, I'm just sitting here thinking about everything.
Do you ever wish we could know the future?

SAM (hostile voice)
And why would I want to know that?
I mean, what kind of question is that?

Awkward pause.

SAM, cont. (softer voice)
I'm here for you. Why don't we go out tonight?

KRISTA
That sounds fun. I'll be home from work by six?

SAM
See you then.

INT : KRISTA'S APT. – LATER SAME DAY
Krista glances around her luxury apartment. It's up in the Hollywood
hills and very expensive. She has a panoramic view of the city.
INT: RESTAURANT – SAME EVENING
Sam and Krista in a restaurant. They are holding hands, eyes glued to
each other. A waiter removes their plates.

KRISTA

That was really good. Thanks for taking me out.

SAM

Of course. Want anything else?

KRISTA

No, but I do need to run to the ladies room.
I'll be right back. Watch my coat, okay?

Sam watches her walk away, leans across the table, reaches into her
jacket and grabs her wallet. He snaps pictures of her credit cards and
checks from her checkbook.

"Whoa!" I said aloud.

"I wonder who Sam is," Matt pondered.

As we continued reading, a couple of things became clear. This was a girl with plenty of money. Her new boyfriend wanted it. She was making poor choices when it came to men. In the next scene, she returned from the restroom.

KRISTA

There's something we need to talk about.
I wish you would only see me. I want you for
myself.

SAM (irritated)

We've had this conversation before.
It's not happening. I can't promise you that.

KRISTA (wiping a tear)

You can't keep me a secret forever.
I won't have that. I won't stand for it.

Krista grabs her jacket and purse and runs out of the restaurant in tears.
Sam smirks to himself.

KRISTA (turning back from door)

138

I don't know if I want to see you anymore.
I'm tired of hiding who we are.

I stopped and looked up at Matt. "Who the heck is Sam?" I asked. "Clearly, he's not available for some reason. I find it interesting in this last scene she's ready to break up with him. While she's in the bathroom, he steals her credit card and banking info." I paused, then went on. "Didn't we get Sally's bank account info?"

"The Captain has the guys working on it. I'm sure we'll get an update."

I wasn't feeling that patient. So I read some more. I found out that Krista and her unavailable lover kept seeing each other despite the fight. Marco detailed in the script a series of fights they got into involving the same issue over the next few weeks, the last few weeks of her life. Krista became more and more angry and distraught. Throughout that time, Sam kept taking money from her bank account. Krista didn't even notice.

INT: KRISTA'S APT. - NIGHT
Krista can't sleep. She talks to herself.
                    KRISTA
          He loves me. He loves me not. How do I know?
                         Does he love me for me or for my
               money?
                         I wish I had never told him about my
               inheritance.
Krista finally drifts off.
EXT: KRISTA'S APT. – LATE NIGHT
Sam takes the key from his pocket and quietly lets himself in. He looks around. It is completely dark. He walks into Krista's bedroom, looks at her one last time, leans over, and plunges a knife into her throat.

Now, that is cold, I thought. As I continued reading, a chill ran down my spine. How close to the truth was that scene? Matt and I flipped to the next set of short scenes.

EXT : BAR - NIGHT

139

ANNA, blond, mid-20's, and her friends are making their way out of a bar. Anna is very drunk. A friend is on each side of her, holding her up. She can hardly walk.

ANNA (in a slurred voice)
Tonight was awesome! Who wants to party some more?
FRIEND ONE
No way, girl. I think you've had enough.
ANNA
No way. I can have more if I want to.
FRIEND TWO (looking at her watch)
Yeah, okay. But not with me. I gotta get up tomorrow.
It's already after midnight. The three come to a large walk-up building.
Anna's friends slowly and gingerly lead her up the stairs to her third-floor apartment.
Friend One takes the key from her purse and opens the door.
They walk into the small but neat one-bedroom.
They help her into bed. Anna begins to snore immediately.
The two friends lock the door and exit.
ANNA (wakes up – slurs)
Thanks guys.
Her head is spinning. It's like her whole room is one big ride.

Matt groans from beside me. "I think we are going to get a better idea of what happened to CC Garden." I almost didn't want to go on.

INT: ANNA'S BEDROOM – WEE HOURS OF MORNING
The KILLER, dressed all in black, opens the bedroom door quietly. All the lights are on. Anna is sleeping right in the middle of her bed, snoring loudly. He walks to her bedside, pulls out a syringe, and plunges it into her wrist. Several minutes later, he picks up her drugged body and drags it to the closet. He loops the rope around her neck, ties the knot securely to the rod, and watches Anna die.

"This is really creepy," I whispered. It made me feel so uncomfortable just reading it. But we had to go on. What was next? Or, should I say, who was next?

140

EXT: LAURA'S APT. - NIGHT

    Her KILLER looks through binoculars focused on window. He watches LAURA, blond, 20's, for a long time. She is in the kitchen cooking. The longer he watches her, the more intense he becomes. He continues watching while she scoops her food onto a plate and goes to the living room to watch TV. He watches when she pours a glass of water from a jug in the fridge, then returns to the living room. He watches her take out a script and begin to read. He watches her drink from the glass. She's thirsty and drinks the entire contents. He watches as her face grows pale, as she tries to get up and falls back, as she vomits then convulses. He watches her die, gleeful and hyped up.

    Was that how Mini Loash died? I wondered. Could we be getting a glimpse into her last moments on this very page? I breathed in sharply and said, "That was also how Lindsay was supposed to die."

    Matt nodded. "This is unbelievable. Maybe she was being stalked and didn't even know it. I'm glad she's at her sister's house."

    We found the story that closely mirrored the death of our latest victim, Cassie Garrison. In the story, her name was Jill. She was being followed. Her killer was obsessed with her. One particular scene caught our attention.

EXT: PARK - DAY
JILL, blond, mid-20's, is walking with a friend.

JILL

Moving from the Midwest was the best and worst thing I've ever done.
I miss everyone so much. But I'm here now.
Even though I'm homesick, I will make the best of this.

FRIEND

Maybe you should find someone to date.
It might add another piece to your life. I could set you up with someone?

JILL (laughs)

Um, no. I'm not ready for that yet. But as soon as I am…
(winks)

The two young women don't know a STALKER is watching, listening, and waiting to strike.

INT: JILL'S PLACE - NIGHT
KILLER is obsessed with Jill. He's been stalking her for months. She's all he thinks about. Now he's poised to act. He watches through binoculars as she runs through her nightly routine: bring in mail; check messages; fall into bed exhausted. Before long, she is fast asleep. The killer enters her house with a key he had made, creeps to her bedroom, see she's sleeping soundly, leans over her, and plunges a knife into her throat. With a start, Jill's eyes open. She feels the blood and tries to get away. She rolls off the bed and staggers toward the door, knife dangling from her neck. Blood is everywhere. Just when it looks like she might escape out the door, she falls exhausted and close to death.

KILLER
Oh, Jill, that was a nice try.

He carries her back to bed and tucks her in. He takes the knife from her throat and leaves as quietly as he came in.

I was glad to take a break from reading the awful and ironic material. "Even the struggle was in the screenplay," Matt mused. "That really is creepy."

I agreed. "But if Marco has a valid alibi, we have to assume he didn't kill her. Still, he has to know who did. How else could the killer know that detail?" I said in a frustrated voice.

"Maybe it's the other way around. He writes the awful scenes; after that someone else carries them out," Matt questioned. That just sounded weird enough to be convincing. I stretched. After a break, we plowed through the final scene. The strange thing was, it wasn't complete. I didn't know what to make of it.

In the scene, 'Linda' was a blond girl in her twenties. She was happy and bubbly. Her whole face lit up when she smiled. The killer thought that broad smile was her best feature. Like the others, she was chasing her dreams. *It's really too bad she has to die*, the killer thought. *She's such a nice girl.* Nevertheless, he was stalking Linda. She wasn't aware of it. He watched and watched, becoming more and more obsessed. One day, he couldn't just watch any longer.

Matt looked at me and said, "This is different, isn't it? We don't know what happens. In real life, Lindsay isn't dead. In fact, what happened to her isn't yet written."

I sat up straighter and nodded vigorously. "You know, you're right, Matt. So the question is, what happens next?" I thought for a moment and continued. "The killer didn't count on that. Maybe he's adding to the story. It's so crazy."

"And miraculous," Matt added.

Chapter Fifty-One

"Finally," Detective Tamara Case exclaimed. She had just gotten in touch with Mini's mother, who told her she and her partner could come right over to interview her family. They had been out of town and just got the message. That explained the delay, Tamara thought. She walked over to the newest rookies and invited them to come along. It was always good for them to gain experience. She knew John knew that. Their captain did, too. The new recruits jumped up and grabbed their phones and some coffee to go. They decided to drive in one car. John Shields drove; Tamara sat up front with him. Jones and Caplin climbed into the back.

"Where are we heading to, guys?" Ross asked.

"The Loash family lives in Orange County. It's a little bit of a drive," Tamara replied.

"I really am curious to see what her family has to say," Kelsey Jones interjected.

"Out of all the cases, we know the least about her," Ross confirmed.

"I guess she has a mom, dad, and five siblings, plus grandparents, who will all be there. I think we'll start by interviewing everyone together. Then we can do smaller separate interviews, since there are four of us. What do you think, Tamara?" John asked.

"Perfect. Great idea."

During the drive, Ross took his copy of the screenplay out and read aloud to them. "So the girl in this script didn't even know she was being stalked. I find that hard to believe, don't you?"

Ross put down the script and spoke. They were all struck with how true to life this was. It was really spooky.

"Oh, I don't know. Sometimes a stalker is that good. I think for a while at least it could go unnoticed. And that is an awful thing to imagine," Kelsey said. "What I want to know is how this screenplay can be so accurate. It's uncanny how Marco Crane knows all these details." Everyone agreed. "This would make a good story for a movie, if it wasn't so tragic in real life," Shields observed.

"It's like life imitates art. Usually, it's the other way around. Art imitates life," Tamara chimed in.

"Maybe that's the point; maybe the killer wants to bring this story to life," Ross observed.

They all thought about that for a moment and hoped that wasn't the case. "I'll be interested to see where we all are tomorrow at our meeting. I want to compare notes with everyone," Kelsey exclaimed.

Chapter Fifty-Two

The four detectives pulled up to a cozy-looking yellow house with a white picket fence that surrounded it on all sides. As soon as they got out of the car, a pre-teen girl ran out the door to open the gate. "Hello," she greeted them cheerfully. "I'm Macy, Mini's younger sister. Come on in."

The girl looked to be about twelve. She wore her blonde hair in two long braids that bounced when she walked. The style suited her bubbly energy and personality. Tamara smiled at her. She couldn't help but be charmed.

The detectives entered a brightly colored house. The walls were pale yellow, the furniture an off white. Several people were seated, waiting to be interviewed. Young and old, they all had the same startling green eyes Mini had had, although the children's were brighter than the elders.

"Hello, I'm Mike Loash. This is my wife, Lucy. These are my parents, Jan and Joe." He indicated two senior citizens seated next to their daughter-in-law. "And these are my children: Macy, Mike, Jr., Morgan, and Malcolm." The children ranged in age from twelve to twenty-five.

"So nice to meet all of you. I'm Detective John Shields; and this is my partner Detective Tamara Case. These are Detective Jones and Caplin." Everyone shook hands.

"Have a seat, please. We have fresh coffee and cookies if you'd like?" Lucy offered. All the detectives accepted the treats.. They were served from a large, elegantly painted tray.

"Thank you so much. This all looks delicious." John glanced at his three colleagues. He pointed to the rookies and then looked at the four siblings. To the others this silently indicated a change of plans. They nodded in agreement.

"We would like to interview you separately, in groups, if that's alright with you. No one is a suspect. But each of you might have something unique to offer," John explained. "It'll also make the process go faster."

The family consented. Every one of them looked ready to help, which always made the job easier. "Kids, why don't you go into the kitchen with the detectives," Lucy urged. The rookie officers stood up.

"Lead the way," Ross encouraged.

Chapter Fifty-Three

The veteran cops sat with Mini's parents and grandparents. Each of the adults sat quietly. The women held their hands in their laps, while the men tried to remain strong.

"Everyone wanted to be here today to help you in whatever way we can. That's just the kind of family we are," Lucy explained. "Again, I apologize for the delay. We just got back from a mini-vacation at our cabin. It's up in the mountains. Beautiful this time of year. I think we watched the sun set every day."

Lucy was chattering nervously. The detectives could tell this would be hard for her. She cleared her throat and continued. "We are happy to meet all of you and talk with you. We just want justice for our girl."

"I know this will be painful. If you can just try to relax," John explained. Everyone took some slow, deep breaths. "Please," he continued, "don't hold anything back. Even if it doesn't seem important, it just might be."

John Shields was comfortable conducting interviews. An extrovert at his core, he had an easy way with all types of people and personalities. He began the painful process of bringing up memories that this family most likely wished they didn't have to relive.

"Have you always lived in this house? It really gives off a cozy, warm, close family impression."

"Thank you. That's how we wanted it to feel. We value hospitality and want everyone who steps into our home to feel welcome," Mike explained.

"Do the two of you live here as well?" John pointed to the grandparents.

The senior Mrs. Loash was a tiny woman, with large glasses and white hair that looked permed. Her husband was slumped over a little, but his smile was radiant.

"We do. We love it here. It's such a great way to stay connected with everyone. We have our privacy when we want it. We live in a large apartment just off the house," Jan Loash informed us, pointing out a window to a structure at the back of the house. "Our son and daughter-in-law remodeled and made it just for us. We have dinner together once a week. We go to church together. And we try to help out in whatever way we can with the grandkids. Now that Macy is getting older we don't always need to babysit like we used to." She laid her delicate fingers in her lap.

That really sounded ideal, John thought. He had grown up in a series of foster homes and felt inspired by a family like this. He hoped they knew what a luxury it was that they had one another. By their closeness, it seemed like they understood.

"What can you tell us about Mini?" Her father nodded for her mother to answer. His smile was gone. A deep pain took up residence instead.

"Mike and Mini were so close. I swear she was a daddy's girl from the day she was born. She would be screaming and crying, then he would come home, and it would stop. All he had to do was pick her up and everything was okay. It was always like that," Mrs. Loash related, as she took a sip of water. "She was bright, very curious. Always wanted to know why things happened the way they did. As a girl she loved math and science. So much so that we got her one of those kids' chemistry sets so she could figure out how things worked."

Her grandfather gave a tiny chuckle. "She got that curiosity from me. I once was a bio-chemist in a lab. I saw that same curiosity in her. So it kind of surprised us when she decided to become an actress. We supported her dreams, of course; but she had a head for math and science."

"She performed in a school play in seventh grade. That's when the acting bug hit her. She liked acting; but I think she would have gone on to become a fantastic scientist of some kind," Mini's mother explained. Mini had looked like her mom, with sleek blonde hair and smooth skin. She'd also inherited her grandfather's contagious smile.

Mike looked up toward the ceiling when he spoke. "She had just moved out of the house. She worked at a local coffee shop. She could afford a small studio. She was so excited." He stopped to gather his thoughts. His voice was full of emotion as he continued. "I didn't want her to move. She was our oldest girl. I'm sure I was over protective. I couldn't help it. Los Angeles is a big place for a young woman." He cleared his throat again and blinked back tears.

He couldn't go on, so Lucy continued. "She came over for our weekly dinners and would normally come to church with us on Sundays."

"Is that how you knew something was wrong?" John gently asked.

Her mother nodded. "She didn't show up for dinner that night. If she had other plans, she would always call us or send a text. She wouldn't let us worry about her like that." Lucy's voice had gone up an octave with a note of hysteria. It was clear she was remembering that terrible day.

It was hard for the detectives not to feel this family's pain.

"So what did you do?' Tamara quietly asked. Joe Loash looked at her.

"When we kept calling and didn't get an answer, my son, grandson and I went over to check things out. We had a backup key she had given us." His voice faltered.

A long respectful silence fell over them until he was ready to go on.

"We knocked on her door first, calling out 'Mini, Mini.'..." His voice faltered once more. He took a steadying breath.

"We all had a very bad feeling. We opened the door. That's when we saw her. She was lying on her kitchen floor. There was vomit everywhere."

Mini's father took it from there. "At first, we thought she had fallen ill. But the closer I got, I could see... she wasn't breathing and... and her skin was a...greenish-grey color." His wife made a gagging sound.

"If you need a break...," John said gently. She shook her head.

"Mike," his father continued, "is a paramedic. He checked to see if there was a pulse. There... there wasn't one." He started to shake uncontrollably. His wife stroked the back of his hand in a soothing gesture.

"We're so sorry you have to relive this. If there was any other way... " John said.

Mini's father took over again. "I couldn't figure out how she died. It looked like she'd just dropped where she was. The only thing we saw besides the vomit was a half-empty glass of water. So we called the police. Once they did an autopsy, they discovered she hadn't died of natural causes. I've seen patients who've ingested poison. It's terrible. It must have been an awful way to die."

Now both parents and grandparents held one another as tears fell. It was understandable, of course. Just thinking about it gave the detectives chills.

"Who do you think would want to do this to your daughter?" Tamara asked.

Her mother looked at the female detective as she wiped tears away. "We just don't know. She had no enemies. She had a very nice boyfriend. She was living life, chasing her dreams. Who would want to do this to my baby? She never told us anything was wrong. We don't have anything else we can tell you about her death. We don't know anything else."

Lucy ended with a pleading sound in her voice. Both detectives exchanged glances. They hoped their rookie counterparts were having better luck.

.

Chapter Fifty-Four

Kelsey and Ross sat with the young adults in the kitchen. Like the living room, the walls were painted a pale yellow. The kitchen looked comfortable and lived in. Pans were on the stove and dishes in the sink. On the counter sat a large cookie jar in the shape of a teddy bear.

"That used to be Mini's favorite," Malcolm said, laughing a little.

Across the large wooden table from the detectives, Mini's four siblings sat. All had blonde hair and those startling green eyes.

"You're the oldest, Malcolm, right?" Ross asked.

"Yeah I'm twenty-five. Mike Jr. is twenty-two. Morgan is eighteen and Macy is twelve."

"You guys all seem pretty close, is that right?" Kelsey interjected.

"Yeah, we are. I mean, we fight and all. But we love each other," Mike Jr. said.

"Mini had just been in a commercial before she died," Macy announced proudly. "It was one of those makeup ones."

Her older sister added, "She even got free products from the company. It was really cool to watch my sister." This was said with pride.

Suddenly Malcolm's face fell. "She was just getting started as an actress. When we would watch the award shows, we could see how she dreamed of one day getting one of those Oscars."

"Can you tell us about her boyfriend?" Mike smiled.

"His name is Chris. He was my friend from college. He was a little younger than Mini, but a good dude. He really cared about her. He was studying abroad in Singapore when it happened. I think he got a job there. Now he lives on the other side of the world. After Mini died, it was just too hard for him to stay. He had to come back to that news. It was awful for him, too," Malcolm relayed.

"We all knew him and liked him a lot," Macy chimed in.

"I used to say if Chris and Mini got married, I could maybe babysit their kids," Morgan said tearfully.

Mike, Jr. laughed. "They weren't that serious. No one was talking marriage. But they did really care about each other."

Four sets of bright green eyes stared out at the detectives. Kelsey continued, "I'm sure it was really hard on you guys when your sister died." Each head nodded in sorrow and agreement.

"Sometimes siblings know things that maybe parents don't. You know what I mean?" Ross asked, looking each sibling in the eye. "Do any of you know if she was having problems with anyone?"

"She was being stalked. At least, she thought maybe she was," Mike Jr. volunteered.

"When did she mention that to you? How close was it to when she died?" Ross wanted to know.

Mike, Jr. thought for a second. "I'd say about two weeks before. It wasn't anything she could prove. She just said she felt like she was maybe being watched. She was kind of vague. Chris was already abroad, so I offered to escort her to her acting class and to the coffee shop. She declined. She said she was probably being silly."

"She blamed it on the script she was working on in class," Macy jumped in.

"Can you tell us about that?"

"She hated the guy."

"Who?" Ross asked.

"Oh, that acting teacher guy. He made her play the role of a girl who was murdered by poison. She said she was almost afraid to eat food after that," Morgan said.

"Did she ever tell the teacher she didn't want to do it?"

"I think so. I don't remember for sure, though. Do you guys?" Malcolm looked to his brother and sisters.

"I think she did. But he didn't really care. He said she couldn't pick and choose what she wanted to work on because everyone was doing the same scene," Mike said.

"How lame," Macy muttered. Kelsey couldn't help but think the same. "She told me that after the class was done with that scene, she was going to quit," Macy spoke animatedly.

"She was counting the days," Mike Jr. added.

"But she didn't know for sure if anyone was after her?" Kelsey questioned.

"I don't think so. She never said she felt like someone was out to get her. Just that she thought she was being watched. But I don't know as much as Kara."

153

He then went on to tell the detectives about Mini's best friend, Kara. "She wasn't in the acting class. But Mini told her everything."

"I know she'll help, because we told her about the interview today. She told us to give you this," Morgan handed Kelsey a note with Kara's phone number on it.

"Can I ask you a question?" Malcolm asked.

"Sure, what is it?"

"It's so weird that she was poisoned. It was almost like the words in the scene she was practicing came to life in a very creepy way. Have you ever seen that before? Have you ever had a case like that?"

Truthfully, neither Ross nor Kelsey wanted to tell the kids that they were rookies and that they hadn't seen anything like this, let alone many cases at all. "No, we haven't. You're right. It is really strange how your sister died."

"My mom and dad aren't the same anymore," Macy said. "My dad is just quiet; and my mom has this sad look on her face most of the time."

Kelsey took a breath. "I'm sorry to hear that. I'm sure it's tough on all of you." Especially, she thought, since their littlest sister was still so young. "Murder is traumatizing. Everyone deals with grief differently." Kelsey felt that her answer wasn't good enough. Still, it was the best she had to offer.

"So did the guy commit the perfect murder or what?" Mike, Jr. asked.

"He might have thought so. But that's why we're here. There are three other cases we're looking into that may or may not be connected," Ross explained. Normally, he wouldn't say something like that. But he could tell this family needed hope. They needed to know that the Homicide squad cared and were on the case.

The kids and rookies joined the adults in the living room. The family seemed relieved that the interviews were over. They all looked exhausted. Kelsey looked at the kids and gave each of them her business card. "If any of you think of anything else, please don't hesitate to call, text or email, okay?" They all agreed and took the laminated cards she slid toward them.

"One more thing," Macy said. "I'm praying you solve the murder of my sister. I know God will help you if you ask him. Will you?"

Kelsey looked uncomfortable. Ross jumped in right away. "Sure, I will. He's always helping me out. I'm sure he'll help us solve your sister's case, too."

"Thank you, everyone, for being so helpful. We know it was tough for you."

"We can't thank you enough," John added. He shook hands with everyone. Then the four detectives walked out of the house.

Chapter Fifty-Five

The four detectives sat together in a corner booth at the Robin Cafe. It was one of those 24-hour places that served good-sized portions.

"After this, I'm going to need to go to the gym. My burger is almost too big for just me," Kelsey said as she took a bite.

"These are not lunch-sized portions for sure," Ross added. He was one of those guys who could eat and eat and then eat some more. He was always hungry and had a lean, thin frame.

"I'm sure it's not a problem for you, Ross," Tamara teased. He grinned and shook his head.

John joined his partner and their colleagues in the booth with his own large Mediterranean-style sandwich. "So let's talk shop. That was such a nice family. It's really awful that they have to face this every day for the rest of their lives. I'm sure, like mine, your hearts go out to them. How were the interviews for you guys?"

The newest members of the division exchanged glances. "It looks like
her boyfriend was studying abroad in Singapore when she died," Kelsey began. "After her murder, he was so crushed that he ended up finding a job and moving there."

"That's relevant because...?" Tamara asked, then added, "The more specific timing of him being out of town?"

"I see what you mean, Tamara. The Loash sibs told us Mini thought she was being stalked but couldn't prove it," Kelsey said, smiling.

"Now that's something that didn't come up in our interviews. Good work, you guys," Ross chimed in. "Her brother offered to escort her when he could, but she doubted her own hunch and said she was probably being silly." The young detective had a sad look on his face. "She must have been so scared and so stuck. I can't imagine." Ross had so much empathy for others. He was one of those people who could put himself in someone else's shoes, or at least try.

"The Loashes gave us a lead on her best friend, Kara. She wasn't in Marco's class. But I guess she and Mini talked about everything. Maybe she can be of help. Right now all we know is that, like the others, Mini was uncomfortable with the scene she was playing out for Marco

Crane," Kelsey said. They all wished they had more details on that. Hopefully, they would soon.

Ross took a sip of his chocolate milkshake. It went perfectly with his burger, fries and onion rings. "I was thinking, since we have her contact info and she's not too far from here, we should give her a call. Maybe she can meet us today. I know it's short notice. It sounded like she might be expecting a call from us, though." Everyone thought that was a good idea.

The call was made. After some juggling and negotiating, Kara agreed to come to the diner and meet.

"Just our luck! Thank you, God," Ross praised.

"You reassured little Macy with your faith. That was a really great job, Ross," Tamara said.

Ross nodded sheepishly. "I meant every word of it."

The detectives had brought their paperwork with them. It was always a good idea to have something productive to do. The paperwork was the worst thing in his mind. John felt, as he stared at his laptop and began typing his report, that he never seemed to have enough time to finish it They spent the next hour working on it while they waited for Kara Jaben to arrive.

Tamara glanced at her watch and looked up. Time had flown by —and that's when she saw her. An average-sized woman with wavy hair was glancing around the restaurant, her head on a swivel, obviously looking around for them. Tamara waved her over and tapped her partner, who was in the zone as he typed. John stood and motioned Kara over as well. The female detectives slid over and made room for her to sit. She introduced herself. "I'm Kara Jaben. Nice to meet you, Detectives." She extended a long, manicured hand to each of them. She had a low, raspy voice.

The foursome offered Kara a drink or something to eat. She politely declined. "I just finished a latte, thanks. How can I help? Malcolm told me you might want to speak with me."

"I'm Detective Kelsey Jones. This is my partner, Ross Caplin. We're with these two, Detectives Case and Shields. We hear you and Mini were best friends? When did you meet?"

"In the fifth grade. It was such a hard year for both of us. We weren't in with the popular crowd of girls. I guess you could say our friendship was meant to be. She loved math and science and was really

157

good at it. Way better than me," Kara said with a chuckle. She stared straight ahead, almost at nothing.

"I can't begin to tell you how hard this has been on everyone. I miss her every day." Kara's voice was tinged with sadness as she remembered her friend. The detectives' hearts broke for her.

"What can you tell us about Mini? What was she like?" Kelsey wanted to know.

"She was fun and energetic. She has… I mean, had a big family and loved them so much. When we were in college, we got an apartment together. I'm not sure if we spent more time there or at her parent's house. I'm still in college. Even though she was super-smart in math and science, Mini chose another path. She ended up loving acting. I moved in with some other girls. That way I could pay less rent. She kept the apartment. That made sense, because it was right in Hollywood. That was exactly where she wanted to be. We still saw each other often and talked almost every day."

"What can you tell us about her boyfriend, Chris?" Ross asked.

"He was a really nice guy. He was crazy about Mini. When she… um…" Kara was having trouble getting the words out. "He was out of the country." Her voice trailed off for a second. "I was the one who told him. That was one of the toughest calls I have ever made in my life. He cried and was so devastated. He flew back for the funeral. I remember that." She reached into her purse and took out some tissues. Carefully, she pulled one out and dabbed at her eyes.

"He met with the police and helped them as best he could. After that, he moved away for good. He said he couldn't stay." She thought for a second. "I think he felt bad that he wasn't around, that maybe if he had been, she would still be… " Kara dropped her head to her chest. They could tell she was starting to panic.

"Take deep breaths. In and out," Tamara coached, putting her hand on the young woman's back.

Once Kara regained control, she apologized. "I'm sorry. This is just so hard. I don't normally have panic attacks. Remembering how her life ended is the worst. I've never experienced anything like it before and never ever want to again."

"We understand that. Your help means so much to our case, and, I'm sure, to your friend. We just have a few more questions," Kelsey gently said. When Kara agreed, the rookie continued.

"What can you tell us about her death?"

"She loved life. It isn't fair. You know she was poisoned, of course. What a terrible way to die. The crazy thing was, she was doing this horrid scene about a girl who was poisoned. It totally freaked her out. She hated it. So much so that she was actually going to quit her acting class. She didn't want to. But Mini told me the teacher wasn't listening and made her keep doing it." Kara suddenly went silent.

"What else, Kara?" John asked. He could tell she was holding something back.

She took a deep breath. "I know she felt like someone was watching her. She just couldn't prove it. I had to pry the information out of her. I was scared for her."

"Can you tell us more about that? What did she say?" Ross asked.

"She said one night a black Chevy followed her halfway home after a late night shift at work. She said he would turn when she did. She tried to let the driver pass. He wouldn't do it. She never got a good look at his face. Eventually, he realized she'd caught on to him and sped off. It scared the daylights out of her, I know that. She called me crying around midnight."

"Did she tell you anything else?" Kelsey asked.
Kara thought, then took a shaky breath. "Well… once Mini said she got the sense that someone was watching her. So she pulled back her blinds. She said all she saw was an outline of a person standing across the street holding binoculars that were aimed toward her window."

"So she never saw a face?" Kelsey asked, feeling frustrated.

"I'm afraid not. As soon as the person noticed her, whoever it was ducked and ran away."

"Did she ever report this to the police?" Ross asked.

"No, how could she? I mean, what would she say? I think there's someone stalking me, only I can't tell you anything about the person," Kara said, a note of hysteria in her voice.

Kelsey couldn't blame her. It was probably true. Their hands would have been tied. What a frustrating situation, she thought. Ross, as if reading her mind, expressed that to Mini's best friend. It seemed to calm her.

"I think Mini began to think she was paranoid. Maybe she was just imagining things, I don't know. But I do know she was scared. She was not the type to exaggerate; so I believed her, as did her family. I'm not sure who she told. I know Malcolm, for sure, but probably not her parents because she didn't want them to worry." The detectives sat listening carefully, taking notes. "I still think there was something to it. Soon after, she was poisoned. Obviously, someone was actually out to get her." The four cops had to agree.

"We will do whatever we can to solve her case," Kelsey assured her. They took out business cards and gave them to a grieving Kara. She took them gingerly and put them in her purse. "Thanks so much for taking time to talk with us. We know how difficult it was for you. Again, sorry for the short notice. Thanks for making time."

"Mini was important to me—to a lot of people. The world lost a great treasure that day. I'll miss her forever."

Ross offered, "If you have anything you'd like to add, or have any questions, please don't hesitate to call."

With a quick shake of her head she said, "I won't have anything else to say. I'm sure of that. But I'll keep it in mind."

It was the best she could do under the circumstances. The detectives understood that. Talking about her best friend's murder had brought up all the bad memories for her. That they could see. She blinked back tears and tried to look at them. She couldn't. She shook their hands and quickly walked out of the coffee shop.

Chapter Fifty-Six

Night fell on the City of Angels. Each detective felt their own level of deep frustration with the slow progress they were making. There was so much to analyze and understand.

The Shields family gathered for dinner like always. It was rare to have the teenagers all home. For a while, John lost himself in the chatter of the day. Tonight his wife had opted to order pizza instead of cooking. It was too hot anyway, he thought. Still, John was having a hard time concentrating on what his family was saying. He tried, of course. However, his heart was with the four dead girls. After dinner was over, he excused himself and went into his office. He would go through the files again. Maybe he'd missed something.

Ross Caplin walked out of the theater with his long-time girlfriend. They hadn't been on a date in ages. Both had busy jobs and full schedules. The movie they saw was okay.

He was falling in love fast with Martha. Her smile, her way with people, charmed him more every day. He was so lucky, he thought. She leaned into him as they walked to his car. The case was really getting to him, but tonight, even though he didn't feel like being around anyone, he took her out anyway.

At least she was enjoying herself, he thought. He wished he could detach and escape into the present moment. That wasn't as easy as people thought. There were so many pieces to this story that seemed hidden to him. He mulled it over as they ate dinner. After she left, he sat down to review his notes again.

Tamara Case finished cooking dinner for her family. That night she served lemon chicken with corn and roasted potatoes. Everyone commented on how good the food was. It made her happy to care for her family. Tonight, however, she felt zapped of energy. At least the meal was a big hit. Even her four and six-year-old girls ate it without complaint. The teenage boys would eat anything. She was glad everyone was satisfied. As they all ate, she couldn't help but think about the young women's families. Their lives were needlessly ended. Their loved ones changed forever in ways they didn't ask for and couldn't imagine. They needed answers. After her little ones were tucked in and homework was checked over, she too reviewed her files and the screenplay, hoping she could find some link she might have overlooked.

George Mendoza didn't even go home. He sat reading the murder books. He read his copy of Marco's work again. *How could the police have missed so much?* he wondered.

He often worked late. There wasn't anyone for him to go home to. After his wife had died, home felt like an empty place. It was so quiet - too quiet for him. So staying at the station, eating a vending machine meal at his desk, wasn't a problem.

Eventually, he looked at the clock. Time had flown by. His brain was fried; his nerves were frayed. He packed up his briefcase and left for home.

Matt and I read the screenplay again. "Aah," he fumed in frustration. "What are we not seeing, Emma?"

"Your guess is as good as mine," I said. I closed the heavy binder. The third read-through didn't bring any more answers than the first two. The words were starting to blur. It had been an exhausting but productive day. I felt like we'd jammed a lifetime into those twenty-four-plus hours.

"Let's call it a night. Maybe with some sleep…" Matt just laughed.

"You sleeping? I doubt it. I know how you get when you're on a case." I smiled and rolled my eyes.

"Okay, okay. You know my secret," I said, lifting my arms up in mock surrender. He laughed. Then he touched my cheek and looked into my eyes.

"We're going to solve this, Emma." His words and gesture of reassurance made me believe that we would. *Hopefully soon, Matt,* I thought.

Chapter Fifty-Seven

June 24th

The following morning everyone gathered for another conference. A kind of buzz and high energy was in the atmosphere. Matt brought in bagels and the captain, donuts. I started the coffee pot before the meeting. It would be another long day. We all needed the caffeine.

"How was your date last night, Ross?" Kelsey asked. He shrugged.

"I don't know that I was the best company. It went well enough, I guess. To be honest, I couldn't wait to get home and go over that screenplay again. I can't tell you how many times I scoured that thing last night. I practically know it by heart. What the heck are we missing, guys?" There were nods from everyone around the table.

"I'm willing to bet, knowing this group, we all had that kind of night," Tamara chimed in. Everyone laughed. She was right. We were all very dedicated to our work.

"Okay, so does anyone have anything new to add, any new theories, any questions?" Our boss asked, taking a big bite of a jelly donut, followed by a gulp of coffee.

"This case is obviously tearing at all of us," I responded. "Marco may have a verifiable alibi. Since the screenplay so closely mirrors the murders, I'm wondering if he has a partner? Maybe he killed some of the women, but not all of them." I let out a sigh, then took a sip of fresh hot coffee.

"I was wondering that, too," John added. "But say he didn't kill any of them. What's in it for him?" Several heads nodded in acknowledgement.

Steve looked over at his partner. "Yesterday we got a hold of Scott and Juliet Hall and set up an interview with both of them this afternoon." He looked around the room and continued. "We ran IDs on the vehicles registered by everyone we've interviewed so far, as well as those of their spouses. Guess who has a black Chevy? Scott Hall."

His partner filled in the blanks. "It sounds like the couple has been friends with Marco for a long time. We'll talk to them. See if we can shake something loose. If he brings the Chevy, I'll snap a picture of the license."

I almost jumped out of my seat as I remembered something. Matt looked over at me knowingly. I loved that our minds were so in sync. "The bartender we interviewed said that CC Garden and her friends came to his bar every Friday. He also said that one night there was a man suspiciously watching CC, or at least that was his impression. After CC left, the guy came up to the bartender and started asking questions about her. The bartender told him nothing. However, he did follow the guy outside and took down his license number. He said it was a black car and remembered the first three letters were A C T. He wasn't sure if he still had the note with the entire plate number but said he would look." Everyone smiled. This could be a big break, and we all knew it. "Even if he isn't able to find the note, he might recognize the man. Why don't you guys call him in to look at the books and see if he can identify anyone," our boss said.

A lineup is a set of photos. We ask a witness to look at the photos to see if they recognize someone. If they do, we ask from where and when. Often, in court, lawyers will dispute the accuracy of the identification. That can be valid. It is not an exact science. Still, it's a start.

"Davis, Cameron, have you guys been able to get a hold of the Haze girl's bank records?" The captain inquired.

"Still working on it, sir. We have a warrant in to Judge Banks. We're just waiting for the okay. We should hear back soon. Once we get it, we'll head straight for the bank," Mike said.

We knew this was important. The screenplay had the first victim's boyfriend stealing her money. I wondered if anyone had taken funds out of Sally's account without her knowledge, maybe even after her murder.

"How were the interviews with the Loash family?" Captain Mendoza asked the veterans and the rookies. John cleared his throat.

"With the parents and grandparents, we didn't get much. Apparently, she had a nice boyfriend who was out of town when she was murdered. He's now living abroad in Singapore, because he was too devastated by what happened to her."

The captain turned to Ross, who continued. "In talking with the four siblings, we found out that Mini felt like she was being stalked, although she couldn't prove it. Her best friend later told the four of us that Mini told her she saw a black car following her after work one

164

night. Her brother offered to escort her to work and class after that, but she turned him down. The siblings also told us, as far as the acting class went, their sister was uncomfortable with the screenplay. Crane had told her to deal with it. She was getting ready to quit."

"Remember that she was poisoned, just like the girl in the screenplay," Kelsey said.

"Speaking of that, Jesse Smith told me to tell you that they compared the poison from both murder scenes. It's the same type," Captain Mendoza informed us. There were gasps from around the room.

"I think Mini thought she was being paranoid and didn't act on her instincts," Kelsey ruminated. "When we asked her siblings about a possible police report, they said she didn't feel like she had anything concrete to give us." Kelsey sighed heavily. "What a shame."

Our hands would have been tied anyway. Still, maybe we could have done something, or at least had it documented. Stalking cases were the hardest to prove. They often went unreported.

Then it was our turn. Matt set down his coffee. "We now have four homicides. The ME noticed a bruise that looked suspicious on the wrist of CC Garden. We went to the exhumation. He found an injection mark. They're now running toxicology to see if they can figure out what she might have been injected with."

"In a way, it was such a relief to let her parents know. They were sad, of course, but happy that their daughter didn't kill herself. I reassured them we would do everything we could to solve her case," our boss told us. He continued. "Caplin, Jones, Case, Shields… help out where you can. But keep on your other cases. Ross and Kelsey had a busy night with two new homicides I'll need you to look at. You guys are not off this case altogether; however, I need you elsewhere, too. Matt, Emma… get that lineup ready and check with the bartender. See if you can nail down Marco's alibi. Also I'm going to need your paperwork on the interviews on my desk asap. Steve, Mike… I'll be anxious to hear about what you find in the bank records, and your interview with the Hall couple."

We all stood up. It didn't surprise me that we had more homicides to work. Often, there were more murders than cops to work them. It was frustrating and often meant juggling several cases at once. As we walked out of the room, I almost grabbed Matt's hand but stopped myself. No one knew about our blooming relationship. I wasn't sure how that would be received. Matt smiled at me again - almost reading my mind.

Chapter Fifty-Eight

Detectives Cameron and Davis stood by the fax machine. They watched the old machine as pages were spit out. "I wish this thing moved faster," Steve muttered, as he pounded on the aging contraption.

His partner laughed. "It's almost done. This is the last page." He took out the final page of Judge Bank's warrant for Sally's bank records. They walked into the captain's office to show him the document and to let him know they were off.

They pulled up to the bank at a good time. As they walked in, they could see there were only a few customers in line waiting for the teller. A man in a navy blue suit and red tie walked over to them. His name tag read: Charles Ridell. "Can I help you gentlemen?" he asked, as he looked at their uniforms and the badges they extended toward him.

"Sir, we're LAPD. We need to speak to the manager."

"That's me. How can I help you?" They showed him the thick stack of papers and explained what they needed.

"Come with me," he said, gesturing to a hallway with several offices. His was the biggest. He sat behind his desk and read through the thick stack of papers. The detectives looked around, enjoying the gorgeous view out the window, before taking their seats. Charles Ridell noticed.

"That view is one of the things I like best about this branch. You can see almost all of downtown from here."

"Mr. Ridell, how long have you been working at this location?"

"About four years now. Why?"

"Did you know Sally Haze?"

He continued to study the warrant and looked up. On top they had placed Sally's headshot, hoping it would jog his memory.

"You know, I did actually. She was and still is one of our best customers."

The detectives exchanged confused glances. "*Is?*" They spoke in unison.

Now it was the bank managers turn to look confused. "I'm sorry. Am I missing something here?" he asked.

"Sir, Sally was murdered about three years ago. Isn't her account closed?"

The manager's face grew pale as he responded. "I think I remember hearing something about that. I'm not sure which customer anymore. It was a while ago. As for her account, let me check. I probably just misspoke. I'm sure it's closed."

The detectives didn't know what to make of the manager. His fingers tapped the keyboard as he searched through the records. The shocked and embarrassed look on his face told them everything.

"Her account has remained open and is active." A bead of sweat dotted his forehead. The detectives tried hard to remain impassive. "Miss Haze had no family left. The notes say here that her parents are deceased. Hmm... they left her a rather large inheritance," he went on.

Then, as if finally seeing what they were getting at, he became angry. He started to put the pieces together. "So if she hasn't been drawing from her account, who has?" he pondered. "We need to get to the bottom of this."

"No, Mr. Ridell. *We* do. We'll let you know what we find out, alright." This was not a question, but a command from Detective Cameron.

The manager nodded and started to bring up Sally's records. "I'll print them out for you now. How far would you like me to go back?"

"How about four years," Steve answered.

"One thing in my purview is to close down her account now. That I know," Mr. Ridell informed them.

"Actually, please don't do that just yet. Any rogue charges made might help us find her killer," Mike said, playing the role of good cop.

The manager thought about it. "Well, I do want to help the police. But at the same time, the bank can't allow fraud. How about this? I can leave the account open for the next five days. Then I have to close it. Can we agree on that?" They did. In the meantime, everyone hoped the short time frame would be long enough to draw out the killer.

Chapter Fifty-Nine

"You've got to be kidding me," I exclaimed. "How could the bank not know about Sally's murder? And how could they keep the account open this long without seeing her?" It seemed unreal to me and was maddening.

"You should have seen the look of shock and horror on the bank manager's face. We all had the same reaction, Emma," Mike said.

"Let's all sit down and go through these records together. We need to figure out who's been using her account," Matt said, a note of urgency in his voice.

So that's what we did. Each of us took a huge stack of records and went into a conference room and sat around the table. I had the first year in front of me. I looked through pages of normal expenditures: monthly gym membership payments, rent, groceries, etc. There were charges for acting classes. They were not for Marco's class, however. I wondered if he took lessons from the same teacher. I highlighted it and jotted down my question for a future interview.

As I kept reading, I noticed that there were four significant withdrawals of over fifty thousand dollars right around the time Sally's death. "Look at this, guys," I said excitedly as I pointed to the charges. "It looks like the money was transferred into someone's account."

"But whose?" Matt questioned, as he read over my shoulder. "I don't think the bank, or a judge for that matter, is going to give us access to that person's account. I think they will investigate it."

"Judging by his reaction, I'll bet the manager will take his time in giving us any information, if he does at all," Mike said.

"Where is Marco Crane's alibi?" Steve asked, as he began to flip through the murder book.

"I got it. There's a copy of a check he wrote to cover his bar tab." He glanced over my shoulder. "Nope, it doesn't match the final four digits on the statement." That was true. It ruled him out in these instances.

Matt looked up at us and said, "I have the most recent transactions over the last year. It looks like someone made regular cash withdrawals of around ten thousand dollars every month. There's even one from a week ago. So whoever this is, they would have to have her pin. Maybe knowing that, a judge will let us look at this person's account, or at least get the name. This is illegal. Mike, can you call the manager now and see if we can get the security tape from all the cameras in and around the parking lot of the bank?"

"Yes. And Steve and I will hit the businesses around the bank to see if they have any tape from the last couple of weeks." Often, businesses keep their footage for up to thirty days. The more we could get the better off we would be.

"We can cover some of that ground with you. Would you mind if Matt and I went with you to interview the Halls?" I asked. "We met Scott briefly. It would be nice to meet his wife. Plus, if you need us to interview one or the other of them, we can certainly do that." They agreed.

"The interview isn't scheduled until tomorrow after lunch, around one p.m. Davis and I are going back to the bank to look at the footage. We also need to go back and talk with our bank manager again. We only have an hour before close of business, so this'll stretch into tomorrow. Why don't you give us all the statements so we can look them over before we leave? Let's put our heads together again with the security footage tomorrow after lunchtime. Let's meet back at the station," Steve said.

"Great, I'm already looking at Google Maps to see what businesses are around the bank. Emma and I will go check them out and try to get the tapes," Matt said, a note of excitement in his voice.

Chapter Sixty

Cameron and Davis returned to the bank. From the cars in the parking lot, they could tell it was busier than when they were there before. A woman with a stroller exited, while a business executive held the door open for her before he entered.

"Weren't we just here?" Mike joked. His partner laughed. Before they could get to the counter, one of the tellers noticed them and said she would get her boss. A few minutes later, a weary-looking Charlie Ridell approached them.

"Back so soon, gentlemen?" He was irritated, although they could tell he was trying to hide it.

"Hello again, Mr. Ridell, we have a couple more questions for you. Can we talk in your office?" Mike asked politely.

"As if I have a choice," he muttered, walking briskly ahead without uttering another word. As soon as they entered his office, he slammed the door loudly and sat behind his desk.

"Sir, could we trouble you for some water or coffee?" Steve asked. It was easy to see how upset the manager was. Steve wanted to stall for time so he could calm down. Ridell sighed, pressed a button on his intercom, and asked the voice on the other end for three cups of coffee. A few minutes later, the door opened. A pretty young woman dressed in a black skirt with a white sweater walked in with their beverages.

"Thank you, Natalie," her boss said. "You can go now. Shut the door on your way out." She nodded and quickly left.

"Who was that?" Mike asked.

"My long-time secretary and assistant. Surely you didn't come by to ask about her, now, did you?"

Mike took a breath and got right to the point. "Mr. Ridell, what we can't figure out is how come Sally's account was not shut down? We looked through the file. It shows the bank was notified." The manager cleared his throat uncomfortably.

"I have been giving that some thought. I wasn't the man in charge at the time of Miss Haze's murder. I was a supervisor at that time."

"Well, then we need to speak to the previous manager. Where is he or she now?" Mike asked.

"And that's where it gets tricky. Um… he, Martin Lopez, disappeared a month or two after Sally died. I think the police have a report."

The detectives knew that if there was a report, Missing Persons would have it.

No detective liked being blind-sided during an interview. "Why didn't you tell us about Mr. Lopez and his disappearance before?" Mike sharply asked.

"It was a really difficult time for the bank. One patron had been murdered; then, soon after that, the manager of said bank disappears. Why would I want to bring that up? Even though it looks strange, it might be a coincidence." The partners doubted that.

While Mike asked the next few questions, Steve stepped out to call their boss. He asked Captain Mendoza to pull the report and have the officers assigned to the Lopez case interviewed as soon as possible.

"Do you remember the police coming in and notifying you?" Steve questioned Mr. Ridell.

"Since I wasn't the manager then, I wasn't in on that conversation. However, I do remember the email that went out. I just assumed the account was closed. I never checked. So when you came in earlier today asking for the bank records, I was shocked and horrified to see that someone has been stealing from her estate. I don't know how it happened. I alerted our Fraud Department right after you left. They are opening an investigation. I also found an estate lawyer's contact information among her paperwork and I asked him to come in later in the week to close the account and transfer the funds to her estate. I explained about your request. He agreed to keep the account open for the next couple of days in hopes you will catch whoever did this."

"We understand it's not your fault, Mr. Ridell. No one is saying it is. We just need to connect all the dots," Mike said soothingly, taking a slow sip of his coffee and waiting for a response. His tone worked. Ridell visibly relaxed. He took a deep breath.

"I know I've been difficult this visit. You are bringing up some very unpleasant memories for this bank. It was just such a shock to find out what was happening with the Haze account. It never should have. How else can I help you?"

"We need as much security footage as possible for as long as you kept it. Then, we'll take the footage and compare it to her statements to help us figure out, and hopefully catch whoever has been coming in and withdrawing funds." They showed the manager a statement. After he examined it more closely, he noted that the thief was using a different bank to transfer the funds. They hoped for now they could use the security footage to catch their killer anyway. Mike worked hard to explain this.

"We have four cameras altogether: two on the entrances; one over the ATM machines outside; and the other at the edge of the parking lot. Footage is kept for maybe thirty days max, so it might not help you. I'll have my security team get what you need and drop off the DVD at your station. It will probably take him an hour or so."

"We would be happy to wait," Mike said. The manager agreed.

"Again, I'm so sorry this happened. If there's anything else you need, let me know. I'll do everything I can."

"Thank you for your cooperation. As soon as you hear anything from the Fraud Department, please let us know. Once we look through the footage, we'll get another warrant for the other bank account listed at the different bank. I'm guessing the person will know something's up once he or she tries to access Sally's account again. So if someone shows up asking about it, call us right away." That was an advantage they had on the killer. So far, he didn't know the police were onto him.

Chapter Sixty-One

It was nice to be outside again. The air was cooler in the morning. The sun was shining bright. The bank was located in a busy area. A school stood on one corner and across from that was a local fast food joint. The large bank building took up half a block. We watched a group of people cross the street as I parked the car in the popular gas station lot. We hoped they had good security cameras.

Chips, cookies, crackers and soft drinks sat on shelves and in coolers. Two young men worked behind the counter. One wore a Dodgers cap and the other a UCLA hat. They both looked up as Matt approached. "Hi, guys, I'm Detective Parker. This is my partner, Detective Blade. We'd like your help." Matt showed them his badge. "What are your names?"

"I'm Jack. This is Moby." Neither looked particularly excited to talk with us. I smiled broadly at them. "I don't know what you want from us," UCLA said.

"We're looking for copies of security footage you have from the last month or so from all the cameras the gas station has," Matt explained.

"Why, what's going on?"

"We're from Homicide. We're investigating four murders. Any footage you have over the past month might help us," I said.

"Is the killer around here?" gasped Jack, the kid with the UCLA cap.

"We don't know. That's why we need to look at the tapes. Hopefully, they can help us solve these cases."

"Whoa! That's kinda scary," Moby said. "We save tape for up to twenty days, and the main camera records for seven days. Then, it gets transferred onto backup DVD's that we keep for up to sixty days," Jack said. "I could get the tape and drop it off somewhere later today if you like? It might take all day to pull together what you need." He gestured to the customers coming in to buy gas.

We agreed and gave him the address of the police station. We then took down their contact info and thanked them for their help and time. It was hard to know if they had anything that could help us. I hoped so.

"Onto the next business," I said.

We scanned the street, deciding where to go next. We certainly had plenty of choices. "How about that coffee shop over there?" Matt suggested, pointing to a medium-sized cafe. I nodded.

"Let's show Marco and any other pictures we have of potential suspects to the cashier and other workers. Maybe they'll know them."

"Good idea," Matt said.

It wasn't a lineup, just a hunch I had to point us in the right direction. It could be a tricky maneuver for the prosecutor to get around later. Still, we had to do something. As long as we weren't suggesting anyone, we might be okay.

As soon as we opened the door, the smell of coffee and food hit us. I took a long deep breath. "Well, it *is* way past our lunchtime," I said, after noticing Matt looking at me with a grin on his face.

We stood in line behind a group of four friends. They were talking and laughing with one another. They wrapped their arms around each other trying to decide what to order. Once they had ordered, it was our turn. I got a latte and a roast beef sandwich. Matt got a smoothie and a tuna melt.

"I'm Detective Blade. We're here because we need your help," I said, showing my badge. "What's your name?"

The cashier behind the counter looked to be in his mid-twenties. His brown eyes were wide. He had a long, angular face and tugged nervously on the strings of the uniform smock he wore. "I'm Rafael. What's up?"

"What kind of security cameras do you have here?" I asked nicely, attempting to ease his nerves.

"The owner just got a new system. We had a couple of break-ins late at night; so he wanted to protect everyone and everything here."

"I see. That's good."

"I don't really know security…" Rafael said, his voice trailing off.

"Who's the owner? We can call him and get what we need."

"Actually, he should be here in half an hour if you want to wait?" We nodded in agreement. The joint was jumping at lunchtime. We could see how busy the young cashier was.

"Tell you what, Rafael. We'll be sitting right over there." I pointed to a table. "When it dies down, would you mind coming over for a second and answering a few questions?" He agreed. We took our food to a medium-sized table.

A little while later, things were quieter. Rafael joined us. "We need you to look at a couple of photos. Have you ever seen any of these people here before?" I laid several pictures on an empty space on the table. One was of Marco. One was of Scott Hall. Another was of his pretty wife, Juliet. The rest were photos of Cassie Garrison's friends from the diner we had interviewed.

Rafael pulled out a chair and sat down. We could tell he was tired. To his credit, he took time to study each face. He took in their features and clothing. After a while, he said, "Yeah, this guy and his wife and that guy were in here just last week. I think they're actors or something. They seemed nice. Are they in trouble or something?" he asked, a concerned look on his face.

Matt cleared his throat. "Not necessarily. We're just doing some investigating. When did you say they were here?"

"Usually, they come in once a week. Last time was… hmm, maybe three days ago."

"All together?"

"Yeah, that's why I remembered. Sometimes they come by themselves or those two come in together." He pointed to the pictures of Marco and the Halls.

Now we had a specific time to look at on the security cameras. We thanked the cashier. He left us to continue eating our lunch.

"I'm starved." I almost whined, taking a healthy bite of my roast beef sandwich.

"Me too. It's really good." Matt smiled and took my hand. My heart began to race. I smiled back. I squeezed his fingers and relaxed.

"Let's just hope one of them went to the bank before or after they came here," I said.

We took our time eating. We needed to unwind a little and take a break from the case. Besides, there was something I needed to talk with him about.

"Oh, no, Emma. You have that serious 'we need to talk' face going on." I sighed. I guess I was an open book.

I took a breath and began. "Matt, I'm kind of afraid to move forward with you. I mean, what if it doesn't work out between us. Could we still be partners, or even friends? We have such a good thing going, I

176

don't want to mess it up. What if we break up? How would we remain friends or partners? I'm not saying we will break up. It's just…" Matt squeezed my hand and saved me from my rambling, anxious self. I must have looked as nervous as I felt. I probably sounded like it, too.

"Oh, Emma. Sweet Emma. Your concerns are valid. I've thought of that, too. I love what we have now just like you do. That's why I want it to be more.—because it's so good, I think it can be even better. Don't you?"

When he put it like that, I understood and couldn't help but agree. He was right, of course. I felt the same way. Then he did the most considerate thing. I began to protest, still thinking worst-case scenario.

"Yes, but 'sweetheart,'" he whispered. The word sounded so lovely to my ears. It kind of melted my heart a little. "What can I do to help you to feel more comfortable with all this?" Matt sincerely asked.

I thought for a moment. "Even if this doesn't work, I would still want to be partners and friends to the best of our ability. Promise me that no matter what happens, we will be okay." I knew I was asking a lot of him. Still, I couldn't help it. I valued him so much. At that moment, not remaining friends and partners was my biggest fear. His face became serious. It was his turn to sigh.

"Emma, you know I don't like hypotheticals. That would be hard, of course," he said honestly. My heart sank a little. Maybe this wasn't going to work after all, I thought.

He continued. "Having said that, I am willing to do whatever it takes. So yes, I promise, if it doesn't work out, we will figure out a way to be partners and have some kind of friendship. I'm telling you, I couldn't be happier with our relationship. I'm excited to see where it goes. And I'm going to be positive and trust that it will work out. Okay?"

In a nutshell, that's who Matt was. So positive. Always thinking the best about someone and determined to get what he wanted. "It's one of the things I like best about you," I said, as I spontaneously leaned toward him and squeezed his hand again.

Chapter Sixty-Two

I looked up to see a tall man standing a short distance from our table looking at us. Matt saw him as well and waved him over. His air of authority and navy blue suit gave him away as someone important. *Maybe he's the owner*, I thought. By the way he was looking at us, it was obvious he had something to say.

"I don't mean to interrupt. I can come back," he graciously said before adding, "New love is a marvelous thing. Who am I to stand in the way of that?"

We both laughed and tried not to blush. We liked him already.

"Please have a seat. I'm Detective Matt Parker; and this is my partner, Detective Emma Blade."

He sat and extended his hand. "I'm Richard Zander, the owner of this fine establishment. Rafael said you needed my help?"

We shook hands and Matt continued. "We'd like to have a copy of your security footage from the last thirty to sixty days if possible."

"Sure. We have nothing to hide. What's this about?"

"We are investigating some local crimes and thought your surveillance footage might give us a clue."

As with Rafael, we then pulled out the lineup and showed it to him. His face brightened. "Those are a few of our regulars. I saw them here a few days ago." He pointed to the Halls and Marco.

"What can you tell us about them?" Matt asked.

"Not much. Scott and Marco are actors, I know that. She does something with plays, too," he said, sounding less sure. "I've only seen her a couple of times."

"You have a good memory," Matt said. He shrugged, waiting for the next question. "How often do they come here?"

"They're usually here once a week. Sometimes they come in together, sometimes not. I can't say for certain, though. I'm not here all the time. I own three more shops in the area. I travel between them."

"Your food and coffee are delicious. If the other shops are anything like this one, we can't wait to try them."

"Thanks. This is the first one I opened; so I'm a little partial. But I guarantee you, the others are every bit as good."

"We'll be sure to try the others," Matt promised. "How can we get the security footage?"

"Every week the system backs up to a DVD. I recycle them every four to six weeks. Let me grab them for you now. If I could get them back at some point, though, I would really appreciate it. Also I appreciate what you do to keep our community safe." He pulled out a gift card and handed it to us. We thanked him. "You're welcome. I'll bring you fresh cups of coffee or whatever you're drinking for the road. It's on the house." We both thought it was a nice gesture and told him so.

A few moments later, the owner returned with our promised drinks and a large manila envelope. "There are six DVDs in here." He set them on the table. I picked them up and slid them into my bag.

"Sir," I said with some hesitation. "Did you know this woman?" I pulled out the picture of Sally Haze. I can't tell you what made me pull it out. Instinct, I guess. It wasn't planned. Richard Zander sat down heavily.

"Know her? She did a little work for me at the shop. Sally was a doll. Her murder broke my heart. She was such a sweet girl. She worked here until…" We exchanged glances.

"For how long?"

"For about a year. Come to think of it, can I see those pictures you showed me earlier?"

I almost jumped out of my chair when he asked. I wondered what was coming next. I didn't have to wait for long. I grabbed them excitedly. Something important was about to happen.

"I think he used to date Sally. Nothing too serious. They saw each other on occasion back then. One day he came into the coffee shop. I saw him looking at her so intensely. I joked with her, saying something like, *I think he likes you.* Sally began to blush and told me he was her new boyfriend. At least that's how I remember it."

We sat in stunned silence. He had pointed to the picture of Scott Hall. Not someone that suspicious to us, but now…

Zander continued. "I didn't know him that well back then. His hair was lighter then; but I could swear that's who it was. Honestly, the intensity of his stare made me uncomfortable for her. It seemed like too much for a new relationship. Sally didn't mention him often. Actually, it was just that one time when I brought it up. She loved being here. Even after her parents died and she inherited all that money, she still wanted to work. I thought she would quit; but she didn't. The last time I saw her was three days before she was murdered." His hands began to shake in anger.

"Is that what this is all about? Finding Sally's killer? Whatever I can do to help, I will. She was a lovely girl and didn't deserve to die like that." Then tears filled his eyes. He blinked them away and looked at us. "Please, find whoever did this to her," he begged.

Chapter Sixty-Three

Captain Mendoza got the call from Davis and Cameron about the missing bank manager. He first took out the old file on Sally Haze and scanned it. He saw that Detective Flagger, one of his now retired officers, had in fact notified the previous bank manager, Martin Lopez, of the murder of Sally Haze. He breathed a sigh of relief. *Thank goodness for that*, he thought. He then turned to the Lopez file. He picked up the phone and made a call to a friend of his who was in charge at the Missing Persons Division.

"Hi, George, how's it going?" Captain Moses Justin asked. Captain Justin was in Mendoza's class at the academy. They had worked their way up the ranks in their respective divisions. Moses was a smart, shrewd and by-the-book captain. Not that different from himself. He was a friend. Mendoza knew he would help in whatever way he could. "Moses, we are right in the middle of the Garrison case. Now, it looks like there are three other cold cases connected to this one."

"So I've heard. It sounds like a big one. How can I help?"

"Do you remember the Martin Lopez case? He was a former bank manager who disappeared. It turns out, he was the manager at the bank where our first victim, Sally Haze, was a client. He disappeared shortly after she died. I'd like to interview the officers who worked the case. See what insights I can gain."

His friend surprised him when he said, "That's me. How can I help." Normally, captains didn't work a case hands-on every day.

Moses read his mind and said, "One of my officers was on maternity leave. So I partnered with my new rookie back then to work the case and give him some hands-on experience." That made sense to Mendoza. He liked his job supervising; but he loved being out in the field even more.

Moses put him on hold while he went to grab the file. A few minutes later he came back on the line. "Alright, here it is." A long silence fell between them. Mendoza could hear pages turning as his friend skimmed through the file. "It's coming back to me now as I look through it. Martin Lopez, thirty-nine, went missing three years ago. His bank became concerned when he didn't show up for work. He didn't have a history of that."

"What did you find out?"

"There were no clues in the case. I admit that's odd. We caught him on camera leaving work at around eight p.m. When we went to his apartment two days later, his car was still there. His keys, wallet and cell phone were on the counter. Nothing looked disturbed. Dishes were drying in the rack. There was food in the fridge."

"So you uncovered nothing, even with the help of the media and the usual tips?" Normally, the press was very helpful to the police. "No, we didn't. He was divorced. The ex-wife was remarried and living out of state. They had no kids. It was just him living alone. His family plastered his picture everywhere. We searched for him. Unfortunately, the case went cold. I remember that a year afterward, the family again went on TV and held a press conference. We got nothing."

There was a silence between them as each thought about the case. Then Moses asked, "Can you explain more about what you think this has to do with Sally Haze?"

Captain Mendoza took a sip of his water and spoke. "Sally's account remained open even after the police notified Lopez of the murder. He only let his bank employees know via an email memo." He took another sip of water and went on. "From what my detectives tell me, they all thought he closed the account. But he hadn't. And there's been activity on it for three years."

Moses let out a sharp intake of breath. "What? Three years? How can that be? No wonder you guys are looking into this." His former classmate caught on fast.

"You got it, Moses."

"I can have my detectives help your guys and gals take a fresh look at it. Otherwise, if you have too many cases, I think this would qualify for the CCU."

The CCU, otherwise known as the Cold Case Unit, looked at cases that remained unsolved. They usually would only take another look if new leads or evidence were presented. There were so many that it was hard to get them all looked at no matter how good the chances were that the police could solve them. Mendoza hoped that between the two squads, they could get justice for Martin Lopez.

"The way I see it, either he took the money and ran, or someone got him to keep the account open and shut him up for good. You haven't come right out and said it; but I'm guessing Sally Haze had some money. Otherwise, who would care about the account?"

"Right again, friend. Let's work together on this. If you could have your people take a fresh look at it… If they could re-interview colleagues or anyone connected to the case again, that would help a lot. See if there was any peculiar activity on his accounts or in his life we could find out. That would be great," Mendoza said. His friend agreed. They were equally competent in Missing Persons, and he knew the last thing they needed to do was tell each other how to do their jobs. His friend didn't mention it. After talking a while longer, they hung up.

Chapter Sixty-Four

Lindsay Jones was feeling ill. She normally didn't get sick. Lately, she had been feeling rundown and tired. Maybe it was the case. Maybe it was Cassie's death. She couldn't be sure. She knew that when she felt stressed her body got sick. Just one of her crosses to bear, she thought.

Her sister Amy had been amazing throughout all of this. She had opened her home and heart to her without question or complaint. The good that was coming out of all of it was they were actually becoming closer. They hadn't shared a room since elementary school. After they moved out and left home, they just grew apart. *Life is like that sometimes*, she had told herself. What a copout excuse that was, she now realized.

As much as she loved her sister's apartment, she needed to sleep in her own bed, if just for a little bit. She loved her sister but craved her own space. She would go back to Amy's later tonight so no one would worry. *I'll be back there by dinner*, she told herself.

Her boss had let her leave early today. It wasn't normal for her to ask or for him to grant such a request. Would he give her a hard time about it tomorrow? She really wasn't feeling good. It wasn't like she was faking it or trying to get out of work. Sometimes her co-workers did that, and it just made everyone look bad. He saw how rundown she looked and practically sent her home himself. So here she was in the middle of a hot June afternoon, and it was only one p.m., all she wanted to do was sleep. When had she ever been home in the afternoon? she wondered. She took the familiar roads and drove to her place.

Just a couple of hours at my own place, in my own bed won't kill me, she thought. It might not be safe at night, but she figured during the day it would be no problem. She could almost feel the anticipation in her heartbeat as she parked her car inside the parking garage and got out. She walked through the lobby and grabbed the huge pile of mail that spilled out of her box. She pushed the elevator button for her floor. She slowly, quietly opened her door and peeked inside. All was quiet.

Her apartment looked just like always. She quickly walked in and closed and locked the door. She glanced at everything: the counter, the couch, even the coffee table. She even took a moment to look behind doors and furniture just to satisfy herself that it was safe. Nothing was out of place. She no longer felt scared to be there, despite what had happened. She opened her fridge and saw that the lethal water jug was gone. Should she grab a glass now, she asked herself. *Nope! Can't do it*, she decided. Lindsay didn't feel that brave. She breathed a sigh of relief. She jammed her mail in a drawer and walked down the hall to her bedroom.

She opened the door and walked inside. Her head was aching now. She crawled in bed. The feel of her sheets was wonderful. She took a few slow breaths. She let her eyes wander around her room. Her favorite Olympic posters hung on the walls. Her old-fashioned alarm clock blazed bright digital red numbers on her bedside table. All was peaceful and familiar. She felt calm and safe and she stared lovingly at the picture of her family across the room on her dresser. Her breathing slowed. Within minutes she was fast asleep.

Chapter Sixty-Five

Matt and I went to one of our favorite places for lunch. The Indian food they had was the best. It was a tiny restaurant that you wouldn't know about unless you were a native or lived here for a while. The owners were kind and the food authentic. Time flew by as we talked and ate. Our conversation was light and easy. We both needed a break from the case.

"So what was your favorite memory growing up?" Matt asked, as he took a big bite of his chicken curry. I thought about that for a second.

"Every year around the Fourth of July, we would go to this carnival. My entire family went. Cousins, aunts and uncles, even our friends who we considered family. It was a huge event that lasted all day. All we ate was junk food. All we did was go on rides. And it ended every year the same way, watching a huge fireworks show." I couldn't help but smile as I remembered. Matt laughed as he enjoyed the memory with me.

"That does sound like fun, especially since you're an only child."

What a smart man, I thought. So observant; always thinking ten steps ahead.

"And yours?" I asked. Now, it was my turn to dig into the curry we shared.

"Hmmm, every year at Easter my parents would hide eggs with money and candy in them, maybe two dollars in each egg. When we were little, that felt rich. They hid dozens of eggs. It took at least an hour to find them all. I can't even begin to tell you some of the crazy places they'd be hidden. We always competed for who would find the most." I smiled just a little. "And I bet we both know who usually found the most eggs?" I teased.

"I tried hard. Sometimes my brother and sister would team up and find more," he laughed. "There was one year when several were placed in a tree that we normally climbed. We had so much fun getting them down." I loved seeing his sentimental side. He continued: "Then we would eat a bunch of candy and get ready to go to a big church service. It was all really nice."

Family memories and experiences were so good for every kid to have. Looking back, those were little things but felt like the world to both of us.

After that, my thoughts wandered back to the case out of habit. The case!

"Shoot!" I said, looking at my watch. The time had flown by and we were already late for our next briefing. We raced back to the station. It was getting close to the time to meet up with Cameron and Davis to interview the Halls. We had overlooked them, but for good reason, I thought. Until today, they were not really on our radar. I wondered what they would say.

I steered the cruiser into a tight parking space in the Police Department lot. Matt and I jumped out at the same time and ran into the station. The main lobby, like always, was crowded with people waiting to see loved ones in lockup or for a scheduled appointment. As we raced by, people cried out to us looking for updates, asking questions about cases that we knew nothing about. The receptionist was doing her best to answer every question and check them all in. What a champ she was, I thought. I smiled at her as we quickly jogged by.

Our offices were on the fourth floor. Normally, we would take the elevator. Today that would take too long. We burst through the door like a tornado. It was quiet and empty. *Where is everyone*? I wondered. We stopped and looked around. Then, we went and knocked on the captain's door. He quickly opened it and ushered us in. It looked like Cameron and Davis had just come in. "There you are. Welcome. Have a seat." Our boss motioned us toward chairs. Honestly, I didn't want to sit. I wanted to go and work on the case. But I knew we all needed to meet and connect and be on the same page.

"So we have some new info for you," the five of us said almost in unison. Then everyone laughed at how excited we all sounded.

The captain smiled. "Why don't you start, Matt and Emma?"

"We checked a couple of businesses for surveillance footage. We're getting some from the gas station across from the bank and from a local coffee shop nearby. Then we went to the businesses and showed photos of those involved in the case to see if it would spark some kind of recognition or memory." I heard intakes of breath from everyone.

I continued. "It worked. Not only that. The owner of the coffee shop recognized Scott and Juliet Hall and Marco Crane. He said they

186

had been in together and individually. Later I just thought on a hunch that I would show the owner the pictures. I included one of Sally. That's when we discovered Sally used to work at the coffee shop and that once he saw Scott Hall looking at her. When he asked her about it, she admitted to dating him. She only mentioned it that once, but it stuck with him." Now everyone collectively seemed to exhale.

Cameron jumped in. "Wow, that's some great work. We went to the bank and got the footage. We talked with the bank manager again. He said at the time he was not in charge, that he was still working his way up. He got a memo about the murder but assumed the account was closed by the then manager. That would have been Martin Lopez, who, a few days after Sally was murdered, disappeared without a trace." Now it was our turn to be surprised. That was a curveball we didn't see coming.

Mendoza began, "I think that's my cue to take over. I talked with Captain Justin in Missing Persons. I've known him for a long time. He's a good cop who runs a good department. He actually ended up assisting on this case. He told me that Martin Lopez was responsible and always showed up to work on time. His employees at the bank notified us when he didn't come in for work one day. It was like Cameron said. He disappeared without a trace. I couldn't have said it better myself." Our captain leaned back in his chair and looked at each of us as he finished his update.

"But how is that possible? Usually there are some leads to follow, even in a missing persons case," I asked, confused.

"Yeah, I know. When LAPD went to his house, they found his keys, wallet, cell phone in the apartment, but no sign of Mr. Lopez," Mendoza said. "Justin told me posters and local news stories brought nothing useful. The family even did a couple of press conferences asking for the public's help. They got nothing. There was no unusual bank activity, and no one seemed to think he ran off," Mendoza explained.

"Yeah, but what about the other car?" I asked, still confused.

"So either Lopez was part of it or someone killed him," Matt said. "Maybe to cover up their actions. I mean, it does seem strange that her account would stay open after her death. I think the missing car is the clue we need to solve this mystery."

"I agree. The problem is, it was never found. To this day, it's still missing," the captain said. That detail about the missing car was left out on purpose. It's not uncommon for the police to hold something back in a case in hopes that later on a tip or a confession that included the information would help us solve the case or be a good lead toward that end.

"Did it say anything about a missing bank manager in the screenplay?" Steve asked us. We all laughed. "I'm afraid not, bud," Matt said. "At this point, we have more questions than answers. So, Captain, we're off to interview Scott and Juliet Hall. Hopefully, they'll be able to shed some light on all this. Depending on the timing, we'll try to start sifting through the security footage from the businesses. I'd like to see what that has to offer." Matt stood.

"Alright everyone, great work. Keep me updated. I wish I could assist more. But with four other murder cases to deal with, that's not possible. Just keep me in the loop," our boss said as he dismissed us, signaling an end to our meeting.

Chapter Sixty-Six

We were set to meet Scott and Juliet at a coffee shop near her work. I wished we could have met them at home. It's always a good idea to see how someone acts in their personal environment where they are most comfortable. Davis drove himself and Cameron quickly through the streets of Los Angeles. I followed with Matt in the passenger seat. We passed by schools and office buildings. Kids played in front yards with parents keeping a close eye. The lunch crowd made their way back to their offices. Many were on foot. That slowed us down a little. I banged the wheel with impatience as yet another jay-walking group of people crossed in front of us. "Could I please get out and give them a ticket?" I asked. Matt laughed.

"While I agree they deserve one; in case you haven't noticed, we're in a hurry. Relax. If we just keep our pace, we'll be there on time." *It's lucky for them*, I thought. Still, I had to agree. So we stopped and started in the busy part of LA until a theater came into view.

It was a white building with a red set of double doors. "I think that's the place where Sally acted in that play," Matt observed, as he looked at the old building. It looked like a small community theater. We turned right into a parking lot where a bustling small coffee shop sat next door.

Davis and Cameron got out of their car and walked toward us. We met them halfway and went in together. The place was as busy on the inside as it looked on the outside. Almost every table was full. It was not exactly the quietest place to conduct an interview. *Be positive, Emma*, I chided myself. At least you have the chance to do this. Matt tapped my shoulder and pointed to the menu.

I nodded and looked it over. So many selections. In the display case pastries and desserts called to me. The menu had every kind of black or green tea you could want. My mouth was practically watering. My three amigos laughed at what I didn't say but could have with my expression. "She'll take one of everything," Matt joked to the cashier behind the counter, who joined in the laughter.

"She's not the first to feel that way, I can tell you that," he said. His voice had a light southern drawl to it. His eyes were a light green, similar to my own, his hair dark brown in a short military-style cut.

"I just had lunch. But I wish!" I was already thinking about what I could get the next time we came here. Maybe it would be a nice date place, I thought. At that, I started grinning like a kid.

"What?" Matt wanted to know.

I winked at him. "Oh… nothing," I said.

Matt, who often ate healthier than yours truly, grabbed a protein box and a cup of water.

Cameron and Davis carried their cups of coffee to a table where a couple sat. They flagged us over. Right off the bat, I liked Juliet Hall. She had a petite frame and red hair. Her smile seemed genuine. "I kind of wish I could try it all," I joked with them. She laughed and smiled at me.

"Everyone says that. It's a cool place."

Scott Hall just looked on. He didn't say anything. His look was a cross between boredom and annoyance. "Can we just skip the chit-chat and move on?" he snapped. Right away it was clear he wanted to control this interview. He turned his head to the left, displaying a tattoo of the Coral Reef on the back of his neck.

"Interesting tattoo," Cameron observed. "It must be an important place for you." When Scott just sat there, Cameron went on in a laid-back way. "I have a few of my own," he said. When Scott didn't respond in any way, we all looked his way.

What struck me was how different he'd acted in this interview so far. When we talked with him at the studio, he didn't say much but seemed cordial enough. Maybe he was just having a bad day, I cautioned myself.

Matt jumped in and switched gears, going back to the first and only statement Scott had made so far: "Of course, sir. Let's get on with it. Nice to see you again. You remember Detective Blade, my partner. I'm Detective Parker. We interviewed you at your acting class the other day." Matt then introduced the other two homicide cops. Still, Scott sat coldly, not offering a hand or a greeting of any kind to either of them.

Scott's wife Juliet smiled and said, "It's nice to see you again, Detectives." Her husband glared as she asked how they could help. It was clear she would be more willing and cooperative than her husband.

"How long have you been married?' Matt asked.

"A little over six years," Juliet responded.

"How did you meet?"

190

"At that time, I was the Stage Manager at the theater next door. Scott was in a play," she said, gesturing toward her husband. "He was so cute and so talented. I considered myself lucky to date and then marry him. I now work as a court reporter. From time to time, I do some volunteer managing and help with the theater."

"What do you do?" Matt asked, turning to her husband.

"I'm an actor, as you know."

"I do know. What I meant was, do you have any other jobs?" Matt asked, with grace and patience in his voice. Scott shrugged.

"I work in the auto industry." *What does that mean?* I thought.

Matt abruptly stood up. "If you don't mind, we would like to interview you separately. Mrs. Hall, do you have access to the theater next door? If so would you mind going with Detectives Cameron and Davis to be interviewed there?"

In unison, they gave opposite answers. He said, "Absolutely not!" And she said, "Yes, of course." She stood up, and Davis and Cameron did too. Her husband looked hard at her and shook his head *no*. Quietly, she sat back down.

"We are a couple. We do everything together. We are not about to be separated for some interview by strangers," he said firmly.

"He's right," Juliet said in a tiny voice. "I would rather we be interviewed together. I would feel more comfortable."

It was sad to see her abrupt transformation from a strong and sweet woman to timid and terrified under his control. It was obvious she didn't agree, but also that she had no choice in the matter. We couldn't force them. Even though it would be better to interview them separately, we didn't have that luxury. Davis and Cameron also sat back down. "Alright then, let's start with a simple question. What kind of cars do you drive?" Matt asked.

"I drive a white Toyota. My wife has a red Honda."

Juliet started playing with her hair and wouldn't look at her husband.

"The DMV has a black Chevy registered under your name, Mr. Hall," Matt asserted. It was not a question, but a statement to which he expected an answer. Scott gave a casual shrug of his shoulders.

"We used to have one. I sold it for parts so I could get my new car. I guess I need to update the DMV records. Sorry about that. I'll get on it." By the tone of his voice, it was clear he was anything but apologetic. If anything, he seemed surprised that we had that information.

Just then Juliet looked down at her feet. "Remember that, honey?" Scott said, addressing his wife. She nodded almost too quickly.

"When was this? Matt asked.

"A while ago. I don't remember the exact date," he responded with a smirk.

"Did either of you know Sally Haze?" Matt asked. Scott's jaw dropped briefly before he regained his composure.

"We both did," Juliet volunteered.

"Well, you knew her better than me," Scott said.

I could tell Matt was not ready to bring up the bombshell we received from the owner. If he brought it up right now, it could end the interview. So he just nodded and went on. "Can you tell me about how you knew her?"

"She was in one of our plays. I was managing the cast and crew. Scott was another lead in the play - the narrator, I think."

Scott looked sharply at his wife. The look conveyed that she'd better shut up right now. It was a fierce and threatening look. She understood it, too. It made us all uncomfortable having to watch their exchange. It contradicted what he'd just told us, that he didn't know Sally well. Then, Juliet said it, as though she'd wanted to help us along.

"I would say, Scott, you knew her very well. You spent more time with her practicing your lines than I did."

That wasn't all they were doing, I thought.

Scott shrugged. "I guess so."

"You two frequented a coffee shop near her bank and place of residence, we were told."

"Yeah, so what? Is that a crime?" Scott angrily spat out.

"No, but we do need you to be honest with us, sir. We are investigating four murders and would appreciate your help." The patience was gone from Matt's voice. It was replaced with icy intensity.

"I will tell you what I want to tell you. I don't even have to be doing this interview. I'm here taking time out of my day, as is my wife. So we *are* helping," he said with similar anger.

"And we appreciate that, sir. We really do," I said in a soothing tone. "But what my partner is saying is that the more information we can get from you, the sooner we can solve these crimes. And I know you

192

want to help us with that." As with Marco Crane, I was trying to calm the situation.

Matt smiled over his protein box and took a bite of cheese. He continued. "How well do you know Marco Crane?" The question seemed to relax Scott and his fiery anger.

"Well, he's my acting teacher and, I would say, friend. He also used to act at the theater where Juliet worked. So, pretty well, I guess."

"What do you think of his screenplay?"

"It's creative and suspenseful. I thought it was interesting to act out the part of the killer." As he said that, a chill ran down my spine.

"Did you act out all the different scenes of murder as the killer?" Matt asked. Scott looked confused.

"All the scenes?" he asked.

"Yes, Marco gave us a copy of his screenplay to read to help us solve the murders." He looked surprised and somewhat troubled.

Just as quickly as that emotion had crossed his face, it was gone. "I don't know. It's not like I've read the entire thing. So maybe. Who knows," he said flippantly.

Scott sipped his drink slowly before he asked, "I have a question for you. What do you think of his work?"

"I see enough murder in real life. The last thing I want to do is read about it," Matt said convincingly. Scott nodded.

"What about you; what do you think of his work? From what you've read?" Steve Davis smoothly asked. He just shrugged and didn't answer.

Mike Cameron broke in: "What's odd to me, Mr. and Mrs. Hall, is that every time a woman in his screenplay would be murdered, someone would be in *real life*, a week or a few weeks later. Doesn't that also strike you as odd?"

Scott looked at the detective and shrugged. "It does seem strange. I'm sure there's a good explanation for it."

"Like what?" Matt asked.

"As if I know," he shot back.

The interview was turning hostile pretty fast. Scott Hall was becoming more defensive by the minute. It was only a matter of time before he would end it, so Matt pressed him hard.

"Tell me about Martin Lopez."

For a minute Scott said nothing. He was speechless.

"Who? I don't know who that is." Matt clenched his fists under the table.

"I don't believe that for a second. He was the bank manager at Sally Haze's branch, the one across the street from the coffee shop. And you know what, he just happened to disappear right after her murder."

Juliet's face went white. It looked like she might throw up. "I have to go to the ladies room. I'll be right back." And with that she dashed out of the booth and ran. I stood, giving the guys a nod, and headed for the ladies room after her. I wanted to know what had made her react that way. Perhaps she knew something.

Chapter Sixty-Seven

Upon entering the ladies room, sounds of vomiting came from one of the stalls. "Juliet, are you alright?" I asked. I leaned against the sink and looked at my own tired reflection in the mirror. I smoothed my hair back and kept my back to her.

"Leave me alone. I don't have anything more to say to you," she said in a half cry.

"I'm here to help. Please come out and talk with me," I said. I waited in silence. A few minutes later the stall door opened and out she came. Her face was streaked with tears. Her skin was pale. She looked sick. She leaned her head over the sink, letting the water run through her hands and onto her face. I grabbed some paper towels and handed them to her. She took them gratefully and began to clean herself up.

There was a seat that was just big enough for two. We sat on it together. My heart went out to this poor woman. She knew more than she was saying but was obviously afraid to tell me what it was. What a bind she must be in. I conveyed that sentiment to her. She just nodded and started crying again.

"Juliet, you knew these women. If you know something, please tell me. We really need your help. We need to put a killer behind bars," I pleaded.

That's when I saw it. Wiping her tears and cleaning up had washed all her makeup off. I could see that one of her eyes was blackened and a little swollen. There was a dark bruise that her long bangs no longer hid. When she saw that I had seen the bruise, she smoothed her bangs over her forehead, effectively covering it.

"Oh, Juliet, I'm so sorry," I breathed. "How long has he been hurting you?" She looked down at her feet. She wouldn't meet my eyes. "Look at me, please." She did, and her eyes told a story that her mouth could not. She just sat and cried for what seemed like forever. I said nothing. Sometimes, that's the best thing you can do. Even if she wasn't willing or able to give me information, she could still listen.

"If you would just hear me out for a moment…" I began.

She nodded for me to continue. I didn't want to say too much, just enough. There was a fine and careful line to walk. I took a breath and looked her directly in the eye. "We think that your husband may have had more to do with these crimes than we'd originally thought.

Maybe he was working with Marco; maybe not. Now, Juliet, I need to say something that will be hard for you to hear. I'm so sorry to have to tell you this; but we suspect he may have been having an affair with one of the victims." Sadly, she just nodded. She didn't look surprised at all. It was clear she already knew.

"I'm sorry. I can't help you. I need to go. Please don't make me stay," she begged. Even though I wanted to continue, she needed to choose for herself. She deserved that. She wasn't ready to go any further that day. I took out a business card and slid it into her hand. I also carried around crisis information hotline cards. I gave her one of those, too.

"You are not alone. When you're ready to talk, I'll be there to listen. There are some really good resources listed on that card, too. The Domestic Violence Hotline is 24/7. They can help you form a safety plan to leave him," I explained. She looked at me with big grateful eyes and put the cards in her handbag.

To my surprise, as we stood up, she gave me a hug. For a moment I held her, wishing I could do more for her. Into my shoulder, Juliet whispered in a tiny voice, "He's dangerous."

"Yes, I think so," I agreed. Then I offered to drive her to a shelter. She declined. "Alright then, you stay safe, Juliet. And please call soon."

Finally, she freshened up her eye liner and turned to go. She had obviously done this before. By the time she was finished, she looked made up and pretty again. All traces of tears were gone. She nodded at me and walked out the door.

Chapter Sixty-Eight

The time had flown by. Mrs. Hall and I had been in the restroom for almost an hour. When I got back to the table, Matt sat alone sipping a cup of coffee. "Where is everyone?" I asked. He looked up at me.

"Shortly after you left, Scott beat a quick path to the door. Then Cameron and Davis did, too. They wanted to start looking at the different security tapes."

I nodded in understanding and took a seat beside him. I noticed there were two cups on the table. Matt pushed one towards me, grinning sheepishly.

196

"I figured you might need a cup after that."

What a great guy, I thought. At that moment, like many others, I felt lucky. Sometimes for me it's the little things people do that touch me the most. I winked at him and took a grateful sip.

Matt smiled. "So… how did it go?"

"I think I had about as much luck as you did. Juliet was throwing up when I walked in. When she came out of the stall, I saw that she had a black eye. I broached the subject of her husband and the possibility of domestic violence. She didn't say he did anything, but her silence spoke volumes. I also sensed she knew something, but was too terrified to say just what it was."

We had both sadly seen what abuse could do and how harmful it could be. I went on.

"At the end when we were leaving, she surprised me by giving me a hug. In the softest whisper she told me he was dangerous I could tell it took a lot of courage for her to admit that I gave her my card in the hopes that she'll reach out."

"There's more?" He asked, as if reading my thoughts.

"I did tell her we suspected Scott might have had an affair with one of the victims. I know it was a risk. I just had to let her know. Not surprisingly, I think she already did. At least that's what I gauged from her reaction. I also gave her a hotline card and encouraged her to use any of the numbers listed, especially the ones regarding domestic violence. I don't think she's ready to take that step just yet. So we wait, and remain available to help her whenever she is." As I said those words, they felt like the right way to go for now.

Matt put his hand in mine and gently squeezed. "You are such a good woman and a sweet soul. I'm glad you went after her and that she knows she has an ally in you—in us really. I'm not at all surprised she hugged you and confided as much as she did. You have a real gift of empathy and compassion with victims and their families. It's authentic. They can feel it. I'm glad you gave her the information. That's all you can do, Emma. I know… I know you wanted to do more."

"She's in a tough spot. I mean, can you imagine?" He shrugged. Matt was such an encouraging force in my life. He saw the good and continued to let me know it. That, too, went a long way with me. I squeezed his hand back in thanks.

We sat for a few minutes more, enjoying our coffee and each other's company. Finally, I stood up and grabbed my purse. "Let's see what the tape says, shall we?"

Matt laughed and stood, too.

"Hey, officers," the cashier said. "Thanks for your service. I hope you stay safe and solve your case. And don't forget to come back and use that gift card." He winked at me and said, "Maybe try everything on the menu. I recommend the banana cream pie myself." We laughed.

"I'll have to remember that for next time. I'm so full right now, I'm lucky I can still walk." Now it was his turn to laugh. We thanked him in unison and walked out the door.

I thought about what the cashier said and how he had thanked us for our service. Appreciation from the public was such an encouragement. To some, we were the enemy. But most of us were good people who wanted to serve everyone in the community. Unfortunately, there were some bad apples, like in any job. I believed that fair and impartial hearings should happen. If the bad apples were found guilty, they should be punished just like everyone else. I hated it when I heard of awful misconduct on the part of a police officer or detective, anyone associated with the department. On behalf of the good apples, I hoped we could show the public the opposite of all that. It started with treating everyone with compassion, toughness at times, dignity, and fairness. These were my thoughts as we drove back to the station.

Chapter Sixty-Nine

Horns blared around him as he drove. Rush hour traffic was the worst, the killer thought. He wondered if he should have waited. But he couldn't. His plans had changed after all those detectives started closing in on him. He punched the steering wheel in frustration. Usually he liked the daylight. Today he cursed it. He'd thought he had more time. He resisted the urge to do it again. He honestly hadn't thought they were that smart. He had underestimated them, and he knew it. There was only one thing he could do. Accelerate the plan. All he needed to do was stay one step ahead of everyone. He could do that. He was smarter and quicker than all of them put together.

A loud horn blared at him from the car next to him. He had drifted into the wrong lane. He glared at the driver and swerved back into his own lane, almost clipping a passing truck. He felt rushed; and it was showing. He took several deep breaths as he tried to calm himself. "The last thing I need to do is make a mistake," he said out loud to himself. The easiest way to be noticed was to act irrational or unreasonable on the road. He slowed the car down to an acceptable speed and kept driving. After all this was over, it was time for him to run. He couldn't let himself be caught. The police were suspicious; however, speculation was just that. *There's no proof*, he told himself.

Did he regret his actions? He felt he should. But instead of feeling remorse, he felt nothing at all. He figured that wasn't normal. Well, what was normal anyway? He had never experienced it. No-one had ever wanted him. With an alcoholic mother and a father in prison from when he was just a small boy, he hadn't had a real chance to learn what normal even was. As he thought about his childhood, unexpected tears filled his eyes.

He slapped at his cheeks and scoffed at his useless show of emotion, then quickly blinked them away. He glanced at the apartment numbers, even though he could drive to the destination in his sleep. It was getting close.

His thoughts strayed back to what was normal. It was only when he'd met her, that sweet Sally, that he started to feel… well… some sense of happiness, he guessed. If only it could have lasted. He knew she had to die. *That* he felt remorse for. He convinced himself he had had no other choice.

"AHHH!" His scream filled his car. What was wrong with him? *Get a hold of yourself*, he scolded. He had things to do. He couldn't let a little thing like his feelings get in the way of his final act. In order to keep from dwelling on it further, he thought about what was coming next. His fingers slid across the syringe full of tranquilizers he'd brought for the occasion. The latex gloves were in the bag on the floor under the seat. His nine-millimeter rested snugly inside the holster on his shoulder. He felt the shape of the large, round roll of duct tape in the bag. He had not forgotten a thing. "It's show time!"

If he could say anything to the cops, it would be, *"Game – set - match."*

Chapter Seventy

Even though the blinds were closed, and it was half past three in the afternoon, the sun still managed to find its way into Lindsay Jones' apartment. She half smiled as she felt the warmth and saw the light trying to peek in. She rubbed her eyes and blinked the sleep out of them. What time was it anyway? she wondered. A quick glance at the bedside clock told her it was three thirty on the dot. She had only meant to sleep for half an hour. Somehow more than two had flown by. She yawned and rolled over—she definitely wasn't ready to get up. She sat up anyway. Remembering she wasn't supposed to be at her apartment, she glanced at the lock screen on her phone. No new texts or voicemails. That was good. At least no one knew she was gone. That way they didn't have to worry. The last thing she wanted to do was upset Amy or her friends.

Brushing the blond hair out of her eyes, Lindsay pulled off the blankets and got to her feet. She walked over to the blinds and opened them wide. The sun that freely streamed in delighted her. She stood basking in its warmth and brightness. A sob came suddenly to her throat as it dawned on her that her friend Cassie would never see or feel another blast of sun like this again. She stood by the window, her back facing the door, letting the tears fall and the sobs echo throughout the brightly lit room. It was all so awful. How could this happen to someone she knew? Why would anyone want to take that precious life? It was at times like these she wished she had more answers. Deep down, she knew suffering and all that came with it was just that… a mystery.

Finally, her crying slowed. She took a breath. Her hair and shirt were soaked. She walked into her closet and found a new outfit to wear. She changed and threw her old clothes in the laundry basket. Then, she walked back into her room. She picked up her phone from its usual spot on the nightstand by her bed and slid it into her jeans pocket as she made her way toward the bathroom. Just then, her phone chimed with an incoming text. "Lindsay, where are you?" Her sister's message read. She quickly typed out a response.

"On my way back to your place. Should be there in an hour or so. Was at my apartment to grab a few things. Everything is fine. Don't worry."

"At your apartment??? Why didn't you tell me? That's not smart, sister."

Lindsay was irritated. She was fine. She was an adult. So instead of answering the direct questions, she asked one of her own. "Want me to pick something up for dinner?" She waited and saw her sister's response asking her to pick up some chicken and mashed potatoes from the deli. She told her she would be back by six-thirty at the latest and agreed on dinner.

She knew just where she would go: Amy's favorite cafe that served the best fried chicken and mashed potatoes. If she left in an hour she could get there and back to her sister's place, even though she'd hit rush hour traffic. She smiled to herself. Lindsay put the phone back in her pocket. Then she leaned over the sink and washed her face. No traces of tears remained as she looked in the mirror.

It was in that moment that she saw a shadow reflected in the glass. She jumped, startled. What was that? She laughed out loud at her reaction. It was three in the afternoon. No-one was here - were they? A shiver ran down her spine. She felt tiny goosebumps on her arms. She wanted to run but couldn't.

She reassured herself, saying aloud, "You're seeing things. Calm down, girl."

It wasn't working. She knew what she had seen. Slowly she turned around, and to her horror, saw him, that threatening man, just for a second. She was about to scream when she saw it. A gun was pointed straight at her heart.

Chapter Seventy-One

Lindsay wondered if the man standing before her with the gun could hear her heart pounding. It sounded so loud to her. Maybe she was still dreaming, she thought. She hoped so. *Some kind of dream*, she thought. As a shiver ran through her, she realized this wasn't a dream at all. It was real. It was very real.

Her eyes were locked on the huge gun pointed at her heart. It was hard not to stare at it. She knew that she had to look away to see who and what she was dealing with. Slowly, she moved her eyes from the gun to his face. She gasped when she saw who it was. She knew him. How could he?

"Am I going to die," she asked in the tiniest whisper. At first there was no reply. She wondered if she had even spoken.

Instead of answering her question, he said, "Hello, Lindsay. Nice to see you again". His teeth looked so perfect, and yet so evil, as he smiled malevolently at her. "Are you going to die? Well, that depends on you. Are you going to make this hard, or easy? Perhaps if you do what I say, you won't. Or… maybe you will. At least then it would be quick. Let's go. We don't have a lot of time."

"Wh… Where… are we go…" she stammered. He took a step forward and with a gloved hand grabbed the long blonde hair that she loved and pulled her toward him. She was like dead weight. She couldn't move. Her legs felt weak and shaky. She wondered if she was going to fall over.

"Come on," he hissed. "I don't have all day. Don't make me hurt you. I don't want to have to do that. But I will."

When he said that, she believed him. She tried to move, but still could not. The terror she felt was like nothing she had ever experienced before. Hiccupping sobs erupted from her body. He grasped her hair tighter. This time when he pulled her forward, a clump of it ripped from her scalp. She bit her lip hard to keep from crying out.

To her shock and horror, her legs gave out. She hit her head on the corner of the sink as she fell to the floor. She heard the crack of her head on the sharp corner and felt dizzy. Fight… fight, she tried to tell herself. Her body was not listening. She was aware of something sticky on her cheek. Several spots of blood dotted the floor and sink. She heard the intruder cursing angrily. She had not meant to fall. His eyes angrily glared down at her.

As the pain overtook her, her eyes became blurry. Then she saw the man put the gun down. He put it down, she thought. I have to run. Now it was not only her legs that wouldn't move. The room was spinning around her. Through her haze she saw him pull something from his pocket. What was that, a pen of some kind? No, it was too small for that, too skinny. Oh, my… Oh, no! It was a needle. Just then something hard poked her in the neck. A shooting pain went through her. Then her whole world went completely dark.

Chapter Seventy-Two

Amy Jones paced her two-bedroom apartment. The time was six-fifty-two p.m. Lindsay should have been back with dinner by now, even if she had stopped somewhere. *It's not that far between her place and mine*, she thought. She wondered what to do. Should she call for help? She didn't want to overreact. Still, her sister had told her in a text almost three hours ago she was happy to pick up dinner. "She also told you that she might not be back until six-thirty," she reminded herself aloud. That calmed her nerves a little. Hopefully, she was worrying over nothing. This was LA after all, and sometimes six-thirty meant seven pm. She took a breath and looked forward to the meal ahead.

Amy thought about how shaken Lindsay had been lately. That was understandable. Amy had never known anyone who was murdered. Even though she didn't know Cassie Garrison, it shook her to the core that she was killed. The eulogy her friend's mother had given was stirring. She admired their willingness to forgive and keep living life. The funeral was made even harder because some maniac had tried to murder her own sister, sweet Lindsay. Why? she wondered. Everyone liked her. She was an open book.

Ever since she'd found God, her life had changed. She'd loved more, laughed more and was becoming increasingly more self-aware. It was wonderful to see her transformation. It had brought the sisters together in a way neither had thought possible. She picked up her cell phone and dialed Lindsay's number. *Ring… Ring.* She waited. That cheerful voicemail came on instead. She hung up and redialed. It rang again. Once again, she was instructed to "leave a message after the beep".

Amy reread the text conversation from this afternoon. She realized with a start Lindsay had texted that she was at her own apartment. At the time, she'd said everything was fine. Was it still? What was she doing there anyway? A surge of anger and panic went through her. What was so important that she had to stop home? Lindsay was smart, not impulsive. Why would she? Tears filled her eyes. She tried not to imagine the worst as the time ticked by. The police were concerned enough about her safety to ask her to stay with her sister. So why in the world…? *I'll give it one more hour*, Amy thought. *If she's not home by then, I'll have to call the police.*

Chapter Seventy-Three

The traffic was brutal as Matt and I drove back from the coffee shop. For an hour we had not even moved. One of the lanes on the 5 was closed, causing infuriating backup. We seemed to crawl along. Like every other LA driver, I was impatient to get where I was going. The afternoon with Scott and Juliet had rattled us both. We were anxious to look at the security footage and see what Cameron and Davis had come up with so far.

"You could turn on the lights and sirens," Matt remarked. I had to admit it was tempting. I shrugged in response.

"Do you want me to?"

"No, but just looking at your face tells me you want to." I couldn't help but laugh. I was such an open book sometimes.

Matt stared out the window for a long moment. "I was wondering what the killer might do next?" Just then his face grew pale. "If I were him or her, I would want to tie up loose ends. Not have any witnesses left to worry about. And then just disappear."

I thought about who the loose ends might be. "Oh, no. You're thinking Lindsay Jones, right?" A sense of panic set in.

"Right. I'm going to call her just to make sure she's fine. I'm sure she is, Emma," Matt said as he took his cell from his pocket.

A few minutes later, he set it down on the dashboard. "I've tried to call her three times. All I get is her voicemail. I even sent her a text. She hasn't returned it."

"I'm sure Cameron and Davis can handle the video for a little longer. It would make me feel better to know she's okay. She's probably at her sister's. We're only twenty minutes from Lindsay's apartment, though. Let's go take a look," I said, turning on the lights and sirens as I sped toward our destination.

Chapter Seventy-Four

It was just after seven p.m. when we finally reached her apartment. The first thing we noticed was Lindsay's car parked in the lot. My sense of urgency was growing. "Let's call her sister before we do anything else," I said.

Matt agreed and phoned the station to get Amy's number. We sat in the car as the dispatcher connected us through our radio to her cell phone.

"Hello," a worried voice said.

"Amy, this is Detective Parker. My partner and I met you at the funeral for Cassie Garrison." Before he could continue, she cut him off.

"Oh, thank goodness you called! I can't seem to find Lindsay. She texted me earlier in the day that she was at her apartment and things were fine. Then, she offered to pick up dinner on her way back to my place. She said she would be back by six-thirty at the latest. It's after seven. I was going to call you in half an hour if I hadn't heard from her." Her sobbing voice echoed through the speakers.

"And she isn't back yet?" Matt gently asked.

"No! I keep trying to call and text her. I was about to drive to her place. Maybe something happened." Her voice was now hysterical.

"Just sit tight. If she comes back, we want you home so you can let us know right away. We are near her apartment and will do a welfare check just to make sure she's okay." Matt didn't want to make her more afraid, so he didn't tell her we were right in front of her sister's apartment. He just calmly continued. "We'll take care of it right away and let you know. I'm sure she's fine, Amy. The best thing you can do is sit tight and wait for our call. Let me say it again: if she does come home or get in touch, please call me as soon as possible, okay?" He said this firmly. She muttered an okay and begged us to do the same. We agreed and got off the phone. By the time the conversation ended, we were standing next to Lindsay's empty car. I peered in the windows. Nothing looked out of place.

Next, we rang the super. Luckily, he was home and agreed to meet with us. He was a tall man with graying hair and wide-set eyes. He told us that he had seen Lindsay's car and thought it was strange that she was there given everything that had happened. He told us Lindsay had mentioned to him that she was staying at her sisters for a while and would hopefully be back soon.

"Maybe she just needed to pick something up," he said, "and fell asleep or something. Obviously, she has to be in her apartment since her car is there," he added hopefully. Finally, after more time-consuming conversation, we got him to give us the key.

"I can go with you and unlock the door," he feebly said.

"No need, sir. In light of everything that's happened, we're doing a welfare check. If we need you, we'll come get you," Matt said firmly. He was good at being both reassuring and authoritative at the same time. When he spoke, people listened. We assured the super we would give him back the key, along with news of Lindsay's wellbeing as soon as possible. We also made sure he understood we would only go in if we felt it was necessary. He finally agreed and went back into his own apartment.

Chapter Seventy-Five

We raced up the stairs to the third floor. It reminded me of the night we were there after the poisoning. Matt pounded on the door. "Lindsay, it's the police. Open up. We need to know you are okay." We waited and got no response.

"Lindsay, it's Detectives Blade and Parker. Open the door, please," I tried. Still silence.

"I'm going to say it one more time. This is the police. Open up!" Matt yelled. Nothing.

Finally, after several attempts, we exchanged glances and Matt took out his revolver. "Cover me," he said. I stood behind him to one side, my gun aimed straight ahead.

Slowly and as quietly as possible, Matt slipped the key into the lock and opened the door. He burst into the room yelling, "Police." I followed after him, doing the same. "Clear," he shouted as he looked into the kitchen.

"Clear," I echoed, as I swept the living and dining room off to my left. He said the same as he went into her bedroom. Everything was clear as I opened the closet doors wide.

Matt called out, "Emma!"

I ran into the bathroom where he stood. My heart did a flip as I saw the blood on the white tile floor. A small clump of blonde hair was mixed in. It was clear that a struggle had occurred. I glanced in the trash can and saw more hair, now turned red from the blood. I pointed at it as Matt looked my way. What had happened here? I wondered. Our quick first impression was that someone had kidnapped Lindsay.

"Maybe she fell and hit her head," Matt observed, pointing to where the blood started, right there on a sharp corner of the sink. It had dripped and was now almost dry on the floor.

"Yeah, but where is she now?" I asked in a puzzled voice.

"I don't understand why she came back here," Matt said, frustrated.

I nodded and let out a sigh. "I know."

Slowly we backed out of the bathroom and called our captain to give him an update. Then we notified the crime scene team so they could come and collect evidence, which would hopefully give us some clues as to what happened. We re-entered Lindsay's bedroom. Her phone was charging on the nightstand. Her bed looked slept in. Her purse sat on the floor, seemingly undisturbed.

"Where could she be?" I wondered aloud.

I put on gloves and unlocked her phone. I saw that she had been writing a note to herself. It looked like a grocery list. I saw the missed calls from Amy and relayed the context of the text messages out loud to Matt. "So it looks like she got here around one p.m. She was texting Amy around three, talking about dinner, telling her everything was fine."

I picked up her purse and went through it. "Nothing out of the ordinary in here. There's a little cash in her wallet. The credit cards look undisturbed. So obviously it wasn't a robbery," I said.

"The windows and doors haven't been jimmied. So whoever got in must have had a key," Matt said after examining all the windows and the front door. "It's almost eight. So this all happened around four plus hours ago," he reasoned.

"That's a long time," I muttered. Despair washed over me like rain. I saw Matt standing in a corner silently saying a prayer. He looked over at me and whispered, "I believe we can find her in time."

Chapter Seventy-Six

The crime scene team had arrived. We had turned the scene over to them. The car couldn't go fast enough as I drove like a mad woman, siren blaring, back to the station. "I wish we could just drive around and look for her," I yelled over the siren.

"Me, too," Matt yelled back.

We all sat helplessly around the conference table at the station. We had to figure out where Lindsay was. Events were happening too fast.

"He has a major head start on us," our captain said. We all joined together to find Lindsay. Cameron, Davis, Case, Shields, Caplin, and Jones looked as distraught as Matt and I felt.

"Why did she go back to her apartment?" Cameron said in a frustrated tone. Matt shrugged helplessly.

"Was someone waiting for her when she got there?" Jones asked.

"I don't think so," Matt said. "Half past three p.m. she was texting her sister telling her everything was fine."

"He had to have a key, or she let him in or left the door unlocked," Shields surmised.

"Doubtful she left the door unlocked. She is a careful girl," I said. Matt agreed.

"We know," Kelsey said, approaching the white board, "that whatever happened took place between three and seven-thirty p.m." She made a note of the time and summary of the text conversation between the sisters. She also noted the time of our interview with Scott and Juliet Hall.

"Scott left right around two p.m. I added that Juliet went into the bathroom and didn't leave for another hour. So either one or both could have driven to her apartment by three-thirty without traffic, maybe four with," Cameron said.

Our captain cleared his throat. "Matt, Emma, find and interview Juliet Hall again. Since she told you her husband is dangerous, let's believe her and dig deeper into their lives. Go hard this time and get what you need. I think she will tell you what she knows," he urged.

"Shields and Case, you two find Marco Crane. Find out where he was all day today. Make him prove it. Again, push hard. We need answers," he said, turning to the remaining officers.

"The rest of us will keep watching footage. There's so much of it to go through. We need to work fast. We will also put out a BOLO for the cars registered to the Hall's. That way, everyone on the streets will be looking for that vehicle. I will clue in the other divisions and get their help. It goes without saying, if anyone has anything, call me. I'll make sure everyone gets the message. Jones, Cap, before you look at the tape, go ahead and canvas her neighbors. She had to be taken out of there somehow. I can't believe no one saw anything suspicious. How can you kidnap someone during the day? I'm no psychologist; but that shows a boldness on his part." We agreed and then got up, racing out of the station, determined to find Lindsay Jones.

Chapter Seventy-Seven

Matt looked through the DMV records and located the address for Juliet Hall. The GPS told us we were about a mile away. The neighborhood was peaceful. Several large oak trees had been planted and provided shade from the hot sun for the residents. The houses all looked mid-sized as we drove by. My heart was in my throat. Worry was written all over my face.

"Emma, we could not have stopped Lindsay from going to her apartment."

All I could do was nod, as my eyes started to fill with tears. I quickly blinked them back. "I know that. I just hope she's okay." Thoughts of the other murders flooded my mind. Matt reached over and squeezed my hand. Just then the GPS voice instructed, "Arriving in 500 feet on the left."

I sat in the car for a moment, gathering myself. I wondered how we would get this scared woman to help us.

"Emma, you take the lead with Juliet since you know her a little better. I'm wondering if she knows what happened to Lindsay," he said.

"She wears her expressions all over her face; so it probably won't be hard to tell," I responded.

We got out of the car and started toward a light yellow house with flowers planted on either side of the porch. Decorations hung from the door that reminded me the Fourth of July was the next big holiday. It was easy to see the Hall's took pride in their home. It seemed so normal. I wondered if maybe we had this all wrong. But the thing about killers is they can often appear quite normal. Their homes or friends or standing in the community can fool anyone and sometimes does. Matt took the last step onto the porch. Once I joined him, he picked up the brass knocker and began to use it.

Chapter Seventy-Eight

Knock. Knock. Knock. The brass continued to pound loudly against the door. "Mr. and Mrs. Hall: police. Open up!" Matt's voice

214

boomed. "Police!" he said even louder. Despite the knocking and shouts, there was no response, which was strange because Juliet's car was in the driveway.

After a few minutes passed, I suggested we split up and see if there were windows we could look into. I found one off the kitchen. Everything seemed normal from that view. Dishes were drying in the drainer. The garbage looked ready to be taken out. I peered closer. That's when I saw it. Underneath the window in a little slot sat a key.

"Matt, I found a spare key," I yelled. Matt joined me immediately. I held the key in my gloved hand. He took a moment to peer into the kitchen window.

"Something's not right. I can feel it. All the other windows are shut tight."

Just because we felt something wasn't right didn't give us permission to go in. The one exception to that rule is if someone's life may be in immediate danger. If Scott Hall was the killer, a case could be made for that. We discussed it from all angles. Maybe she was sleeping. Why invade her privacy without evidence that something was wrong? Finally, since Juliet had told me her husband was dangerous and there had been signs of abuse, we decided to go for it.

Matt looked my way and said, "Alright, let's go in." We both pride ourselves on doing things by the book. So this was a hard decision to make. I hoped it was the right one.

We made our way back to the porch. I slipped the key into the lock. It opened quickly into a small but cozy kitchen. For the second time that day, we pulled out our guns and informed anyone who was there who we were. I walked into the living room. Leather coffee-colored sofas lined the large wall. On either side were shelves of books. The room looked neat and well kept.   As I ran deeper into the house, I smelled the odor of blood. I knew something wasn't right. "Clear," I shouted as I ran through the living room and checked closets. Matt motioned that I take the bedroom while he rushed toward the bathroom and two guest rooms. I turned down a narrow hallway. Closets were on either side and the one door at the very end made it clear I was at the right spot. Slowly, I pointed my gun ahead of me. I stepped to the side and opened the door.

The first thing I saw was all the blood. No! No! No! I thought in despair. Blood was spattered on the walls. The once light-gray carpet was transformed into a deep crimson. I didn't take another step into the master bedroom, because it was obviously a crime scene, but I opened the door wider and let my eyes roam around the room. On the bed, the body of Juliet Hall lay motionless. By the large gash across her throat and the blood dripping from her wound onto the covers, it was clear she was dead. I stood in stunned silence, just staring.

A hand grasped my shoulder. I almost jumped, but then I felt the reassuring squeeze of my partner's hand. For just a moment, I turned into his embrace and let him hold me. His arms wrapped tightly around me. It felt like hugging a strong rock. I leaned in even more, letting the scent of his soap fill my nostrils. Then I took a step back from him and cleared my throat.

"Thank you. Now let's get to work," I said in a firm and calm voice.

About twenty minutes later, the medical examiner and crime scene team showed up. "What a mess," Doctor Locking observed as he surveyed the scene. He leaned over the body of Juliet Hall. "Judging by her body temperature, this happened recently."

"How recently?" Matt wanted to know.

"This is just a guess at this point, but I would say in the last four to six hours or so."

"That makes sense. The last time I saw her was between two and two-thirty. We interviewed the couple this afternoon," I said for Dr. Locking's benefit. His time estimate made sense, as it was now going on ten.

"This looks like an unprovoked quick attack," Jesse Smith said as he approached us. "My crime scene team has already located three bullets." He pointed at the headboard and the wall near the bed.

"It looks like she was shot in the face," Dr. Locking added, pointing to a small hole near Juliet's left eye that leaked blood. I almost gagged as I looked again at the blood and tissue all over this once lovely woman's face.

"We are going to let you guys do your thing. Come on, Emma, let's go search the rest of the apartment," Matt said as he steered me away from the bedroom.

Walking back into the living room, we noticed a tarp had been laid on the floor and one of the techs was checking the carpet, taking any hairs or fibers he could find. We stepped around him and walked toward the desk. Matt snapped on a pair of latex gloves and opened the first drawer. Inside were file folders of bank statements and income tax records. We flipped through them.

"All this looks pretty typical," Matt observed as he put down the first folder.

"They were organized," I remarked.

We kept looking for what seemed like forever. Looking through income statements isn't my favorite thing. I opened the next drawer and pulled out folders of more paid bills and receipts. I then opened a third drawer and found what I was looking for. Inside was a back panel that was loose. Matt leaned over and started to work the panel with both hands. After a while, it came free. We found more folders and a computer.

"Yes!" Matt exclaimed as he piled the contents on the desk. Inside we found bank statements from Sally Haze's account showing transfers of large sums of cash from it to Scott and Juliet Hall's account. There was even a copy of her credit cards and driver's license. Matt let out a slow whistle. He used his phone to take snapshots to use as evidence when we found Scott Hall. We needed to turn over this valuable treasure trove to the Crime Scene Unit.

Matt waved one of them over and showed her what we found. She took out a large plastic evidence bag. We helped load the contents. Our tech team would need to look at the laptop and give us more information.

"Would you mind if we have a quick look at the computer?" I asked. I wanted to find any leads we could.

"Sure, that's fine," the CSI investigator agreed and put it on the desk. Before we got our chance, she dusted the computer for fingerprints. She also dusted the top of the desk so we could set it down without contaminating the scene. Once we finished, they would dust for prints again and take the large drawer as well. It was pretty obvious to everyone that the Hall's fingerprints would be all over the place, since the evidence was found in their home.

"I'll just use this corner here. Please keep working," Matt said as we stepped to the side. She smiled at us in appreciation and laid the computer on the plastic evidence bag.

Just then a loud ringing came from somewhere. At first, it didn't register that it was my phone. Matt tapped my shoulder and pointed to my ringing purse. Quickly I dug into my large bag and grabbed it. As I did, I saw the captain's number filling the display.

"Hi, Captain. What's up?"

"How is it going at the Hall place?" he asked. Oh, no, I thought. He didn't know yet. He was going to be angry with us and had a right to be. Our first call should have been to him.

"Um, I'm sorry, Cap, we should have called right away. Are you sitting down?" He cut me off sharply.

"I already know, Blade. I was with Jesse when he got the call." I sort of breathed a sigh of relief.

"We were just about to call you once we had more information."

"I got it. This time, it's no problem. In the future, you would be advised not to let me hear first-hand information again from anyone else but my officers on scene. Are we clear?"

I gulped and said, "Yes, sir. Sorry sir." I meant it.

Then, just like that, Captain Mendoza moved on. It's one of the things I love about working for him. "Okay, what's up? Fill me in," he said. So I did.

"You or someone else will need to look through the evidence later," he ordered. "Do a quick read and turn it all over to the crime scene team. They will process everything."

I then told him about the computer that Matt was getting ready to boot up. "Captain, this could be important. We need to look at it more closely."

"Blade, listen to me. You have more pressing and immediate matters to attend to."

"Like what?" I wondered what could be more important than a fresh crime scene.

"Shields and Case went over to Marco Crane's apartment to interview him again, remember?"

"Yes," I responded.

"When they got there, they found him with a gunshot wound to his head. He's dead."

Chapter Seventy-Nine

For the third time in one day—actually in several hours—my partner and I went to another crime scene. This had to be a record, I thought. Unlike the other two victims, Marco Crane had lived in a really nice neighborhood. His house had a security system and would have been hard to find if you didn't know where it was. It was tucked away on a dead-end street. The driveway was long and curved. I made the last turn toward the house. It was a sprawling ranch-style, two-story home. As soon as we got out of the car, a patrol officer met us and led us inside. Mike Cameron spotted us, excused himself, and came rushing toward us.

"It looks like Marco was shot in his living room," Mike said, as he led us to the crime scene.

We knelt over the body of Marco Crane. As I did, a wave of guilt came over me. I'd thought he was the killer for a long time. Now, he was a victim. "How many bodies is this?" I asked wearily.

"Six in total, maybe seven if we don't get…" Matt answered, his voice trailing off. A lump formed in my throat as I perused the scene. Marco's hair was matted with blood. Three bullet holes were visible.

"All shots to the head and face," said Doctor Mora London. She was a top assistant to Dr. Locking. Even at a crime scene like this, she stood out. With her auburn hair tied back and her large green eyes, she was surveying the scene. She leaned over the body and touched a pulse point.

"He's still warm. This didn't happen too long ago," she observed. "Dr. Locking is at another scene. That's why I'm here."

"We just came from that one, Mora," Matt said.

"Are they related?" she wanted to know.

"It's a pretty high possibility. Just treat it individually, keeping that in mind, okay? The victims knew each other; that we know for sure," Matt said.

"Sure thing, guys. Once I know more, I'll call your captain." We thanked her and moved back toward our fellow detectives.

Davis was standing in the bathroom. It looked like a guest bath, since it was off the kitchen. He pointed to the laptop that sat in a plastic evidence bag on the counter.

"Look what we found. It was floating in the tub when we got here." Inside the bag was a laptop drying out with some rice in the bag, which was supposed to help.

"There goes that evidence," Matt said sarcastically.

"Our techs are talented. The computer is destroyed, but maybe not the hard drive. I'll be taking it in as evidence so they can have a look at it," Davis said.

"We found a laptop at the Hall's place. We were just about to look at it when we got the call to come here," I said. Now I wondered what was on both of them. "Was there any other evidence?" I asked.

"Crane had a security system with a camera. Mike's on the phone with the security team to get the tape emailed to us as soon as possible."

Just then, as if on cue, Mike walked in. "Done. Let's have a look, shall we."

Every police unit has a mobile command center. We walked out to their car and Mike pulled up his email through the WIFI connection on his computer. Davis sat in front while Matt and I stood peering over his shoulder, waiting for it to load.

Chapter Eighty

An image of Marco's house emerged on the screen. "This is a good camera system, very clear," Matt observed. The tape started five hours before. Mike hit the fast forward button until we saw movement. The time stamp showed that it was around two hours ago. That would have made it around eight p.m. This really was recent, I thought. A black Chevy showed up and made the final turn into the driveway. The driver parked the car in some dense bushes. He faced it away from the camera and used it as a shield to get to the front door. He wore a hooded sweatshirt and sunglasses.

"He knows there are cameras and is trying to hide his face," I said. The others nodded in agreement.

In the video, his hand reached up to ring the doorbell. As he waited, he pulled down his hood for just a second to scratch the back of his neck.

"Got him," Matt said excitedly. There on the back of his neck was the Coral Reef tattoo that we noticed earlier in the day.

Just then the door opened. Marco's image appeared in the frame. The two men embraced. He opened the door wide, ushering Scott Hall inside. Then the door closed.

The cameras only captured the outside. "I wish I knew what was happening in those moments inside the house," Davis said, an edge of irritation in his voice.

We fast-forwarded the tape until we saw it. About twenty minutes later, Scott Hall was seen racing out the door. He had blood all over his clothes. A gun was sticking out of his side pocket. He ran to the car and slammed the door shut. He drove like a bat out of hell down the driveway. "Just enough time for him to kill his friend and destroy the laptop," Davis said.

"What made Marco dangerous to Scott all of a sudden," I wondered aloud.

"See at the end there? He wasn't even trying to hide his face, like he had nothing to worry about," Matt said grimly.

"Not only that, he just got sloppy," I remarked.

"Now that we know who he is, we need to figure out where he is and where he has Lindsay. And we need to do it fast," Davis informed us, urgency in his voice.

Chapter Eighty-One

We stayed at the crime scene for another hour. Marco's office didn't hold any more clues. Our captain had put out another BOLO for the make and model of Scott's car. That told all police and highway patrol troopers to *Be On the Look Out* for a particular car and to stop it and proceed with caution.

"Let's go back and look at some more security footage," Matt suggested. "I want to see if Lindsay shows up anywhere."

I replied, "Of course, you do. I do too. But where do we begin?"

"I guess we could drive around looking for his car," Matt said a little sarcastically. It wasn't personal. Like me, he felt frustrated and helpless. I knew that thought was ridiculous as well. This was a huge city. We wouldn't have a clue where to begin. If she wasn't in Hollywood, our chances at randomly finding her were slim to none. Los Angeles is way too big. And if he took her out of the city, well… I didn't want to think about that.

"I think the best way to use our time is to build an airtight case against Scott Hall and find out as much about him as we can. Maybe that will lead us to Lindsay," Matt said. I had to agree.

"I'm not going home tonight. I'm working until I find her," I said, with determination and stubbornness.

"*We're* going to do that, then. It's not just you. We are partners, remember?" Matt said as he walked toward the door of the late Marco Crane's home.

Chapter Eighty-Two

Lindsay Jones woke to hear a moaning sound coming from somewhere. At first, she couldn't identify from where. She felt groggy. Everything hurt. With a start, she realized it was from her own lips. She tried to move her hands, but they were stuck. She tried to stand but couldn't. She felt weak all over. "Hello," she croaked. She was met with silence. She couldn't hear her own voice. She tried to open her eyes, but they felt glued shut. She found herself in total darkness. *Where am I?* she wondered. What happened? Slowly, as her body began to wake up, it all started to come back. The scene in her apartment - Scott pointing his gun at her and then sticking her hard with something. That's when the world went black, she realized. Was she going to die? To her the scariest part was that she knew him. How could he?

What a silly and unnecessary mistake she had made. Was she going to pay for it with her life? She had thought her apartment was safe enough to go home to, just for a couple of hours. She was so wrong. What time was it? How long had she been gone? Had anyone noticed? Was anyone out there looking for her? As she thought about her situation, hot tears slid down her face.

"Please, God," she prayed, "get me out of here alive."

Lindsay Jones definitely needed a savior.

Chapter Eighty-Three

June 26th

The light of dawn came as I slowly opened my eyes at my desk. Despite my *"I'm staying awake and not going home until we find her"* sentiment, I was still human. I'd needed to take a couple hours for sleep.

At first, I'd protested. How could I sleep if Lindsay was still missing? Matt reminded me that I wouldn't be good for anything, or able to help, if I didn't rest for just a little while. I knew he was right. And now, I was glad I'd listened and taken his advice. We had been working very late into the night. I looked at my phone. The time read eight-thirty in the morning. I inhaled the smell of fresh coffee and grabbed a cup.

At my desk, I had Juliet Hall's diary in front of me. The crime scene team had found it and brought it to us. By the time they did, I was so tired my vision was blurring. Later this morning, the bartender was coming in to look at our lineup. The office was filled with the hustle and bustle of the morning. Cops were ending their shifts while others began.

I looked at Matt, whose head was on his desk. I wanted to brush back a lock of his hair that clung to his forehead. Instead, I just looked at him. Once this case was over, we would do that courting thing he talked about. I was excited to get to know him on a whole different level. Not Matt the police officer, but Matt the man. He always knew the right thing to say. He could make me laugh with a sarcastic word or a corny joke. He was steady and calm. To think I was going to have the chance that many women I knew wanted made me kind of giddy.

I turned my head away and looked back down at Juliet's diary. What did you want me to know but couldn't say? What, Juliet, were you trying to tell me? I opened to the last entry. It was dated June 24th:

"I told Scott I couldn't put them off any longer. The detectives kept calling, wanting to interview us together. He was dead set against it. I knew that if we didn't, he would look guilty. Maybe I would too. A few nights back, while Scott was once again out late, I looked through his desk and found the back panel in one of the drawers was loose. I opened it. That's when I found it all. I had always thought Scott was being unfaithful. Just the way he flirted with and looked at women when I was around was enough of a clue. But then, I found real proof of not just infidelity, but worse. Scott dated our friend, Sally. She was my friend; and he dated her right under my nose just a few short months after we were married. He never really loved me after all. How could I have missed all this? Because I wanted to. The signs were there. I chose to ignore them. I knew it was a mistake to marry him. Now I have something I can hang over his head when he gets

home. I can't wait to see the reaction of my so-called actor husband when he finds out that I know what he's been up to. Stealing money and being unfaithful."

The entry ended there. I turned to see Matt reading over my shoulder. "Good morning," he said in a low sexy voice. Despite the serious subject matter, I looked up at him and grinned. Then I breathed my coffee breath in his face. He laughed.

"Yummy. I need a cup."

Once he got back, he pulled his chair alongside mine and glanced at the entry again. "I hate to say it. But I think that's what got her killed," he said. I nodded in agreement. "Perhaps she wanted a good divorce settlement."

"Perhaps she wanted control," I countered.

I flipped back several pages, and we continued to read. The date of this entry was June 10th, which was just before Cassie was killed:

"Marco invited his whole acting class over to a party he was having. We got all dressed up. The stress of everything is making me lose weight. Almost nothing fit. I managed to find a long black dress that still did. Marco was such a good friend. Scott sees him now more than I did. So I was excited. We went to his lovely home. I hope to have a place like that one day. It seems so peaceful. Everything was going fine until later in the night. Scott was across the room talking with some of the students in his class. I was sitting on the couch with Marco and another group of students and their significant others. I saw the way he was looking at her. The way he touched her arm, and the way he slid his hands on her back as he turned her toward him to say something that I couldn't hear. Cassie didn't seem to notice. Or, if she did, she appeared to like it. That just upset me more, the way she flirted right back, how she laughed at everything he said and leaned her body into his. I had just met her that night. She was young and talented and beautiful, just Scott's type. Marco saw me staring and tugged at my arm. He had the nerve to suggest that my husband was just being friendly. You've got to be kidding me! I wanted to scream. I was so angry. I took an Uber back home without even telling Scott goodbye. He probably wouldn't notice I was gone anyway."

226

We kept reading her story. It was both heartbreaking and fascinating. A couple of nights later she wrote:

June 15th

"Scott didn't even come home last night. I didn't wait up for him either. I used to, but not anymore. What was the use? Tonight was the first time we saw each other since my quick exit from the party. He was not happy. He screamed at me about leaving without telling him. Then he hit me. It was worse than usual. He was so angry. When I mentioned Cassie, he flew into a rage. He punched me. My eye will be black for at least a week. He was so angry he broke my favorite lamp in the living room. Then he picked up the glass end table and threw it with everything on it against the wall. Did our neighbors hear all this? I kind of hoped so. After that, he threw me against the wall and spit in my face. He threatened to kill me if I left. He said he might do it anyway. He has said it before. But this time… I believe him. I'm scared, really scared… I have to leave him. But how? I can still hear his words. If I do, he said he would kill me."

Chapter Eighty-Four

As we read on, it was clear that Juliet Hall thought her husband had murdered Cassie Garrison and was beginning to wonder about the others. I wished she had told us instead of confronting him. A killer like that would do anything to keep her quiet.

As if reading my mind, Matt said, "She probably thought she could handle it."

Her mistake, I bitterly thought. That wasn't fair; and I knew it. Blaming the victim was not right. I was just so angry and sad that she couldn't turn to us. I was so angry at Scott for what he probably did to her. I was so angry that he carried out his threat so quickly after our interview. I was lost in my angry thoughts when our captain's voice brought me out of it.

"Rise and shine, folks. Let's get back to it and find Lindsay Jones. Matt, Emma, the bartender is here to see you."

We offered Jason Castro a cup of coffee. He shook his head and tried to rub the sleep from his eyes.

"We're sorry we had to wake you. Things are moving fast, and we need your help."

"Sure, no problem," he yawned.

Matt placed the photos in front of him.

"Just take your time," I urged.

He did, looking at each one carefully. "I've met this one. But it's not the guy I told you about. I think he came in once or twice with CC."

He had just pointed at a picture of Marco Crane. We nodded our understanding and waited as he continued to study the photos. He then looked at the picture of Scott Hall. "I think it's this one. He looks a little different. Back then he had a beard and his hair was longer. But it's the same guy."

"What do you mean?" Matt asked.

"That's the guy I saw watching CC Garden. After she got scared and left, he was the one who tried to ask me questions about her."

"So you didn't think they were romantically involved?" I asked.

"It didn't look like it. More like she recognized him and got spooked." That was a wrinkle I wasn't expecting.

"Actually, I got something for you guys." Jason reached into his bag and pulled out a scrap of paper. "I found that partial license number."

I wanted to leap across the table and hug him. I kept my cool and said, "Thanks so much for your help, and for finding that."

"I'm sure it'll be useful," Matt said.

We stood and shook his hand. Once we walked him out, we went back up to the office to run the plate.

Mike Cameron tapped on his keys and did a manual search for the numbers we had from Jason. He scrolled through listings of partial plates matching what we had. "No luck yet," he said.

I crossed my fingers as I read registration after registration. Maybe this is a dead end, I thought. It was always possible that Jason copied down the wrong partial plate or that it was stolen or unregistered. Just when my eyes began to blur after all that scrolling, my colleague looked up with an expression of surprise. He pointed to a listing. We all looked at it together. You could have heard a pin drop in that moment. Our stunned silence said it all.

"This car doesn't belong to Scott Hall," he said. "This car is registered to Martin Lopez."

Chapter Eighty-Five

Everything still hurt, Lindsay thought as she tried to move. She opened her eyes but couldn't see anything. It was then she realized everything was dark. She was in a place that was pitch-black. Where am I? A feeling of panic washed over her. Again, the question came. Where am I? Her thoughts were all jumbled and frantic. Then she heard - Click. Rattle. Rattle. What was that? She moved her arms and realized that's where the sound had come from. The sound was so loud. She wanted to plug her ears. Her head hurt so much.

That's when she realized she couldn't. She stretched out her arms and realized she could only move so much. She wondered what was making it so dark. There was a heaviness around her face, and something was covering her mouth. In the darkness, she wondered what to do and began to pray. That calmed her down.

It was in that stillness that it all started coming back to her, sleeping in her own bed, then waking up. The killer came to find her. He broke into her apartment and pointed a gun at her. What other choice did she have but to go with him? Then she remembered the needle. That's when everything went dark and her memory ended. And now she was here. But where was that?

She had a vague memory of waking up in this place before. But she'd quickly gone back to sleep maybe? Lindsay slowed her breathing and made her body become very still. She listened. She strained her ears to hear. She took in a deep breath through her nose and sniffed several times. The smell was musty and dank. She put her fingers on the ground and felt dirt. It was hard and compact under her touch.

Even though her muscles felt weak, she reached back and felt the chains that had made the rattling sound. A thick chain was wrapped around her waist, another around her arms. Her legs were not chained but felt weak. This was all too much, she thought. Hot tears began to fall. Did anyone even know she was here? How am I going to get out? She longed for water.

Slowly, she stood up on shaky weak legs. She took one step and fell hard on the ground. Maybe her body wasn't ready for this, she decided. So she scooted herself forward until something stopped her. She scooted back, once again hearing the rattling of the chains. She felt around until her hand found the post. That would be her landmark of sorts. Now she could judge how far she could go. In horror, she realized the limitations brought on by the two chains that held her. No wonder she was having trouble moving.

Drugs, plus chains, don't make for a good combination. Since standing was out of the question, she began to stretch out her legs. She had once injured her knee playing soccer. The tedious exercises she once hated doing in physical therapy were coming back to her. She hated to admit that over time, they'd worked. It was painful, but her knee did heal. Now, she was thankful for those memories and the many hours she'd put into getting well. She knew she had to escape, and she could only do that if she could move.

The pain was intense. She cried out as her muscles screamed in protest. Although she couldn't move her arms very far, she did what she could to stretch them out. She pulled them in front of her body, then to the sides. She clenched and unclenched her fists while wiggling each finger and toe. She was not hurt, she thought. She thanked God for that. When she stopped to take a break, she heard a sound coming from somewhere, maybe outside, maybe above her. She couldn't tell. She froze. Then slowly, as quietly as she could, she moved back into the position she woke up in. If the killer was coming back, she didn't want him to think she could move at all.

She heard several locks click and knew it gave her the cover she needed to make just a little noise as the chains rattled. Her bonds caused her to move at such a slow pace, she hoped she could get back to her original spot in time. Although it wasn't far, it felt like a hundred miles. She got her opportunity when she counted: one lock; two lock; three locks. Then the door opened.

Chapter Eighty-Six

Even though the blind fold covered her eyes, Lindsay could faintly see the light pouring in as the switch was flicked on. She heard footsteps coming toward her and sensed his presence in the room. "Hello, Lindsay," he said.

She tried to speak but found her lips were taped shut and her mouth very dry. "I'll take off the tape if you don't scream. But the second you do…" He let his words linger.

She sat quietly and waited. Then, a painful rip as the tape came off her mouth. It was all she could do to keep from screaming, it hurt so much. Tears filled her eyes. She quickly blinked them back. He continued, "I'm going to hand you a bottle of water and some crackers to eat. You are chained, but you should be able to move your arms enough."

He handed her the water. She took huge gulps. It felt like a fountain of refreshment sliding down her throat.

"Thank you," she said in a whisper. Her voice didn't sound like her own. It sounded raspy and weak. She wondered if he even heard her. He handed her half a pack of crackers. She ate slowly. Despite her circumstances, she couldn't help but feel a tiny tinge of gratitude.

"What's going to happen to me?" She hadn't wanted to ask but knew she needed to.

He sighed, "Oh, Lindsay. You're my favorite. So talented you are, so beautiful." In that moment, he sounded almost sad. Was that remorse she was hearing?

"I wish," he went on, "I didn't have to kill you. But soon I will. So say your prayers and enjoy what little time you have left."

She wanted to beg, wanted to reason with him. She knew it was pointless. The evil she now heard in his voice, the menacing quality, was unmistakable. A feeling of helplessness washed over her. The fear she tried to keep at bay was bubbling up to the surface.

He continued, "There are some things I need to take care of first. But don't you fret. I'll be back."

"What time is it?" she asked. She couldn't tell with the blindfold duct tape being so tight.

"I guess you could say it's a very late breakfast or early dinner." He spoke in a sing song voice, as if this was all a game to him. *What a sick, evil man*, she thought.

"That's why I brought you the food and water," he cooed. In some ways, that was scarier than his menacing tone. If it was lunch time, she had been gone for probably twenty-four hours at least. Surely, Amy must have called the police and they were looking for her right now. She opened her mouth to speak again, hoping she could keep him there and distracted for a while longer.

It was no use. Before another word passed her lips, he stood up. She heard his footsteps getting farther away, then the click of the light switch and the closing of the door. One lock, two locks, and then the third lock clicked into place. She was plunged into darkness again.

Chapter Eighty-Seven

Scott Hall clicked the last lock into place and headed for his car. He needed to get rid of the blood-soaked clothes he was still wearing. He had to give his car a thorough cleaning before… He smacked himself on the side of the head. *Don't even think like that*, he told himself. He was always worrying about this or that. Maybe that was what gave him away, he thought.

Scott thought about Juliet. He didn't want to kill her. He had had no choice. She was putting the pieces together. He didn't think she would. He sighed in annoyance. Clearly, he had underestimated her.

She'd found the back panel of the desk and looked through his papers. The scene had been ugly. Her threatening and screaming at him. He flew into a rage and shot her.

He would be more controlled with Lindsay Jones, he told himself. He had looked carefully at her when he gave her the food and water. The chains were secure. Actually, it didn't even look like she had moved from the spot where he had originally dropped her drugged body. The tranquilizer he had given her was strong. She might not even remember most of the day. As he walked down the long and winding road into the woods, he noticed the sun setting fast. It would be dark soon. He needed that cover in order to do what needed to be done.

And after that, what? Could he really kill her? Out of all of them, she was special. He wished he didn't have to do it. Still, she could not be left alive to tell anyone who he was or what he had done. No one would be looking for her for a while, he thought. That was a good thing. She was staying with her sister. Even if the worst case happened and the alarms were sounded, the police always waited more than twenty-four hours before declaring someone missing. So who would worry? He still had a few hours, he decided.

He wanted to get rid of the bloody clothes and all the evidence; but as he walked, he felt weary to the bone. When he got tired, he stopped thinking straight. This was a plan he couldn't mess up. If he just slept for a few hours, he would have the energy in the dead of night to go forward. He touched the envelope in his pocket. Inside was a new identification and passport. He glanced at the plane ticket to anywhere but here and smiled to himself. No one would find him. He knew the three hundred thousand he had in cash would be more than enough to live on for quite a while. Maybe, once he got settled, he could invest some of it. He knew he couldn't risk getting more money out of Sally's account. The last thing he wanted to do was draw attention to himself by making a big cash transaction. Still, his weary mind thought, the more money the better.

Scott reached his car and opened the trunk. He pulled out his tent and sleeping bag, and walked deeper into the woods, allowing the large trees and the cover of night to hide him.

Chapter Eighty-Eight

Lindsay stretched out as far as she could. Her legs still felt weak. She must have dozed off after the killer left. Even though she couldn't see his face, she had been around him enough to recognize his voice. She was now sure it was Scott Hall. She had worked on scenes with him. He was a talented actor. She wondered why he would do this to her? Truthfully, Scott was the last person she would have suspected.

A yawn escaped her lips. How long had she slept? How could she have fallen asleep in the first place when getting out of here was what she should have been thinking about? Despair threatened to overtake her as she sat in that dark, lonely space chained up like an animal. She felt more tears forming in her eyes. She didn't know she had any left to cry.

Instead of giving in to the despair, she decided to be still and try to *hear what God had to say.* As she listened, a memory came to her. She was eleven. It was summertime in California, one of the hottest on record. It had been at least a hundred degrees for days. But that didn't bother her at that age. Her parents had sent her and Amy to one of those summer camps. It was a Christian sports camp. They'd spent all day playing dodgeball and soccer. At night they roasted marshmallows, ate really good food, and had fun chapel time. The memory that was coming back to her was something the teacher for that day at camp had said. She told the story of the people wandering in the desert in the wilderness. She told them how Pharaoh would not let the people go; but how at one point in Genesis, God said, *"Be still. All you have to do is be still – and I will fight for you."*

Lindsay wasn't eleven anymore, yet she needed to hear those words more than ever now. A feeling of peace came over her. Truthfully, there wasn't much she could do chained up in the dark in an unknown place. What she could do, however, was powerful. All she needed to do was be still and let Him fight for her. Some people had psychology or philosophy that they drew strength from. She drew it from the word of God. If that's what he said he would do for the people back then, she felt sure he would do it for her now. As she sat praying in the silence, she gained an understanding of what she should do next.

She wiggled her feet, testing out the muscles in her legs. At first the pins and needles were strong, but they subsided. If she could just find something, anything, to help her. She stood up on shaky legs and took steps toward the right. Progress, she thought, as she remained upright and didn't fall flat on her face. She could only go so far. She bumped into something. She reached her hands blindly out and up as far as she could. That's when her fingers brushed against something hard. It was a shelf of some sort. She pushed her hands back, exploring it. Her hands found a hard, large square. Even in the dark, she knew what it was. It was a toolbox. She reached up and stood on tip toe, praying she could grab it and pull it down. After a while she could.

Quietly, she put the toolbox on the floor and sat down. She felt around the box and found the latch to open it. Her heart skipped a beat when she realized it was unlocked. She opened it, hearing the hinges creak. She slowly ran her hands along the tools, surprised that she was able to identify some by touch alone. She wasn't a mechanic and had no talent for fixing anything. She wondered how she knew what they were. She found a hammer and several nails. She knew she had to be careful. As scary as it was, it had to be done. She took a cleansing breath, said a quick prayer asking for help, and began.

She took the nail and put it on her face next to her eye. She pulled the blindfold away from her face as best she could, then used the nail to tear away at the edges of the tape. A flutter of excitement went through her as she heard the tape and some of the fabric finally tear away. The nail was sharp. She was so busy working at it that she didn't notice the cut it made on her forehead near her eye; or how it scratched her face. She didn't even feel the pain. She then moved the nail to the other side of her face, this time going a little faster, as she repeated the process. Again, she heard it… that wonderful sound of tape and fabric tearing. She pulled off the blindfold, but for the moment saw only darkness. Even so she knew how to get back to her corner. The chain wouldn't let her go any farther. She shoved the fabric into the toolbox to hide it. Then she closed the lid. Who knew she could accomplish so much in the dark without any vision. She felt proud of what she had done so far. She didn't want to take the credit. What was happening was beyond her. She was getting help.

Lindsay slowly walked backwards until her back hit the post she was chained to and slid the toolbox as far behind it in the corner as she could. She hoped Scott hadn't catalogued what was on the shelves. Maybe he wouldn't notice. *Yeah, right*, she thought. *A big black toolbox is no longer on the shelf.* Ok, so he might. But if she had made this much progress, she knew she would keep fighting. Whatever it took to stay alive she thought. A surge of hope swept through her. That was step one. She actually felt like she might have a chance to survive.

She wasn't sure what to do next. So she sat down again and became very still. Then she had an idea. She decided that more than anything else, she needed light. Her heart beat fast as she wondered how much time she had. She wished she knew exactly. Her legs ached. Although she was moving, it wasn't what anyone would call at lightning speed. She had to stop for a moment and catch her breath. She breathed in deeply, leaning back against the post.

The killer had come from straight in front of her and off to the left. After a few minutes, she stood again on those shaky legs and began to move in that direction. She hoped she was moving toward the door. The room was so dark she honestly couldn't see a foot in front of her. She found she was able to go approximately three feet. She took a jump in an attempt to pitch herself forward. She felt the tug of the chain around her waist. The force of it was so great it pulled her back and she went sprawling to the ground. She fell so hard, she saw stars. A moan of pain escaped her lips. More tears fell from her eyes as she lay there wondering what to do next. "God, please help me," she prayed.

She stood again, this time focusing on her balance, and pulled on the chain more slowly. To her dismay, the result was the same. She found if she made only small movements the force of it wasn't like before. She felt the chain rubbing her skin raw as she kept trying to move forward and backward to loosen the chains. Her arms were free. She stretched them up as far as possible. That's when she felt it. A string was hanging from the ceiling. She almost cried again as light poured into the room. "Thank you, God," she breathed. For the first time, she felt like she had some control. Instead of feeling powerless, she felt a stab of, what was it?

Hope, she realized. It was hope.

Chapter Eighty-Nine

June 27

The car belonged to Martin Lopez. We were getting closer. Even as the clock passed midnight, the news had surprised me and everyone else. We spent all day and all night looking through records trying to figure out where Scott Hall had taken Lindsay. So far, no luck. Another day had passed and that wasn't good.

"How did Scott get the missing car? And where has he kept it until now?" Matt wondered aloud, once again reading my mind.

LAPD now had a connection between the disappearance of Martin Lopez and Scott Hall. That case was not in our jurisdiction. Once we got Hall, we would need to work with Missing Persons, and possibly Homicide, so they could close their case. I hoped we would get justice for his family, too.

Matt's voice brought me back to the present moment. "We need to look again at property records for Scott Hall, Juliet Hall, and even Martin Lopez."

"Maybe even extend that to their immediate families," I added.

Davis and Cameron went to put out a second BOLO for the missing Lopez vehicle. We decided to add Scott Hall's as well, just in case there was some kind of backup plan we didn't know about. For now, he was one step ahead of us. *Not for long*, I thought. We all started pouring through tax records and property listings. After a while, Matt stood up and stretched. He wrung his hands in frustration.

"So far, we have nothing," he muttered. I felt the same way. We needed to find Lindsay… and fast. Our prime suspect had already killed two more people. I didn't think that was his plan. I floated my theory by Matt. He agreed.

"It was probably surprising to him that we knew as much as we did. So he got rid of everyone who knew anything."

"Do you think that would have happened anyway?" I asked with remorse filling my voice.

"Hard to say. I suspect that may have happened no matter what."

Sometimes that's how it goes. The closer we get to solving a case the more dangerous it gets. It reminded us of Lindsay and the danger she was in. *What must she be going through*, I wondered, *if she's even alive?* It was a morbid thought. I needed to clear my mind.

When I got up, I turned and saw Matt standing in the corner. He leaned against the window with his eyes closed and his hands folded. I just watched him. I could tell he was praying and didn't want to interrupt. If God wanted to help us solve this case, I wouldn't argue. We needed all the assistance we could get.

My partner opened his eyes and noticed me looking at him. He smiled and stretched.

"What were you thinking?" he asked quietly. I told him about being okay with God helping us if he wanted to. Matt laughed and said with complete confidence, "He has. And he'll help us solve these murders and find Lindsay. I just know it."

Just then the door opened, and Cameron ran in. "Hey, guys," he said as he stood in the doorway looking in at us. We turned almost in unison.

"What's up? It's only been an hour. What could have developed so fast?"

"We just found Scott's car in a parking lot. A patrol officer found it on a residential street near the Grove, a busy shopping area in Los Angeles. I was surprised he would leave it near there. He was trying to hide it in plain sight. They called us right away and are still at the scene preserving the evidence. I was just saying a prayer, asking God for help not two minutes ago, and then we got this lead." Cameron had a huge smile on his face.

Matt winked as it dawned on me that my partner had just been doing the same. "Let's go take a look," he said. We all raced out of the conference room toward the parking garage.

Chapter Ninety

The nice thing about working this late at night and into the morning was there were not a lot of cars on the road. LA with very little traffic was a welcome sight as I drove. We wound our way through the streets of Hollywood. The only people who were out on the corners were the homeless and the pimps and pros, and those seeking their services. I felt sad as I passed by one girl. She didn't look a day over nineteen. She had long dark hair with sad eyes and barely anything on. "What must her life have been like?" I said out loud.

Matt saw me looking at her and sighed sadly. "I don't know. It breaks my heart, too. She doesn't deserve this life."

"No one does," I said.

My thoughts were on that girl. I must have zoned out. The next thing I knew, Matt tapped my shoulder. I jumped about five feet and then realized with a start we were near the outdoor shopping center. I spotted the flashing lights ahead of us and around the corner I took the turn.

That's where we found Officer Malcolm, one of the newest members of the Highway Patrol, keeping watch over the car at this very late hour.

"Thanks, man," Matt said as he clapped him on the shoulder.

Even before we asked, Malcolm told us his story. "Sure, no problem. It's kind of crazy. I had taken my wife to a movie earlier tonight and we parked in that same garage. I noticed that car then but didn't think much about it." He smiled at us and continued. "Then I came on the night shift and read the BOLO and remembered seeing that car here. Or at least I thought so. It was worth checking out. So I drove back and spotted it. On taking a closer look, I realized it was the same one."

"Good job. Thanks so much," I said, smiling at him.

"Yep, I'll just be in my vehicle. Let me know when you need me." He turned and walked toward his car.

I pulled out a large flashlight and held it for Matt as he inspected the vehicle. Cameron and Davis pulled up and got out. "We thought you might need backup," Davis said.

We nodded our thanks. "Want to call this license in? I know we know it's his. Let's just be absolutely sure."

Davis copied down the plate and went back to his car. Each police cruiser was equipped with a computer where we could easily run plates or get background information. A few minutes later he came back and affirmed that the vehicle was indeed registered to one Scott Hall. The next thing we needed to do was get a judge to sign a warrant for us to open the vehicle up. We probably could have used exigent circumstances; but upon inspection it didn't look like Lindsay or anyone else was being kept inside.

"That would be too, easy," Matt said.

"How about you and Emma wait here while Cameron and I go to night court and get that warrant," Davis said. We agreed and got back in our own car. Since finding out that the car Scott Hall used when he drove to Marco Crane's place belonged to Martin Lopez, we could establish a connection to both murders.

For a while, Matt and I sat silently with the heat on and the lights flashing. During the day the temperature borders on heat stroke. Then at night, it can get chilly.

"I feel like we're running out of time," I said.

"I know. I hope not," Matt answered. We both knew that the more time Lindsay spent with Scott Hall, the worse her chances of survival became. Based on rough calculations, we concluded it was going on thirty-six hours.

Chapter Ninety-One

Lindsay was surprised that Scott wasn't back yet. Her stomach rumbled letting her know she needed to eat again. Unfortunately, all the crackers and water were gone. She should have split that meal in two; she chided herself in frustration. None of this could have been predicted. Despite her irritation at her own stupidity for going home, none of this was her fault. She was thankful that he was gone, but she was afraid of when he would come back.

She had turned on the light only to discover that she was in some kind of barn. She saw some empty stalls, maybe for horses. She was surrounded by bales of hay and a shelf where the toolbox was. The air smelled damp and musty. Dust was everywhere. The biggest spider she had ever seen made an appearance, and then went behind one of the large bales. She almost screamed. She was not a fan of bugs, spiders or anything like that. She let out a shaky breath.

"If that's the worst thing that happens to you tonight, no problem," she told herself. Strangely, that calmed her and made her laugh.

She had been working on getting out of the restraints. She found some bolt cutters, and with shaking fingers had begun to chisel away at them. The problem was it took so much energy and strength. She still felt weak from whatever Scott had given her. Not as sick or dizzy as before, though, she noted with some hope. Maybe it was the drugs, or maybe the fall she had taken. Whatever it was, it sure made her move slow. She kept at it, even when the strain of it was too much.

Finally, she heard a loud crack as the chain around the post attached to her arms snapped apart. It was so startling to not be held securely that she fell backwards and to the side into one of the stacks of hay. She couldn't help but moan. Her body ached so much. She then remembered the spider behind one of the bales. That got her motivated to get back up and stick to her plan.   She still had one more chain to break, the one around her waist.

She started with the post again, trying with all her might to break the chain from around the thick pillar. Scott had wrapped it several times. It must have been six feet long, she estimated. That way she would have some room to walk a few feet from the post. She turned and faced the post, wrapping herself around it. She used her body weight to push her arms with the cutter into the chain even harder. It made a sawing sound back and forth, back and forth. There were several layers to cut through. Her hands were so slippery from sweat and blood that she had a hard time holding on. With a final grunt and push, she heard the familiar sound of the snap.

Lindsay wanted to clap but was too tired. She sank down on the rough ground, taking in shallow breaths. She was free! The first part of the plan was complete. Now, all she had to do was get up, move toward the door and either figure out how to unlock it or climb the bales of hay and get one of those old windows open. Did she have enough strength? she wondered. Just then she heard it, the terrible sound of footsteps coming toward the door. Oh, no, no, no. What should she do? She reached into the toolbox and grabbed a screwdriver. Maybe she could use that to defend herself. Then she heard it: one lock; two locks; and the third lock being undone.

Chapter Ninety-Two

"Got it," Cameron said excitedly as he and Davis raced back to the scene we were keeping an eye on. He held out a warrant to us.

"Signed and ready to go," Davis said.

"Alright, great, let's get to it," Matt said as we got out of the car.

Scott's automobile sat untouched and locked. Matt slid on a pair of latex gloves and took out a lockpick set he carried with him. He worked it into the small hole. We heard the familiar click. "And we're in," he said as he opened the driver's door.

As he opened it up, light flooded into the car. It was a four-door with a trunk. The outside gleamed. It was obvious to us that the car was well taken care of. Time was flying by. I felt as if we had none left. I raced around to the passenger side and slid on another pair of gloves. Cameron and Davis did the same as each took a side in the back. I opened the glove box. It was jammed full of napkins, a glasses case, insurance and registration forms, and then...

"Well, what do we have here?" I asked as I reached my hand as far back as it could go and pulled out a piece of paper. I unfolded it. "It looks like some kind of hand drawn map," I said. I observed that the starting location was where we were now. I could tell by the major intersection nearby. "I wonder where it leads to," I said to no-one in particular.

Matt came around to my side and peered over my shoulder. "Where, indeed," he mused. "I vote we follow it. Maybe it will lead us right to him and Lindsay."

"Let's hope so," Davis said from the backseat.

As much as we wanted to leave that very moment, we needed to finish our search in order to learn whatever we could about our suspect and his plans. Everyone worked quickly. I heard Matt's low whistle from behind the car and turned toward him. "Look what I found in the trunk," he said. He opened a suitcase and found stacks and stacks of cash all neatly laid inside a large rolling suitcase. He began counting it. "There's got to be more than one-hundred thousand dollars here," he said.

Just then Cameron told us about his discoveries. "I found several wigs, some hair dye, and a few fake mustaches back here."

"It looks like our boy is trying to leave the country," Davis observed as he pulled out a fake identification card and passport. I wondered if that was the set he was going to use or if he had another.

I found one other piece of valuable information jammed between the seats. "It's a crumpled up receipt for one plane ticket to Thailand scheduled to take off tomorrow afternoon from LAX," I said.

Matt handed out evidence bags. We all slid in what we had found. It took several bags, as each piece of evidence needed to be labeled and packed individually.

"We all need to follow the map. Maybe that's where he has Lindsay," Matt said.

It would not be smart to only have two officers. Davis called our captain and gave him an update. After a minute, he came back and said, "Mendoza wants our location once we figure out where we are going. He'll send more units as backup, just in case."

The question now was how do we get the evidence back to the property room? There is a certain protocol for handling evidence that must be followed.

"I'm going to flag down that patrol officer and have him bring it to our squad. They can bring it to the property room," Davis said.

We all took our bags and walked them to the young patrol officer. He had called the impound lot to take the car back to be thoroughly examined by our crime scene team. To our relief, we saw three more patrol cars coming to assist him. Someone needed to stay at the scene, while others needed to get the evidence to the right place.

"I'll drive, if you guys want to follow us," I said. "It's a pretty clear map. I think I can find my way," I added, hoping I was right.

After we explained what we wanted the patrol officer to do, we turned over the scene to him. I was impressed by his willingness to help. He had stayed at the scene and worked on his paperwork while we searched the car. He told us he had been on the job for about six months. *What a baby*, I thought, remembering those days. What a case for him to find himself in the middle of. I was hoping he could handle it.

As if reading my mind, Matt got in touch with his supervisor to come and assist and take charge. Although we both thought the rookie would be fine, we needed to follow protocol. With that much cash, it was important to have a higher-up take possession of it and bring it back to police HQ. We shook his hand along with the other patrol officers, and climbed into our cars. We headed out to catch a killer and hopefully save his next victim before it was too late.

Chapter Ninety-Three

I wondered if Matt could hear my heart beating as I drove. It sounded like a jackhammer that kept getting faster as we went. There was always an adrenaline rush as you get closer to catching a killer.

"I'm wondering what you're thinking, Em?" Matt said. I sighed.

"Actually, I was thinking about how hard my heart is beating and wondering if you can hear it too?" He laughed. I was joking, of course. My face didn't show it.

"We're doing the best we can with what we have. Plus, I've been praying for Lindsay all night," Matt informed me.

We drove through dark streets. I was grateful for my headlights. The night not only was dark, it was silent. Maybe that was because we were driving further away from the city.

In Los Angeles, the map was easy to follow. As we went further out, we were having a hard time figuring out just where to go. The handwriting was sloppy, and the drawing was chicken scratch. I pulled over, puzzling over what to do next. We didn't have time for this, I thought.

We got a call from our captain saying that Kelsey may have hit pay dirt with the property records. Once we got the information, to our relief the hand-drawn map and the cap's report seemed to match up. We were on our way to an old farmhouse more than twenty-five miles out of Los Angeles proper. It belonged to Juliet Hall's great-grandparents. Kelsey said there was a big barn and modest house set on ten acres of land.

To be honest, I was out of my element. I knew nothing about farms or barns. Realizing that made me feel just a little more nervous than usual. At least the captain had sent some local police as backup. They knew the area better than we did. Their help would be invaluable.

"Okay, slow down. Turn here," Matt said as he interrupted my thoughts. He was right. There was a sharp curve to the road. If I didn't hit it just right, we might wind up in a ditch. I slowed the car to almost a crawl and turned on my high beams for a second to have a better view. I glanced back to make sure Cameron and Davis were still with us. I saw they had done the same. I sped up some and took the curve as quickly and smoothly as possible. Once we rounded it, we could see the road came to a dead end. Any sidewalk or street signs were nowhere to be seen.

"I guess we walk from here," Matt said. We saw four officers coming toward us. I was so thankful for the help. We definitely needed it.

"You're right. The road ends here," an officer that looked like a linebacker informed us. The lead introduced himself as Detective Harman Weights. His partner, Grace Campbell, stood beside him. She was exactly the opposite, petite and pretty with dark hair and large brown eyes. The Uniforms were Thomas and Cove. The eight of us stood, huddled together, working on a plan. We studied the map one more time.

"It looks like we go to the right," I said. I could tell that was the last direction Scott Hall had drawn on the map. After that, the trail went cold.

Chapter Ninety-Four

I wished we had made several copies of the map. Everything seemed to be happening at lightning speed. I was grateful for that. Unfortunately, the road was narrow, meaning only one person could walk on it at a time. So that's what we did. Campbell took the lead. The rest of us followed behind her in single file. It was almost like playing train, each of us with a hand on the shoulder of the person in front of us.

If Scott was holding Lindsay there, we didn't want to let him know we were coming. So Weights, Cameron, and I all turned on our flashlights, holding them close to the ground so they would only give off little slivers of light. We stepped as quietly and carefully as possible. There was a ditch on each side of the path. The walk was longer than we thought it would be. Finally, we saw the outline of a car just off the beaten path. Everyone stopped. Matt leaned into the car as I ran a flashlight beam around its interior. Other officers covered us with their guns. Cameron stood at the hood while Davis checked for the license plate. He sent a text to the captain, asking him to run it ASAP. We knew it wouldn't take more than a few short minutes. We waited. It looked like no one was in the car; but even in the faint light the three flashlights provided, we could all see what looked like blood covering the driver's seat. It was dried and had that reddish- brownish tint to it we knew so well. A few minutes later, Davis gathered the group. The license plate had been run. It was the car Martin Lopez once drove. It was registered in his name.

"We got him," Matt whispered.

We explained to the officers who Scott was, and the circumstances. This was a dangerous situation. We were all keenly aware of that fact. My rule-following heart wanted to get another separate warrant to open it. We didn't have time. Lindsay had to be our first priority.

These were emergency circumstances. We stood for a moment by the car talking about what our plan would be. As much as we wanted to look in the car, there was no time right now. Since we couldn't see signs of life in it, we had to keep walking.

Weights informed us that the old farmhouse had never been put on the market. As far as he knew, it was abandoned.

"The perfect hiding spot," I said.

We got back into single file and turned off most of our flashlights. We stepped away from the car and headed deeper into the woods. *SNAP!* The sound was deafening in the silent darkness.

"What was that?" I whispered as I saw both lead detectives fall down. We rushed to them and helped them up. A large, uneven tree root stuck out right in our path. It was almost hidden in the dark.

"Are you ok?" Matt asked.

Weights answered for both of them. "Yes, thanks. Sorry about that. We just tripped over one of those tree roots. We're fine."

I realized we all needed our lights. The path was completely uneven and a safety concern. So we walked even slower and had to risk letting a few more lights shine to guide our way.

And then we saw it. Out of the shadows, the outline of a building emerged. It was a barn. We stopped for a moment, listening, trying to hear anything in the night. Crickets chirped. For a while, that's all we heard. That door probably made almost everything soundproof.

We had decided to break up into teams of two. One team would take the farmhouse. One team would stay in the clearing while the rest of us went in twos to each side of the barn.

A single piercing scream filled the air, followed by a gunshot. Now, we all raced toward the barn. I wondered if it was already too late.

Chapter Ninety-Five

Lindsay heard the locks clicking. One lock; the second lock; and then… He was in the room and the light went out. She couldn't see him. But she could feel the intensely evil presence. He stood for a moment silently. To her it was like a standoff. She wanted to move but couldn't for fear he would hear her. To her dismay, he had seen her and knew she was free. She tried to be as silent as possible, knowing she only had one chance to save her life. He closed the large door and re-engaged the locks.

"Lindsay, you need to answer me now. If you don't and I have to come find you… Well, let's just say you wouldn't want that." His voice was so calm, and so evil.

As she listened, a chill went down her spine. She believed him and responded "Yes," in a tiny whisper. He took several steps toward her.

"It's time for you to die, and for me to get out of here," he said. "Are you ready to die, Lindsay?"

A cold shiver ran through her body. No, she didn't want to die, she thought angrily. She was young and talented and had a lot of life left to live. She had never been asked a question like that before. She had never even thought about it. Lindsay didn't answer.

"I asked you a question, a very important one!" Scott shouted. "I said: Are. You. Ready. To. Die?" She paused and thought about it again. Was she?

"If I must, then I am. I am forgiven of my sins and know that you cannot harm me. Maybe my body, yes, but my soul is not yours to hurt."

Her boldness shocked her. It shocked Scott, too, because there was no response for a while. Then he said, "I don't want to kill you; but you know who I am. There can be no loose ends."

In that moment she realized she should do everything she could to keep him talking. "I wouldn't tell on you," she said hoarsely. She wished she had more food, more water. To think that crackers and water might be her last meal… *Stop it*, she told herself. *Stop it and focus.*

"It's not that simple, love."

"Why me?" she asked. "And why are you hesitating?"

He sighed for a moment. She heard him step toward the middle of the room. "Even though we didn't know each other well, I've admired you from afar. I chose you as my last victim. It was not in the screenplay that Marco wrote, so I improvised."

Screenplay, she thought. What is he talking about? And then it came to her. The police had asked her about Marco's screenplay. "You… you mean this is based on his writing?" she stammered, trying not to sound too hysterical.

"Yes, it is. You didn't know?" Scott said, as a sneer came into his voice.

"I don't understand all this. What do you mean?" she said, hoping to stall him for time.

"I mean, when I saw my friend's screenplay—at least in the beginning stages—I thought it was an intriguing story. I wanted to 'bring art to life,' shall we say. So I spied on him."

"How did you do that?" she asked. "It wasn't hard. All I had to do was install a program, and I could see everything he did and said on his computer. All he had to do was open a simple email from me. He did that almost every day. The more he wrote, the more I followed his plan, almost to a 'T'. It's too bad we don't have more time. If we did, I would show you."

In a sick way he almost sounded regretful, she thought. "But you said I wasn't in the plan. So why me?"

"Because I could. Because your death will throw the police off. At least that's what I had hoped."

Lindsay thought about what Scott was saying. In some weird way, it made sense. He went on. "Then when you didn't drink the poison, I knew I needed to find another way to get you." He laughed. "All it took was a little patience. I figured at some point you would start to feel safe, go back to your own apartment. I just needed to watch and wait." He cleared his throat. "Once you did that, I was ready."

She could have screamed at herself. Why had she been so careless? She should never have gone home.

As if reading her mind, he said, "But you did, Lindsay. You went back home. And that was all I needed." She shuddered and tried not to cry or lash out.

After a few moments of silence, he said. "Now, at the count of three, I'm going to turn on this light and shoot you." His voice was icy calm. "I'll make it fast, I promise," he said.

252

Her heart hammered in her chest. She would try to dodge the bullet. She prayed it wouldn't hurt too much. Like a caged animal, she was trapped and not moving very fast. She was the perfect target.

"If you do move, I'll tranquilize you and make it even easier on myself," he threatened.

She felt panic rise as he spoke. She could try to stab him. She might even be able to. But he had a gun and a needle. What chance did she have? She did have one advantage. He had no idea she had found the toolbox and was holding the biggest screw driver she could find.

"Any last words?" he asked in a sing-song voice.

In that moment, no words came. Lindsay did the only thing left to do. She prayed. She recited the twenty-third psalm, reminding herself in her own voice that the Lord was her shepherd. She did not have to fear evil, for God was with her.

As he turned on the light, a calm came over her. She was right. She had the advantage. He looked at her in shock as he realized his mistake too late. As soon as he turned on the light, she lunged toward him with the screwdriver stretching out her hand as far as it would go. The screwdriver drove into his stomach. He gasped. Despite the shock, his reflexes were fast. He grabbed her by the hair and threw her to the ground. He kicked her again and again. The screwdriver slipped out of her grasp. In that moment, she felt it was over as he kicked it away.

She couldn't help it. She started screaming. Then, he pointed the gun at her. The moment he put his hand on the trigger and started to pull seemed like an eternity. He fell forward onto her ankle as she tried to scramble away. She heard a cracking sound as the bone broke under his weight. She felt the gun pressed into her stomach and heard a loud boom. Searing pain shot through her. She tried to move, to breathe, anything. But in that instant everything faded to black.

Chapter Ninety-Six

We all heard the gunshot after the scream. We ran as fast as we could toward the sound in the pitch-black night. Matt grabbed my hand. While I ran on the path, he valiantly trudged beside me in the ditch. We tried to get to her as fast as we could. *Please, God, help me get to her in time,* I thought. I couldn't believe I had even felt that way or asked a God who I didn't even believe in for help. But I knew Lindsay and Matt did. And I suppose in that moment that counted for a lot. I must have said it out loud, because I heard Matt shout, "Lord, please help us get to her in time." His shout was echoed by everyone else.

We hit the clearing and all eight of us ran toward the bright light. As we did, we saw a figure in black running out of the barn, trying to get past us. "Police! Freeze!" several of us yelled at once.

Drop your weapon," Matt ordered, as he moved in front of Weights and stared at Scott Hall, who was aiming a gun at my partner's heart. "Now! Now! Now!" Matt screamed.

He didn't drop the gun. As Matt ducked, Scott Hall's trigger went off. So did mine. I shot Scott Hall twice. I've always been one hell of a shot. This time was no different. I aimed for center mass and didn't miss. Scott Hall went down. For a moment, the silence loomed large. Everything felt like it was going in slow motion, even though the opposite was true.

Several of the officers rushed forward. As they secured him and called for help, Matt and I ran toward the barn. There we saw Lindsay Jones lying on her back, her head tilting toward her right side. I felt sick to my stomach. Two long chains sat broken on the floor in front of a large pillar. Off to the left, a screwdriver covered in blood gleamed in an ugly color. I saw all the blood. I couldn't tell if she was…

"Please, God, let us not be too late," I begged Him. She didn't deserve to die like this. She was young and sweet and had so much left to give to this world.

"She's still alive, but just barely," Matt said, as he leaned over her body and checked for a pulse. I grabbed a blanket that I saw on atop shelf and rolled it into a ball. I handed it to my partner so he could put pressure on the deep stomach wound that was leaking blood. I turned back and ran to the door.

"Call for a bus. She's still alive, but she's fading fast!" I yelled.

"Two are on their way, Emma," Davis said as he came in and put his arm around me. Together we walked over to Matt, who was now kneeling beside Lindsay. He held the blanket on her wound. I heard him pray.

"The Lord is my shepherd. I shall not want. He makes me lie down in green pastures. I will fear no evil for you are at my side."

Chapter Ninety-Seven

July 1

It took several days and several interviews. Ultimately, it was determined that I was justified in shooting Scott Hall. No good police officer ever wants to kill a suspect. After all, our motto is to protect and serve. Still, I had no choice. He had pointed his gun at my partner's heart. That alone was reason enough. It didn't help that he hadn't followed orders to put down his weapon. I might have been cleared by my superiors, but still, my heart felt heavy. Was his death really justice for the seven victims and their families? Was it really closure? I didn't think so. I had never killed a man before. *It's not something you just move on from*, I thought, as tears filled my eyes once again. I was sitting at my desk, writing my reports, trying to concentrate and failing miserably. What was the point? I wondered, letting bitterness wash over me.

A hand fell on my shoulder, firm but gentle all at the same time. Even though I wasn't facing him, I would know that touch anywhere. I turned in his direction. I smiled through my tear-filled eyes. Matt pulled my head to his chest, letting me have that moment, stroking my hair, and offering what comfort he could. Actually, we'd had a lot of moments like that over these past few days. I had been a wreck. He was struggling as well.

"You did what you had to do. You saved my life and Lindsay's, too," he soothed. "Let's get out of here. I want to take you somewhere."

The workday was long over. That didn't matter to me. I had gotten good at avoiding going home, and sleeping, too. I just couldn't take the silence right now. Matt pulled me to my feet. I started to protest, but he shook his head and led me out of the station. He led me out to his car and opened the door. I slid in and watched him get in on the driver's side. I was so lost in my thoughts that I didn't even ask where we were going.

Finally, I told him I knew he was right. "I guess I've been wondering what the point of all this was. Reminding me was more than enough."

"Yes," he agreed, "more than enough."

Lindsay Jones was a fighter. She would be wearing a cast due to a broken ankle for several weeks. Plus, she had sustained a gunshot wound to her stomach that ripped through her intestines. She had several surgeries over the past few days. Despite everything, she was holding on. She also had several cuts and scrapes from working herself out of those chains. How she did that was still amazing to me. That took grit, fight and determination. In a crisis, she was a clear thinker.

Once she was well enough, I couldn't wait to tell her that the nightmare was over. The cases had been solved. And her life could go back to normal, whatever that was for her now. She would need a lot of therapy. Still, I was confident she would pull through on all fronts. For now, she was awake and breathing on her own. And that was a good start. Once she was well, we would take her statement and tell her what we had found out about Scott Hall.

We had our techs look at both Marco's and Scott's computers, and the flash drive as well. We determined that Scott Hall and Marco Crane had been friends. Probably up until he died, Marco had thought they still were. Marco had shown his friend what he was working on. Scott had decided to make the story his own. He had spied on his friend via a computer program that let him control Marco's computer remotely. It gave him access to everything Marco had written. Once it was installed and working, he put his evil plan into action. I still wasn't sure why Scott had done it. We would probably never have had the answer to that question. Once he found out Sally Haze was rich, he made his move. He had charmed her, dated her, and lied to her throughout. Once he got everything that he needed from her, he killed her and stole her money.

Thanks to our tech team and the missing persons squad, we found emails between Lopez and Hall, detailing the theft. Scott bribed Martin Lopez, the bank manager, to keep her account open so he could take freely from it. We were guessing here; the theory was maybe once the account stayed open, he no longer needed Martin. So he kidnapped him and killed him. There was no evidence that the bank manager was involved in any other crime. Unfortunately, his body was still missing, and now his killer couldn't tell us where to look for it.

Once Scott had killed once, he wanted the feeling of power it gave him again. He continued to monitor the writing of the rest of the screenplay. Anytime Crane wrote a new character and another way to die, he made it happen in real life. Marco was never the wiser. Once he was done with his writing, Marco became just another loose end to him. So just like that, he killed his friend in cold blood, taking his computer and flash drive with him in the vehicle owned by Martin Lopez.

Juliet, too, was a loose end. He couldn't afford for her to tell the police what she had been putting together. We had found some more pages of her diary in his jacket pocket. That last entry I'd read wasn't actually her final words. In the missing pages she detailed her suspicions about the money and whose it was and where it had come from. Juliet wrote that she had decided to confront her husband and use what she knew as leverage. The problem was, she didn't know the danger she was putting herself in.

The real missteps Scott Hall had taken in his plans centered around Lindsay Jones. For some reason, he had decided she should die, too, even though it wasn't in the screenplay. He had used the same method as in the screenplay, thinking the poison would work. Instead, in a miraculous twist of fate, Lindsay didn't drink it. Maybe he had intended to kill more women in the same way. Who knows? We surmised that once he'd found out Lindsay was alive, he made adjustments to his plan. He had to find her and kill her. She was just another loose end to him. Once he killed her, he would leave the country with as much of the stolen cash as he could.

"What are you thinking about?" Matt asked as we pulled into a large parking lot.

"Just the case and all the twists and turns," I said. Most cases weren't as open and shut as you see on TV.

"I'm just glad we solved it and that Scott Hall can no longer hurt anyone."

"Yes, but that wasn't justice or closure for the victims or their loved ones."

"No it wasn't." Matt agreed. He took my hand. "Emma, Lindsay is now safe and we will be able to tell her soon. She survived. At least we got to call the families and explain that their nightmare was over, especially CC Garden's parents. Now they know that their daughter didn't take her own life. And all that counts for something."

We sat in silence for a while as I thought it over. He was right.

"Now, come on. Let's go, shall we?" he asked as he opened his door and slid out of the car. It was another humid evening. A typical scorcher. Matt came around and opened my door. He took my hand as I slid out of the car.

We walked toward a large building. From inside, music blasted. What was this? I thought, as he opened the door and we entered. I wanted to ask; but it was so loud I was sure he wouldn't be able to hear me. We walked into a darkened auditorium. It was packed. We managed to find seats next to each other in the middle. I listened to the loud music, and after a while, I realized they were singing about God.

I had never been to church in my life. I wanted to be uncomfortable. Instead, I relaxed as people sang and swayed to the music all around me. I just let myself get lost in it. We sat down and a man walked onto the stage and welcomed all in attendance. Then he started to speak.

"Hi, I'm Pastor John. If you haven't been to Rock of Ages Church before, let me be the first to welcome you. If you haven't been to church before or in a while, well then, you were meant to be here."

His words gave me pause. He sounded so confident. Was I meant to be here? I wondered. He went on: "I'm here to tell you that there is someone so much greater who loves you, who wants to know you. You've been thinking about Him, wrestling with your ideas of him, maybe even praying to him a little in your time of great need." I froze. How could he know that?

As he spoke, tears filled my eyes. It was like he was talking directly to me. "You were put on earth to do important work. Your life matters. You matter. If you've been wondering who this Jesus is, come to the altar. Stand next to me and come meet him. He wants to know you. It's the best decision you'll ever make."

I felt my entire body trembling. I had seen how Matt, Lindsay, and Dr. Locking, along with others, leaned on Jesus, how they had prayed and believed and hoped for the best. I remembered how the grieving parents of Cassie Garrison had said they would one day forgive their only daughter's murderer. How they had prayed for answers. How, when we called them to let them know what happened, they said their prayers for solving the case had been heard. What surprised me most was that they felt compassion for the murderer and hoped he had repented at the last moment of his life, that even though they didn't know why things happened, they knew that God was still with them.

My thoughts came back to the present. The pastor said I mattered, that what I was here to do mattered, and that Jesus wanted to meet me. I wondered if it was true. I wondered if he could transform my life like he had so many others. I wondered if mine was a life worth saving. .

After the service, I saw Matt looking at me. I nodded to him and pulled him up. We stood and walked toward the front of the church.

I guess I was going to find out.

www.ingramcontent.com/pod-product-compliance
Lightning Source LLC
Chambersburg PA
CBHW052045240626
47153CB00006B/2218